LORNA SCHULTZ NICHOLSON

When You

Least

Expect It

Red Deer Press

Published in Canada by Red Deer Press, 195 Allstate Parkway, Markham, ON L3R 4T8
Published in the United States by Red Deer Press, 311 Washington Street, Brighton, MA 02135

Red Deer Press acknowledges with thanks the Canada Council for the Arts and the Ontario Arts
Council for their support of our publishing program. We acknowledge the financial support of the
Government of Canada through the Canada Book Fund (CBF) for our publishing activities.

 **ONTARIO ARTS COUNCIL**
CONSEIL DES ARTS DE L'ONTARIO
an Ontario government agency
un organisme du gouvernement de l'Ontario

 Canada Council   Conseil des arts
for the Arts   du Canada

Edited for the Press by Peter Carver
Text and cover design by Tanya Montini
Proudly printed in Canada by Avant Imaging & Integrated Media

Library and Archives Canada Cataloguing in Publication
Title: When you least expect it / Lorna Nicholson.
Names: Schultz Nicholson, Lorna, author.
Identifiers: Canadiana 20210209690 | ISBN 9780889956414 (softcover)
Subjects: LCGFT: Novels.
Classification: LCC PS8637.C58 W44 2021 | DDC jC813/.6—dc23

Publisher Cataloging-in-Publication Data (U.S.)
Names: Nicholson, Lorna, author.
Title: When You Least Expect It / Lorna Nicholson.
Description: Markham, Ontario : Red Deer Press, 2021.| Summary: "When Holly Callahan, at 17 a
determined competitive rower, fails to make the team heading for an international competition, her
world collapses. She's also dealing with her single mother's new boyfriend whom she detests. It's only
when she meets a stranger at the local boathouse that she is able to find a new path to rowing success--
Provided by publisher.
Identifiers: ISBN 978-0-88995-641-4 (paperback)
Subjects: LCSH Rowers — Juvenile fiction. | Failure (Psychology) -- Juvenile fiction. | Blended families
-- Juvenile fiction. | Resilience – Juvenile fiction. | BISAC: YOUNG ADULT FICTION / General.
Classification: LCC PZ7.N534Wh |DDC 813.6 – dc23

Red Deer Press
www.reddeerpress.com

To all the rowers and coxswains that I have sat in a boat with.

To all my coaches who instilled in me the toughness, and beauty, of the sport.

To all my coaching mentors who taught me to coach.

To all the rowers I have had the pleasure of coaching.

You all showed me that rowing

is an

art.

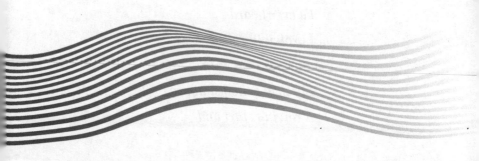

The Start

My mom once
laughed
and told me
that the start of a
rowing race
sounded like
a baby being born.
I was
fourteen,
at the time,
and thought that was
the stupidest thing
I'd ever heard.
I probably rolled
my eyes.
But ... are they similar?
A rowing start and

the birth of a baby?
Heavy pushes and grunting, I guess.
I exited Earth
too early
to experience
birthing a
baby,
and I don't remember
my own birth—
only moms can do that.
I was a lucky kid.
Parents,
two of them,
together,
a family.
Loved.
They wanted
only me,
no other baby.
Now ... I wish there was
someone else,
for them to love
besides me.

Chapter 1

My heart pounded right through my spandex singlet. I sat halfway up my rowing slide, with my oar angled and buried in the water. My entire body vibrated in anticipation of the word "GO!" Water splashed against the side of the boat. The sun beat down. Polarized sunglasses, secured tightly around the back of my head, hugged my face.

Today was the last day of tryouts for the Junior Canadian Rowing Team, and this was the last race of the day. My making the team was down to this one last seat race. I'd made it through three days of racing on the rowing course in St. Catharines—home of the Royal Canadian Henley and Canadian Secondary School Regatta—and now I was fighting with one other rower for the last spot.

One spot was left. That's it; that's all.

And there were two of us competing, our fates still

undecided. After this race, one of us would secure that seat. I sat tall in the boat and focused my gaze on the rower in front of me. I didn't dare look outside the boat.

Breathe, Holly, breathe.

One of us was going home after this last race. The others, who made the team, would travel to the World Junior Rowing Championships in Lucerne, Switzerland, later in the summer. Ten rowers had already been selected, and I'd had to live through their squeals and happy celebrations. I'd also witnessed the devastation of others who were cut and already sent home.

I inhaled and exhaled, trying to calm my rapid breathing. I was sitting bow seat in one of the two coxed four boats, and Keira, who was from Vancouver, was sitting bow in the other boat. Only two boats were racing today. The schedule was two races and, out of the eight of us rowing, Keira and I were the only ones competing. The format was for me to sit bow seat in one boat and race, then Keira and I would switch boats and race again. The two race times would be added up, and whoever had the fastest time would be the lucky one.

I'd already lost the first race.

And we'd already switched boats. I had to win this

race. This was it for me. I needed a win and I only had one more chance.

My body shook. I quickly looked down to make sure I was in the right position. I was good, still sitting only halfway up my slide. Both boats, to make it fair, were starting the race with a half-stroke and had the exact same start sequence. My knees were bent, like I was in a squat, and I sat tall, ready to push back and use my legs to power the oar through the water.

I wanted this so badly. For so many reasons.

I tried to suck in oxygen, to get rid of my jitters.

Stop shaking. You can do this.

I desperately wanted this ... so I could travel to Europe and compete at a high level. Be a national team athlete. But ... I also needed this ... so I could be gone all summer from the new family that had been dropped on me. I didn't want to go home. Home wasn't home anymore.

I had to win. Please let me win.

My hands were clammy as I gripped the oar, but I didn't dare wipe them off. Sweat was already dripping from every pore in my body.

I had this. I could do this.

I blew out air again to stop the hammering in my

chest. I couldn't look out of the boat, at the maple and willow trees lining Martindale Pond, the water we were rowing on. No, I had to stare ahead, keep my focus inside the boat. We were lined up in the starting gates, and the stern of the boat was being held by a boatholder, meaning we were ready to go at any moment.

"Half-slide, rowers." Eleanor Ing, the Canadian Junior coxswain from the year before, spoke into the microphone, her voice coming through the speakers of the coxbox that ran the length of the boat. She'd been the coxswain for the Junior eight that went to the World Championships last summer and won bronze. She knew her stuff. I tried to swallow, but there wasn't a lot of saliva in my mouth. My heart kept thumping, but I exhaled and sat tall.

I wanted the race to just start. Now.

All my training, all my work on the indoor rowing machines, all my focus and dedication and time, and going to bed early and getting up with the sunrise, it all came down to this. One more two-thousand-meter race.

My legs still shook. And my arms. And my upper body.

And my brain.

You got this.

I looked forward, focusing on the elastic in the ponytail of the rower who was sitting in front of me. Oh, God. I wished the race would begin. I had to explode off the start, push, drive my legs. I tried to even my breath, as I waited for the start command.

"Bow seat, touch it up, please." Eleanor spoke to me.

I pulled my oar just a little to help straighten out the boat for her. The wind was tricky today, coming from the port side, so the boat was being pulled. The water also had a bit of chop. My heart still pounded, out of synch with the chop. Even though my throat was dry, I couldn't take a sip of water now.

"Okay, bow. That's good," she said. "Rowers ready?" She spoke in this clear, calm voice, so unemotional. She was following the rules. With her experience, Eleanor had already made the team, so she wasn't in the fight. Not like me. Every coxswain I'd ever known was small, light, and tough as shit, Eleanor included. She would call out our start, then steer the boat with a rudder to make it go straight. I didn't know Eleanor that well, as we didn't even live in the same province. She was from Halifax, Nova Scotia. She had been instructed by the coaches to call the race with no emotion, so there was no advantage. Normally, the coxswains were the motivators, coaches in the boat. Not today.

With my oar in water, I was ready. *Please. Just start the seat race, already!* Beside us, the motorboat chugged, the gas fumes circulating in the air.

"Boats, are you ready?" one of the coaches called out from the motorboat.

"Ready," said Eleanor.

I sat tall. Focused on that elastic.

The next thing I heard was the beep of the starting horn.

"Half!" Eleanor called out.

I drove my legs hard, pushed back. Snapped my knees. Got my oar through the water and out, using my wrist to turn the oar, flatten it. Up the slide again.

"Half!" Eleanor spoke with authority.

Another half-stroke. Again, I pushed back, helping to move the boat forward.

"Three-quarters!"

Longer stroke. The first few seconds had my heart rate in overdrive. The water churned beside the boat, little swells that slapped against the side of the shell. My legs pushed down. My hands moved around and out over my knees. I started up the slide again, following the rower in front of me. Where was the other boat? A look out of the boat could cause disruption, unnecessary movement, seconds on the time clock. Only the coxswain could look.

"Half!" Eleanor spoke rowing language. "Sitting at forty-two," she said.

We had the boat moving at forty-two strokes per minute! No wonder I was gasping. High for a four. That high a stroke rate usually only lasted for the start.

"Full!"

I drove back hard on that first full stroke of the race. My breath was as frantic as the pace. Everything needed to slow down, catch the cadence, so I could breathe.

"Give me ten hard ones!" said Eleanor.

We'd done our five-stroke start, and now the boat needed momentum. And the ten hard strokes would do that. She started at one. Where was the other boat?

Don't worry. Keep pushing. Keep driving.

"Eight!" Up the slide, push back.

"Nine!" Up the slide, push back.

After she called out, "Ten," we settled into our race

rhythm. "We're at thirty-four," she said. "Bow, take over the race." Eleanor talked calmly.

Now I had to call the race. Me. Those were the rules in a seat race. I would call and so would Keira. Eleanor could only give us where we sat in comparison to the other boat. The pace was okay, and I was hanging in there. Was everyone else? After the ten, we seemed to settle too much, though. Sure, the boat took on a rhythm that I was comfortable with, but maybe too comfortable.

"They've got half a boat on us," said Eleanor.

Half a boat? Already!!!! I had to do something.

"Take it up," I called from the bow.

The rower sitting in the stern, in stroke seat, the seat that dictates the pace, accelerated, and I dug in hard to follow: pushing, sliding, pushing, sliding, pushing, sliding.

We hit the five hundred meter mark. There was still fifteen hundred to go.

"They're still half a boat ahead," said Eleanor.

"Twenty!" I called out. Come on, twenty hard strokes. Did I do the right thing? Twenty at the five hundred mark was risky.

Please. Make it the right thing.

We pushed through the twenty, then the boat fell flat. I could feel it. Fatigue set into my legs, my hips, my upper body. My brain.

Finally, a thousand meters. Halfway done. My breathing was ragged. My legs were on fire, quads burning with every stroke. Should I call for another hard twenty? I could see the other boat out of the corner of my eye, but it wasn't good. They were definitely ahead.

Come on. Keep going, Holly. Don't die. Please don't die.

"Twenty," I called out in a gasp.

The boat picked up a little. My legs seared and my breathing was like rapid bursts. In and out. In and out. I kept sliding and pushing.

Keep going, Holly. You can do it! Dig. Dig. Dig.

Fifteen hundred meters.

"Less than half a boat," said Eleanor.

We were catching them! Could we? I had to push just a little harder. Harder. Harder.

"Last two-fifty," said Eleanor.

"Take it up!" I yelled.

We were moving. Pushing. Could we do it?

The horn blared, announcing a boat was across the finish line. Then a second horn.

Our Stories

You're probably wondering
what my deal is
with Holly,
why I'm in her
story.
I was a rower, too.
Rowing raised me up
but it also took
me down
below the surface
because I had zero patience.
Patience is part of
sport,
but more
importantly
it's
a part of life.

I learned the hard way.
Perhaps,
my earthly mistakes
can be fixed
if Holly
listens,
acts,
and doesn't
resist.

Chapter 2

"I'm sorry, Holly," said Coach Fisher.

I nodded. Tears pooled behind my eyes, but I wasn't giving them a chance. Not yet. Coach Fisher was a former Olympian and one of the best coaches in the country. I had desperately wanted to work under her this summer. I hung my head.

"You've come a long way. You're young and you still have one more year as a junior."

I kept staring at the ground.

"Keep training this summer. I remember my setbacks when I was your age, and it's tough to handle, but don't give up. If you can, row at your club this summer. You have potential, and this is your first experience with National Team. It can take time—years. You have years."

I gave one nod. But not one word, because this ball of something was sitting in the back of my throat, blocking my words. I knew that the rowing in my club this summer would be *just okay*. I would be the only one from my high school four in the rec program, and I'd be with the others who rowed for fun. Everyone I rowed with in my high school four had made this team. Everyone but me.

Fun? I didn't want to row *just for fun*.

And I sure didn't want to go home.

Coach Fisher shook my hand, and my meeting was over.

No, I was getting CUT.

I quickly gathered all my things, including my duffle bag that had my high school athletic crest on it, and bolted out of the building to the parking lot. I stumbled as I ran, and my duffle bag slapped against my legs.

I heard the footsteps behind me, but I didn't look.

"Holly!" It was Kash, my best friend, who knew all about my ridiculous home life.

The tears now poured out of my eyes like a full cup of spilled water. She grabbed me in her arms and hugged me and, because she's six-foot-one, my forehead hit her cheek. Kash had inherited her father's Dutch genes, and she was long and muscled, perfect build for rowing. Yesterday, she'd made the team, and today I hadn't. I was happy for her. I really was. But this was not how it was supposed to go down. We were both supposed to make it and have the summer of our lives.

"I'm so sorry," she said.

I couldn't speak. I seriously couldn't utter a word. Only sobs escaped. A ball of phlegm was lodged in my throat and I felt like I couldn't breathe. Oh, God, I didn't want anyone seeing me like this, crying hysterically in a parking lot. I couldn't stop myself, and I cried into her shoulder, tears soaking her singlet.

"You'll make it next year," she whispered in my ear.

I sobbed. "I want it this summer. I want to go to Worlds. I want to race. This summer. Not next summer. That seems so far away." My chest heaved up and down. "And I don't want to go home."

"Oh, Holls, I'm sorry home sucks so much." She hugged me harder. "What am I going to do without you?"

Then she pulled away and held me by my upper arms, staring directly into my eyes. Her gaze was serious, forcing me to make eye contact. "There will be a next year. We have to believe that. Think of the killer high school crew we'll have. We'll totally dominate. Beat the crap out of everyone by boat lengths. Then, next year, we'll both make it. I swear. We will. We'll train hard. And we will go to Penn or UVic together. Be roomies."

I couldn't reply. I was drained of energy. Both Kash and I had been sort of recruited for the University of Pennsylvania crew. This meant that the coach had come to our school and talked to both of us, but nothing was concrete. My mom had been iffy about me going there, even going away to university. Did her standard, we-can-talk-about-it-when-the-time-comes and don't-put-all-your-eggs-in-the-rowing-basket lines. What would she think now?

"What if Penn doesn't want me after this?" I mumbled. "What if my mom says no because I got cut this summer?"

"Listen to me," she said. "We kick butt with our high school crew next year, and we're both good. Plus, your mom's a pushover. You just have to keep wearing her down."

"It's kind of two against one now," I said. My entire body sagged like it was weighted down, heading to the bottom of a lake.

The fall. Next year. Next summer. Those times were still not computing in my brain, because all I could think of was this moment, my now, especially because I knew what awaited me at home, and it wasn't pretty. Not even close. In fact, my home life had recently turned into a bizarre nightmare. With no rowing, and no Kash, the summer from hell was coming in like a hurricane on water, blowing everything into little pieces, and parts of me were floating everywhere.

A car pulled up. It was my mother. She'd been watching my races down at the grandstands in Port Dalhousie, where she could see the finish line. And me lose.

"I gotta go," I blubbered.

"Don't give up," said Kash. "Please. Please." She hugged me again, her strong arms circling me. "I'll text you," she said. "Let's talk tonight."

I nodded. I didn't have the energy to speak. I got in the car, wiping my face.

"Holly, I'm so sorry." My mom put her hand on my shoulder.

I knew she wanted to hug me, but I couldn't move. I felt hollow from losing, and just wanted to be left alone. Plus, she'd been pissing me off recently, so we weren't on the best terms. I couldn't move and I wouldn't move. I remained a stiff block in my seat.

"Drive," I said through gritted teeth. "Just go. Get me

out of here. And don't stop to talk to anyone."

So she did. No words were said. We drove away from the St. Catharines Rowing Club and the boat bays, over the bridge, leaving Henley Island. I stared at the bending willow branches lining the side of the road. Every morning we'd run this road for warmup. Just a kilometer there and a kilometer back. I didn't want to be leaving. I wanted to run this road again tomorrow morning, just as the sun was rising. I wanted to get in a boat, feel the sun on my face, the sweat on my back, the water beneath me.

In less than ten minutes, my mother merged onto the Queen Elizabeth Way. I had a little less than three hours in the car with her. Back to Bracebridge, my sleepy town with the small rowing club and ... my new pseudo family. My life could not get any worse. I curled into a ball in the front seat, feet on the seat, arms wrapped around my legs. I'd never loved any sport more than rowing. I'd played soccer, softball, volleyball, basketball, but it was rowing that did it for me. I had wanted this so badly.

"You hungry?" Mom finally asked.

"No," I answered into my knees.

"Okay," she said softly. "Maybe in a bit."

More silence, and I did appreciate her not asking questions. I'm sure she wanted to.

Suddenly her phone rang, and I groaned. I opened one eye and looked at the entertainment system. It was him. My mom's boyfriend. The guy who wanted to be like my stepfather, some new father-figure in my life. Um ... no thanks. I'd never had a father, and I sure didn't need one after turning seventeen a month ago. For God's sake, I was going into senior year in high school. So. No. I. Didn't. Need. A. Dad.

We'd all had to have one parent with us during the seat racing tryouts, but if you made the team, your parent went home. Kash's mother had left yesterday, and now Kash got to stay in St. Catharines, live in dorms and train until she left for Europe. And here was me—with my mother, heading back to a freaking nightmare. I didn't want to hear *his* voice on the bluetooth.

"Don't answer," I muttered.

She did anyway.

"Hi, Stew," said my mother.

"How'd she do?" Stew's voice boomed through the car.

I closed my eyes. Where were my headphones?

"We can talk at home," my mother told him, with this false cheerfulness in her voice.

Talk at home? Talk at *home*? Yeah, right. It wasn't *our* home; it was his home. We'd recently moved into *his* house, with *his* two kids, *his* things, *his* energy.

I uncurled myself and found those damn headphones in my bag.

Art Form

I looked at rowing
like art,
musical notes
all strung together.
From the first day
I placed the boat
in the water,
the gentle slapping
of wood hitting water
made me breathe,
gave me life.
Which I foolishly threw away.
Rowing makes Holly
breathed, too.
The early morning
sunrises,
pink, purple, orange,

then blue.
The water beneath the boat
gives her
energy,
passion.
I don't want Holly
to throw it
all away,
or worse
give up
because people,
* her family,*
don't
* believe*
in her.

Chapter 3

My real father—as in the guy who donated his sperm to my mother, who was my father for all of three months before he took off—never resurfaced. What a jerk. A piece of crap. That's how I really feel. He knew me for ninety days of my life.

One day, I wanted him to read about me, or watch me on television, his daughter, and how I was an Olympic athlete. Gold medalist. Or better yet, I'd love him to see my smiling face on a cereal box in the grocery store. And even *better than that* would be if he was with his "new" family in said grocery store. I'd tracked him down and found out he had a new wife and two little girls. Thanks, social media. Maybe those little girls would say something about me being their hero, not even knowing I was *their sister*, and he'd look and see *my face*. The other daughter. And then ... if he ever bothered to get in touch with me to say congrats, I would tell him where to stick his congrats. You abandon your kid when she's a baby, you deserve nothing. I didn't even have his last name—which is Bancroft. My mom legally switched us both back to her maiden name, Callahan, when he left her.

Now ... would that ever happen? Would I ever get that satisfaction of ignoring him when he tried to be proud of me? I'd just been cut. The reality kept punching me in the stomach and was getting worse, now that we were almost at Stew's house.

We drove down the street, Stew's street, and I stared at the maple branches hanging proudly, their June leaves swaying in the breeze. Soon it would be July, and summer. Summer, and me with nothing to do. I stretched out of my tight ball and sat up straight. And I sighed. Oh, man. This was not going to be easy.

I am totally for my mother having a boyfriend and being happy—after all, my dad had dumped her, left her high and dry with a baby. But why, oh why, did we have to move in with Stew and his kids? Two loud boys. And Stew was somebody who I really wanted to hate, because the situation just sucked. There had been one other boyfriend before Stew, and I'd kind of liked him. He understood me, let me be moody, let me be happy, didn't bug me, didn't have kids, and didn't want me to be part of his family. He was easy to like because he didn't affect me. But she'd dumped him.

Then along came Stew. He was so annoying, always this super-positive, let's-be-happy, life-is-a-bowl-of-cherries person who drove me to my room, where I closed the door. Life wasn't always happy-happy. Like now, for me. I wasn't the least bit happy. And the worst part was, my mother wanted me completely involved in this new family life. Whoa. Not my deal. Mom and I had always been a unit of two. My mom was an only child, too, and although we spent time in the summer with my grandparents, who lived in Bathurst, New Brunswick, mostly it was just us.

We moved in with Stew and his boys on May fifteenth, and we'd been living with them for forty-two damn days. Yes, I kept count. I hated being thrust into this new posse of people. Since I seriously wanted to hate Stew, I nitpicked and found things about him that annoyed me. Wasn't that hard, actually. Honestly, I don't think he's any better than my non-existent daddy-o, because Stew's a flesh version, someone real and tangible, and in my face all the time.

"Did you have a good sleep?" my mother asked.

"Yeah," I mumbled. I really hadn't slept, just faked it so we didn't have to talk.

My mom and I managed great when I was a kid, but then high school arrived, and I became addicted to rowing and was gone all the time, or sleeping, or eating. So, she had more time, and she didn't worry about me, because I went to bed early to get up early. She met Stew by fluke at some Home Show that was set up at the community center in Barrie. She went to get some decorating ideas. So much for the Home Show giving her tips. I would have taken new blinds, even a cheap glass vase, as compared to moving into *his house*.

As we approached the house, I saw Stew's Audi in the driveway, and I cringed inside. Mr. Real-Estate-Agent drove an Audi to look the part of super-salesman. Super-positive-happy-salesman.

"Stew made a nice dinner for us," she said.

"Of course, he did. He's Super-Stew."

"Holly, he worked hard on the meal."

"Okay, I won't rock the boat." My words were laced with sarcasm. "My boat has been rocked, but I sure won't rock yours."

"I'm here for you, if you want to talk."

"What's to talk about? I got cut. Period. Full stop. *And* now I have to play happy. *And* I don't want to. *And* you know I didn't want to move."

"I'm sure you're disappointed. But give it a little time. It's summer. You're just out of school and ready for some fun."

"Fun? Are you kidding me? I don't want fun. That's not who I am."

"Time does heal."

"Oh, my God. Now you sound like him. And not in a good way. Right now, I want to go to *our* little house. I want to curl up on *our* sofa and cry, and sleep, and have you rub my back. That's all I want. Instead, I have to go inside and face happiness. I never asked for this change."

My mother blew out a rush of air, but she didn't respond this time. We'd been down this road before and had many arguments about Stew, the man in her life, who was now in my life, the man I didn't want in my life. His boys had lived in the same house for their entire life, so it was *theirs*. I got that they were inconvenienced as much as me, and I felt for them. I just wish we hadn't moved in, for all our sakes.

"I understand how hard this is for you."

"No, you don't. You were never an athlete. And you never had to move in *with your mom's boyfriend* when you were my age. You had Grandma and Grandpa. So, you don't understand."

She put her hand on my shoulder. "Come on. You must be starving. Dinner will be ready soon."

"Can I at least take a shower first?" I asked, shaking off her hand.

"Of course. But, please, say hello when you walk in. You know how he is when you just ignore him."

"Why is it always about him and his stupid feelings?" I put my headphones in my bag and gathered up my stuff, shoving everything into my backpack. "Okay, I'll be Little-Miss-Perky to make Super-Stew happy. So ridiculous."

"Holly, that's enough."

I walked into the house and smelled the food. He was a decent cook; I would give him that much. But it was the accolades I had to bestow on him after every meal that drove me insane.

"Hi," I said.

"Hey, how are you doing?" Stew wore a plaid man-apron.

"Okay," I said. "I'm going to take a shower."

"How'd it go?"

I cleared my throat. "I'll talk later."

"Sorry," he said. "But you know, Holly, everything happens for a reason."

In the first ten seconds of seeing him, I was ready to explode, and tell him to shut his mouth, zip the sayings. I gritted my teeth and flashed a phony smile. "I've never heard that saying before," I said as sarcastically as I could. "Wow, are you ever clever. Now excuse me, I'm going to have that shower."

"Join us for dinner, okay, Holly?" said my mother.

"Yeah, I slaved all afternoon, knowing you'd be starving," said Stew. He did some stupid little dance, and I wanted to throw up.

Then he put his arm around my mother, and she smiled up at him, so I left. As fast as I could.

In the shower, the water cascaded from the shower head, falling over my skin, washing the crusty sweat off, but not the sting. I could have stayed in there all day. And all night. As the water cleaned me, I thought about what I was going to do. There was no way I was going to quit. Coach Fisher was right; I was young. I would do this, make it, row in the Olympic Games one day. My ultimate goal. Of course, I knew there were steps along the way. And I'd just missed one. But I would keep going, not give up. I got out, got dressed in my rattiest sweat shorts and tank, and went downstairs.

Stew was whistling away out on the deck, as he turned the steaks over, sipping on his red wine in between each flip. Mom was in the kitchen, tossing the salad. No wine for her yet. The television sounded from the family room because—surprise, surprise—the boys were playing video games. I hated this. Wanted our ratty sofa. Because our furniture wasn't as nice as Stew's, we'd moved very little of our stuff. We brought a few family photos and some dishes. Whoop-de-do. I walked to the cupboard and got the plates to set the table. At least they were ours.

With a platter stacked with steaks, Stew whistled his way into the kitchen. I had to admit, since I'd refused to eat all the way home, they did smell and look good.

"Look at these babies," he said.

"Looking good, Stew," I said.

He eyed my clothing. "Nice of you to dress for dinner."

"I've got a gown upstairs I could put on. Add a little

bling and lace to the party. Could even show cleavage." I placed the forks down and avoided looking at my mother, because I'm sure she was making a face at me, telling me to stop with the snarky comments.

"Always got a smart answer." Stew placed the steaks on the table. Then he called out, "Dinner!"

Suddenly, the room took on a new energy, because Kevin and Curtis barreled into the kitchen. Stew's boys.

"Hey, when did *you* get back?" Kevin asked me. He was the oldest, twelve, soon to be thirteen, and a pain in the butt. He thought he knew everything, and hung with this gang of boys who liked to toss their hair back all the time. Curtis was ten, soon to be eleven, and still okay-cute.

"Years ago," I said.

"Yeah, right," said Curtis. "Like, maybe minutes."

"She's joking," said Kevin, playfully pushing Curtis. "Or being sarcastic, because that's her middle name."

"Yeah, that's what Dad calls you," said Curtis. "*Holly Sarcastic Callahan*."

"Let's eat," said Stew.

We all sat down, and although I'd like to say "as a family," that doesn't work for me. We weren't this big happy family Stew tried to make out we were. They were a family. We were a family. And together we were two families. Not one. Well, sort of, because my mother was like a switch hitter. The platter of steaks made their way around the table, as did the salad, potatoes, and mushrooms.

"Looks good," I said. "Steaks are perfect." This was said without any sarcasm, because they did look good and I was hungry, so it was the truth.

"Thank you, Holly," said Stew.

Silence hovered above the table, as everyone hunkered over their meal, cutting steaks and chomping on lettuce like rabbits.

As I ate, I waited. The life talk was on its way. The Stew TED talk. Stew liked to play a sharing game during dinner, and we had to go around the table and talk about our day. Stew thought that all his dinner speeches could be inspirational TED talks. Um ... no.

It took all of thirty seconds before Stew said, "So, Holly, let's talk about what happened today. If that's okay. We can start with you."

"Maybe not tonight, Stew," said my mother. "Holly's had a rough day."

Great, let's ease into this gently. Thanks, Stew.

"It's okay, Mom. I'm not sure there is much to tell." I cut my steak and my fork scraped the plate, the noise bouncing off the walls. Tears welled behind my eyes, but there was no way I would cry, not here, not at the dinner table, not in front of Stew. If I broke down, there'd be no end to his psychological chatter. It'd be a "you-know-you-can–talk-to-us" kind of conversation. No, thanks. Especially not the "us."

I inhaled a big breath, knowing I'd started, so I might as well finish. "I didn't make it—end of story."

"I'm sorry to hear that," he said.

Yeah, right. "Thanks," I said.

"You got cut," said Kevin.

"Yes. I. Did. I'm done my sharing. Who's next on your hit list, Stew?" My appetite was disappearing, the steaks now looking like slabs of cow.

"I know what it's like," said Curtis, from across the table.

I glanced at Curtis, and it was true, he did know, because he had been cut from the spring lacrosse team he'd wanted to make. I'd felt for the kid, because he genuinely loved playing the sport, spent hours outside with his stick and ball.

"I know you do," I said softly. "Thanks, Bud."

"Sometimes in life," said Stew, ruining the actual real moment I was having with Curtis, "things have a reason for happening."

Here we go. The life conversation is now going to blast off, then just sputter and fall in the dirt.

"Isn't that the cliché—'Everything happens for a reason'?" I popped a mushroom in my mouth.

"What he means," said my mother slowly, "is that sometimes, life has unexpected moments."

"O-kay, Mom," I said, without rolling my eyes, but barely. "Thanks for that insight." What was going on with my mother? Stew was really rubbing off on her, and not in a good way. She used to be fun, and also slightly sarcastic. A much better version of her.

She put her fork down, and I noticed her hands were shaking. "And these moments can be positive or negative," she said. "But life is about twists and turns. Sometimes something negative gets turned into a positive."

"Mo-o-om," I said. "Seriously! You're going in circles."

"Your mother is right," said Stew. "When one door shuts, another one opens."

Oh, boy, did I want to roll my eyes and say something really snarky. Cliché city.

"I'm not a quitter," I said. Somehow, though, I knew this wasn't about me. As usual.

"We have some news," said my mother quickly.

WTF. They were getting married. The steak that had just tasted so good rolled around and around in my stomach, making me want to barf. Today, of all days, I couldn't handle this announcement. Did they think it would cheer me up? Give me a reason to get over my being cut? Make my summer better? Spin my negative into a positive? What if she asked me to be her Maid of Honor?

Stew put down his knife and fork and took my mother's hand in his.

Oh, yeah, it was coming. I glanced at Curtis, and he was stabbing his steak, obviously not clueing in. Kevin kept eating, head buried, hair hanging in front of his face, oblivious to anything around him.

Stew smiled and squeezed my mother's hand. She had this weird, glazed look on her face, and his smile spread from ear to ear. I put my fork down, leaned back, and crossed my arms over my chest. "Okay, you two, get this announcement over with. Spill it."

My mother put a little smile on her face and squeezed Stew's hand back. The nauseating touching I could definitely do without.

"Curtis, Kevin," said Stew. "Heads up. This is important for all of us. This is one of those twists in life that will have a positive effect on each one of us."

They both put their forks down and glanced at their father.

My mother opened her mouth to speak, when Stew said, "We're having a baby!"

I was speechless.

SPEECH-LESS.

"You're what?" Curtis asked.

"Gross," said Kevin. "That means you stuck your penis in her vagina." He flicked his hair. "That's from health class."

"I don't think we need to say it like that at the dinner table, Kevin," said Stew. "Making a baby between two people who love each other is wonderful."

"You had sex," said Kevin, singing his words. "You ... had ... sex."

"Sex?" Curtis howled in laughter. "Sex! That's funny."

"You don't even know what sex is," said Kevin. He

hit Curtis on the shoulder.

"Hey, don't hit me." They started doing their fighting thing at the table and, in the process, a glass tipped over. Stew jumped up to get the paper towels. So much for the announcement. I watched the puddle of milk get bigger and bigger, the liquid drip onto the floor, and I did nothing to clean it up. I just stared at it—drip, drip, drip.

There was a part of me that wanted to laugh at the absolute absurdity of this situation, but I couldn't, because inside I was ready to crack. Finally, I took my gaze off the milk and I stared at my mother, making her look at me. "Mom, tell me this is a joke?" I tried to keep my voice calm.

"It's not a joke, Holly. We're very excited. And hope you are, too."

"Um ... do you guys know there is something called contraception?"

"Holly, this is exciting for all of us," said Stew. "We're bringing new life into the world. A little person who will be a part of all of us at this table. This is a beautiful start for us as a family."

"You're serious? Exciting? No. This is just *fucked* up."

"You swore," said Curtis.

"You guys should have used condoms," said Kevin. "You can buy them in a vending machine."

With everything that had happened today, I couldn't deal with this. My body was shaking; my heart pounded through my ratty old tank top. I threw my napkin on the table, pushed my chair back, and stomped out of the dining room. I was so stunned that I tripped on Kevin's bike helmet that was halfway up the stairs. The boys left their crap everywhere, and now there was going to be a baby in this house.

A BABY!

I kicked the helmet and sent it flying, where it landed at the bottom and skidded across the hardwood. I heard someone get up from the table, but I kept moving up toward my bedroom. I slammed the door and flopped on my bed.

How could she do this?

My mother was having a baby at the age of forty-five. Forty-five! And I had no choice but to have the summer from hell while my mother was pregnant.

You Are My Sunshine

Unlike Holly,
I had a
dad who loved me,
would never have
abandoned me.
Seeing her pain,
because of a deadbeat dad
and a distracted mom,
makes me remember.
I sat on my bed
and I was five, I think.
Yeah, five.
Little teeth still. Wispy blonde hair.
Earlier that day
I'd skinned my knee.
Mommy, sing that song.
You are my Sunshine, my only sunshine.

(I bet you know this tune.)

Mommy sang clear.

Daddy came in my room.

Can I sing, too?

He sat on my canopy bed

and it sank

beside me.

He wrapped his arms

around my

body,

and I felt all warm inside.

I forgot about the

skinned knee

because

he made me happier

than sunshine.

Daddy sang.

My mom and I laughed and laughed.

Daddy stopped singing.

Am I off key? he asked.

Yeeeeeesssss.

He tickled me. Tickles of love.

Now, he hurts

and neither the song
nor sunshine
make him happy.
I want to take away
his pain,
because he took
mine away
when I was five.

Chapter 4

I lay on my bed and stared at the posters of female athletes on my white walls. Serena Williams. Hayley Wickenheiser. Megan Rapino. Christine Sinclair. Silken Laumann. They'd all made it big time. I'd got cut today. I read up on athletes all the time, from all eras, and watched motivational movies and interviews, and I knew that the female athletes on my wall also had their ups and downs. Of course, that didn't stop the throbbing in my heart from being cut. I had to get over it, and I would, somehow.

But getting over the *baby* was another deal.

My posters were tacked onto white walls, because I'd refused to paint them when we moved, thinking this wasn't going to be permanent. *Stupid me.* Posters, I could take with me. I thought maybe the relationship wouldn't work out, and Mom and I would be in our own place again in a few months. I never visualized my mother with Stew forever.

Lorna Schultz Nicholson

But now my mother was having a *baby*. *His baby*. *Stew's baby*. What a nightmare.

My body sank into the mattress on my bed, and I felt like I had a heavy barbell on my chest, one I couldn't push up. I closed my eyes, and tried to drown out the sounds of the voices from downstairs, but they floated up the stairs, anyway.

When my phone rang, I rolled my head, picked it up, and saw it was Kash. Lucky her. She was still in St. Catharines, training, and would be there until she left for Europe.

"Hey," I said.

"Hey," she said back, "How are you doing? I've been thinking about you all day. You okay? How was the drive to good old Bracebridge? I miss you already."

"Am I okay? That's an interesting question for my day."

"So sucks."

"Oh, there's more," I said. "Wait until you hear what's shaking here in the land of Super-Stew."

"Spill."

"You ready for this?" I paused for a split second. "My mother ... is preggers, as in knocked-up. By Stew, of all people."

"Cut the shit! She's what?"

"You heard me. My mother is having a *baby*." I still couldn't comprehend that this was happening, and saying it just sounded so weird. "Apparently, I'm getting a brother or sister, whether I want to or not."

"Did she and Super-Stew plan this? How long have they been together again?"

"Maybe one year, tops. I have no idea if this is planned, or a big fat ooops." I stared at Serena Williams. I loved her tough, no-shit attitude, her style of dress. Good for her for wearing a catsuit at the French Open and a tutu at the U.S. Open. But more than that, I loved how she could smack that green ball. I could smack a ball right now.

"Hopefully, an oops," said Kash.

"I didn't ask questions," I said, "because I was seriously stunned over the *big announcement. And* they told us all at dinner, on today of all days, so thanks for that. I think they actually thought it would make me happy and excited, and I'd forget about getting cut. Are you kidding me?"

"They told you at dinner? Today? After you'd just come home from racing your heart out."

"That's how it went down."

"Your mother didn't tell you by yourself, to prepare you?"

"Nope. They wanted to do it as a family. Give me a break. And you know how Ashif and Cassandra are all PDA in the halls at school—that's how disgusting my mom was with Stew. They actually held hands when they made their big announcement." I groaned. "Why didn't I make the crew? I wouldn't have to be here all summer. Now I have to deal with this every day, all day. And I can't even run away to my grandparents in Bathurst, because they're doing some drive down the U.S. coast in their RV for the summer. They're not showing up here until sometime in August."

"This *sucks* for you. I can't believe it. This is like high school crap. Boy and girl have sex, she gets pregnant, and they ruin both families for life."

"I know, right? My life is ruined. My summer is going to totally suck now."

"What *are* you going to do all summer?" Kash asked.

"Well, I bawled my eyes out in the shower, but I'm not quitting, Kash. I'm not. I can't. I'm going to try the recreational program. And I'm going to have to get a job to get out of this house. Hey, if I save enough money, maybe I can leave and get an apartment."

"Okay, okay, that's a bit dramatic. You can suck it up for one year, crying baby and all. They cry all night, you know. My aunt's baby wailed. But then ... *dun-da-da-dan* ... we're off to Penn or UVic or somewhere, and living in a dorm."

"Can't we go next year, skip senior year?" I groaned. I picked some lint off my gray duvet. Gray and white. That was the color of my room, even though my mom had tried to convince me to get something "bright and colorful." She'd made a point of getting me new bedding for "the move." A fresh start, she'd said. I'd been miserable that day, and got the dullest duvet cover I could find. She'd picked the white eyelet to match. Whatever.

"Hey, good on you for trying the rec program," said Kash. "But, FYI, that program might blow. I know that's not what you want to hear, but just giving you a heads-up. I heard Tessa and Madison might go out for it."

"Oh, great." I muttered. Madison and Tessa were the big-time school partiers, who also posed as athletes. "Any idea who's coaching?"

"Haven't heard a word."

I sighed. "If it doesn't work, I'm going to train my butt off at the Sportsplex on the Concept2. Not the same, but it's all I can do. I'm gonna have to get out of this house, or I'll be in my boring bedroom for the entire summer. God help me. First, I had to move in with Super-Stew and his kids, and now there's going to be a *baby*."

"Hey, if your mom can get some action, so can you." Kash laughed. "Find some guy and have a titillating summer fling. Just remember, I'm the first one you tell when you do the popping."

"Titillating? Really, Kash? Is that like a summer thesaurus word? As if that's going to happen here." The heaviness appeared again, and I squeezed my eyes shut. The last thing on my mind was having a boyfriend. I didn't want to have time for that.

"Plus, you're gone," I said quietly. "How will I ever meet anyone without you? Guys only talk to me to get to you."

Once, when we were hanging at the Yorkdale mall in Toronto, Kash got asked by some man if she wanted to model. She laughed in his face and told him she was an athlete, not a model. She's seriously gorgeous with her Dutch genes. Zits are non-existence on her face. I touched my chin and felt the one that was prime-for-picking.

"That's bull," she said. "I'm the Jolly Green Giant or Big Bird. Guys are petrified of me."

"Yeah, right," I muttered.

"Here's the facts, girl. Our training kills the social life. We go to bed at, like, nine. But you could give it a go this summer. Your one and only chance."

"I'd trade a summer of fun for a summer of rowing, any day of the week. I wish I could have that seat race back, do it over again and win."

"What happened, anyway?" Kash asked.

A knock on my door sounded loud and clear.

"Just a sec," I said to Kash. I pulled my phone away from my mouth. "Yeah," I said to whoever was at my door.

"Holly, it's Mom."

I put the phone back up to my face. "I better go. My mom wants to talk."

"Good luck with that."

"Thanks."

I pressed END, but I didn't get off my bed when I called out, "What do you want?"

My mom slowly opened my bedroom door and stepped inside my room, shutting the door behind her. "I thought we should talk," she said.

I stared at her as she walked toward me, and that's when I noticed her boobs. How could I not have seen that they were bigger? Rounder? Fuller? *Baby boobs*. And that she looked like she'd gained five pounds. She'd always had a bit of a tummy, and she usually wore loose tops, but now that I was staring, it was definitely bigger. I'd been too absorbed in my training to notice anything about her.

"Like talking is going to help," I said. "The sperm and egg have already bonded, Mom."

She sat down on my bed anyway, and tried to touch my hair, but I jerked away. "Don't," I said. "Save it for the *ba-by*."

"Holly, I know this is a shock for you."

"Shock's a good word." Now I stared at my poster of Hayley Wickenheiser. She'd had the guts to go to Europe and play on a men's hockey team. And she'd participated in the summer *and* the winter Olympics. She could shoot the puck as fast as the men.

"I realize how hard this might be for you," said my mother.

Hard. Hard was working your ass off in a boat. Hard was training every single day, lifting weights, running hills. Hard was being tested on an ergometer, seat racing over and over, doing all that work, then getting cut. This wasn't hard. It was just stupid.

"I wish you'd quit saying that," I said. "Find another line." I stared at Silken Laumann. She was a rower from the 90's, and a *huge* hero of mine. She'd been injured in this awful rowing accident ten weeks before the Olympics in 1992. The year before, she'd won the world championships in single sculls rowing. But then she was warming up for her race and had a boat collision that shattered her leg. Silken was told by doctors she might never row again. She had five operations. Five. And got back in her boat and competed at that Olympics, and she won the bronze medal. What a comeback.

"I'm forty-five, Holly," said my mother. "I didn't ever think I would have another baby. And now I've got a new life growing inside me. This is almost like a miracle. It's proof that something can happen when you least expect it."

"Yeah, *shit* happens when you least expect it." I refused to look at her, and just stared up at my white ceiling.

I'd gotten cut and I had a new family. Double crap in my case. I refused to make eye contact because, while her dreams were coming true—even though I didn't know anything about these dreams of hers—mine were being put on hold.

"I only had you for all those years," she said, "and I was happy. But when I met Stew, things changed. He's a good man, Holly. And a terrific father."

"He's annoying." Now I looked at her, right in the eyes. But when I saw the hurt, I shrank a little inside.

My mom's hurt turned pretty quickly to her stink-eye look. "That's unkind, and I didn't raise you to be like that," she said.

I had to turn away from her. "Do Grandma and Grandpa know?"

"Not yet. I wanted to tell you first."

"They're going to freak."

"I think they'll be happy for me. For us, Holly."

"I don't think so. I'm not sure they even like Stew." I kept my gaze on the ceiling.

"Of course, they do. He's a good, decent man and you know it. The two of you, well, you're just different, and that's okay."

"Thank God for that," I said.

"Holly, there's lots of room for different in this world."

"Mom, there's different and then there's, like I said, annoying. I still can't believe you've hooked up with someone like him. He drives me crazy with his *happy-happy* attitude about everything. Let's all chat about this and that, and look at the bright side of everything. Sometimes there's no bright side to look at. He's a self-help junkie, and now he's going to be in my life *forever*. We were *us*, now we're *them*. It's like a little spill became a big blob."

"Holly, I don't need your permission here."

"Obviously."

"But I would, in time, like you to be happy for me, for us. I know that might not happen overnight. And I do know today was a blow for you. I understand how hard you worked to make that boat."

"Neither of you understands what it meant to me. If you did, you wouldn't have made your big announcement today."

She sighed and gave me a sad smile. "I'm sorry," she said. "Stew was just so excited that he blurted it out. I'd planned to wait until after your tryouts were over. You were so down in the car, I just couldn't tell you on the drive back."

"You're probably glad I didn't make it, so I could be home for your big *family* reveal."

"Holly, that's not true. But when you didn't make it today, Stew thought that the announcement would be okay, might start the summer off on a positive note. We've seriously been waiting for a good time. We thought it might soften the blow, give you something to look forward to. And I thought it would be so fun if you were here to be involved, come to appointments with me, hear the heartbeat. I'm truly sorry the announcement hit you so hard, and if I could take it back, I would, and tell you on a different day, when you were feeling ready for the news."

I sat up. "Ready for the news? You should have told me in private. Not in front of the entire clan." I refused to call them family, because they weren't my family.

She nodded. "I understand your point."

"Gee, thanks. Score one for Holly." I stared at my posters of Megan Rapino and Christine Sinclair. Man, could those chicks run. Their moves with the soccer ball were incredible. Behind the back, kick, land it, and kick again. Head it. In-sane. I may have scored one with my mom, but I sure didn't score one on the water today.

A wave of exhaustion landed on me like heavy rain. I lay down on the bed, curled into a ball, facing the wall, away from my mother's gaze. This time when my mother touched me, I let her, for no other reason than I couldn't move. I didn't have a single ounce of energy to bat her away.

"When's the baby due?" I muttered.

"Around the beginning of December. Maybe we'll have a Christmas baby. That would be exciting for all of us."

Math is my strong subject, but any idiot could figure out that she'd been hiding this from me for a month. It was the end of June now. Come to think of it, I hadn't seen her with that wine glass in hand for a while now. And she'd been going to bed at nine every night. Sleeping in on weekends. She'd told me she was busy at work, run off her feet. Why didn't I clue in?

"How long have you known?" I asked.

"I wanted to wait the three months and a little more," she said. "Especially being my age. My chances for miscarriage are higher. But so far, I'm having a healthy pregnancy."

"You didn't answer my question."

"Maybe a month and a bit. It was important to wait."

"You were pregnant when we moved. And you didn't tell me?"

"You were rowing, Holly, getting ready to go to St. Catharines for the Canadian High School Regatta. Then you were writing exams, finishing your year at school."

"Was that Stew's idea? To hold off on filling me in on some really important detail that would affect my life?"

"It was both of us. We just wanted to make sure the baby was healthy and I wasn't going to miscarry. And we wanted you to get through your school year without interruption. We thought the summer would be perfect."

I closed my eyes. "I'm tired," I said. "I can't deal with this anymore."

By Chance

Do you believe in
chance meetings?
That two people can
meet
at exactly
the right moment?
Or maybe
you believe these meetings
have been
orchestrated?
(I might believe this now.)
Or maybe you believe
in none of that.
That's your choice.
Whatever you believe
is what you
believe.

Lorna Schultz Nicholson

Just know,
I'm watching,
hoping
a connection
will
right
my wrongs.

Chapter 5

I woke up in the morning with the puffiest face ever. Too much crying. As I lay on my bed, I heard both Stew and my mom leave for work. The cars started. Backed out the driveway. And still I waited, until I knew no one would run back in for keys, or a forgotten lunch. My mom had taken the boys with her, as she was dropping them off at some summer camp, where they did crafts that neither of them wanted to do. When I was sure they were all gone, I got up, went down to the kitchen, and sat down at the table with a glass of water. And I just sat there, staring into space.

Then it hit me. *What was I going to do?*

My whole summer plan had been focused on making the crew, training in St. Catharines, then traveling to Europe, and now I was back in Bracebridge without my best friend, Kash.

What was I going to do *all summer long?*

Lorna Schultz Nicholson

No rowing. No BFF. No grandparents to hide out with.

One big happy family. Yeah, right.

The minutes ticked by, and I just sat, unable to move. Because I didn't know what to do. For the entire spring, my schedule had been jam-packed. I got up early every morning to row and then, because our coach was driven, he got us afternoon rows and weight room time. We ran, and trained, and every weekend we were off for regattas. Sometimes, we left on Thursday morning, so I missed a lot of school. In my spare time, I played catch-up. Then exam time came, and I hunkered down and studied 24/7. Good grades are important to me as well. Oh, and throw a mid-May move into that schedule. I thought about that move. Mom had rushed us out of our small but comfy house because she was pregnant. I know that now. But I sure didn't know it then. My mom and I had lived in the same small three-bedroom house for fifteen years, which meant we had stuff. It had taken a full month of weekends to sort through our crap, and a gazillion trips to the Salvation Army.

Now, here I was in a strange, much bigger, house with little that looked familiar. Even though I didn't have to switch schools, we'd changed neighborhoods, and it just felt like I'd been dropped off a cliff into a ravine. I glanced up at the clock. I'd been sitting for an hour. This had to stop. I picked up my phone and saw a text from my grandparents.

We heard the news!! How do you feel about it?

Had Mom phoned them about me not making the team? Or were they talking about the *baby*? I quickly phoned them, hoping they'd be able to answer

"Holly," said Gram. "How are you, honey?" Her voice sounded like she cared, and it also sounded like she was in the RV, on the road somewhere.

"I'm okay. I don't know if you've talked to Mom yet, but I, uh, didn't make the rowing team."

"We know. We're so sorry. You worked so hard, too." She paused for a second. I could hear my Gramps in the background, muttering about something. Then Grandma said, "Your mom, she also told us we're going to be grandparents again."

"Yeah," I said. "Kind of crazy, if you ask me."

"You've had a lot of adjustments lately, but it'll be good. Babies are always a good thing."

Was everybody happy about this but me? I thought for sure my grandparents would hate the idea. "Babies cry," I mumbled.

"That they do. What are your summer plans now that you're not rowing?"

I exhaled. "I'm not too sure."

"You'll figure it out. You always do. I might lose you. We're heading through the mountains."

"Okay, I'll let you guys go. I can't wait to see you in August. Have fun."

"We love you!"

I pressed END and sighed. Even my grandparents were having a good summer. This so sucked. I got up and put my glass in the dishwasher. The only thing that might feel good, and give me some perspective on my pathetic life, would be to run. I went back to my room and I pulled on a pair of shorts, a sports bra, and tank top. Threw my boring brown hair in a ponytail and tossed on my ball hat. I stepped outside, did a few stretches, and popped in my earpods.

As I ran, I breathed. Really breathed.

The sun sat high in the June sky, and it was scorching down on me. I liked the heat. The movement of my legs, pumping of my arms, and breathing air into my lungs, were all giving me energy. I lengthened my stride and listened to a random country playlist.

I didn't have a route in mind, but it was like a magnet was guiding me to the Muskoka Rowing Club, my home away from home. No one would be there at this time of day—the summer Learn-to-Row program hadn't started yet. And anyone going out, like the adult recreational program, would have completed their morning practice, and the afternoon rows wouldn't start until later in the evening. There might be a few mothers in the park, but that would be it.

How was I going to go from rowing every morning before school and every afternoon after school, in a boat that flowed, with a coach who cared, to recreational rowing?

And how was I going to deal with my mother's expanding stomach?

A baby? Seriously. What was she thinking?

Sweat beaded on my face, trickled down my chest and back. I kept running. Seven more minutes and I would be at the club. All I wanted to do was sit by the Muskoka River to cool off, outside and inside. Mostly inside.

I rounded the corner to Kelvin Grove Park, and ran down the road to the rowing clubhouse. When I got there, I stopped running and wiped the sweat off my brow.

Quiet. Serene. No one was at the park this morning.

The boathouse was small and housed the few boats our club owned, some used for the high school program. There were also singles that were privately owned. I walked by the front of the boathouse, and that's when I saw the poster for summer recreational rowing on the locked door. I stopped and read it. It started tomorrow morning.

I walked down to the water, sat on the end of the dock, and watched the river water move. How could one body of water be so different, every minute of every day? It intrigued me. Even in winter, I would put on my winter running gear and come down, just to be close to it. It slapped against the wood. Ducks quacked as they floated their way across the water, bobbing with the waves, ducking every now and again to stick their butts in the air. In May, the fuzzy little baby ducks swam behind their mother. Now those babies were older, and mama duck wasn't so paranoid about where they were going.

Maybe I should have been a duck.

I could have left my mother a lot earlier.

I took off my shoes and socks and dangled my feet in the water. I leaned back and lifted my face to the blue sky and morning sun. The slight breeze created a little chop, so the sound of the water hitting the side of the dock was rhythmic, hypnotizing. Questions circled my brain, like the hawk above me, hovering over the water, looking for a fish to jump. It swooped down. And missed.

One thing for sure was that I needed a job and I needed to train. Would that occupy sixteen hours a day? Sleep would take care of eight to ten—or twelve, if I pushed it. Training could take up a good three hours, if I went morning for the recreational program, and night at the Sportsplex for dry land training.

What about friends? It's hard to keep friendships when you're an athlete, training all the time. I missed parties, because I was too tired or had a race coming up. My friends were my rowing buddies, and I had no other real friends to call and say, "Hey, let's go out." And I most certainly didn't want a boyfriend like Kash had suggested.

My mind swirled.

I had to work and save money, because who knew what would happen when that baby arrived. They were going to need a crib and stroller, and all that "stuff" that went with babies. Where would the kid sleep? I'd already taken over the spare room. The boys had their rooms. I'd probably get the kid in mine.

I had to go away to university now, somewhere far, so as not to be in that house. But Mom had been stalling on that one lately, and now with the baby, and Stew, maybe we didn't have the money for me to go away. Maybe she gave her money, my school money, to her new *family*.

First, though, I had to endure Stew all summer long.

All. Summer. Long.

Super-happy-Stew, always wanting more from me than I could give.

I'm only trying to help.

Everything happens for a reason.

Things have a way of working out.

Life is about experiences.

Yada, yada, yada.

We're having a baby!

My stomach was knotting into a big ball. It clenched in and out like an elastic being snapped. Everything DID NOT happen for a reason. What a stupid, stupid, stupid saying. What possible reason was there for me being cut? To make me sad? Hurt? To be home for the news of my mother's pregnancy? My body started shaking. The stomach clenching continued. My breathing became shallow.

I couldn't catch my breath.

What was happening to me?

Without thinking about what I was doing, or where I was, I screamed.

It started in the bottom of my stomach and came up through my lungs, picking up air, and more air, up my windpipe, and then it just exploded. Shrill. Piercing. A noise I had never made before in my entire life.

And when I was finished, it left me breathless.

My shoulders shaking, I started sobbing again, feeling like I was drowning in the water in front of me. I closed my eyes and I tightened my fists. Every muscle in my body was tense. I wasn't giving up, no matter what. I was going to fulfill my dreams, and that was all there was to it. I would find a way.

I tried to scream again, but this time it wasn't the same, and the scream actually hurt my throat. It was as if I'd let it all out, had my time, and this was an afterthought.

All I could think of now was that I was a fighter.

My stomach hurt. My lungs felt depleted. I exhaled, stale awful air.

"Are you ... okay?" The voice behind me was gravelly.

I sat still, like a steel post.

"Are you okay?" the low voice, obviously male, asked again.

Connections

Sometimes
you know someone
for years,
maybe you even
spend every
day at school
with them,
maybe you work on
projects together
or live in the
same neighborhood
but there is
zero
connection.
Like no sparks.
And then
you meet

Lorna Schultz Nicholson

someone

in some random

place

and you're

totally different personalities,

maybe not even the same age,

and something clicks,

wires are

zapped.

Chapter 6

"I'm ... I'm fine." I managed to get the words out.

The man looked at me and nodded. One little nod, his scraggly graying hair moving slightly. Was he homeless? Looking for money? Bristly face, sunken eyes, weathered skin, gray hair. But clean-ish looking clothes: cargo shorts, the ones with the massive pockets on the sides, and a golf shirt, and Nike flip-flops.

I stood up and wiped off the dock debris that was now sticking to my legs, just to look casual, and not like an idiot who had just screamed. I quickly put on my socks and shoes to get ready to leave.

"I better get going," I said, hoping my voice didn't sound shaky. This was so embarrassing.

Again, he gave me one nod.

I started to walk toward him, my head lowered, but still glancing at him out of the corner of my eye. Once I got close to him, he moved aside and let me pass.

I was well past him when I heard his voice.

"I hope you're okay." He said the words so softly, I almost didn't hear him.

I turned to glance at him, just to see if he was following me. But he wasn't. "I'm fine," I said. I took another step, moving away from him.

"I know it's none of my business, but you didn't sound okay."

I kept walking forward, but I also kept looking back. He hadn't moved toward me. Not even an inch. I don't think he'd even moved a muscle. He was just so still, standing there with his hands in his pockets, his shoulders slumped, staring into space like a zombie. I got that. I'd sat for an hour this morning.

I turned away from him. Time to run home. I was sticking my earbuds in my ears, when I saw that the boathouse door was open. How had I not heard him opening the door? Those doors squeaked all the time. Maybe he hadn't seen me, either, until I screamed.

Then I saw a single boat cradled in the stretchers. It hadn't been there when I arrived. He was the only one who could have taken it out. It must be his. If he was stealing it, he wouldn't have put it on stretchers.

Was he a member of the Muskoka Rowing Club? I sure as heck didn't know everyone, especially all the adult recreational rowers.

I turned around, just to see where he was. He still hadn't moved. Now he was staring out at the water, and he had this dull, sunken look on his face, and it just punched me in the gut. It was like his emotions were oozing from his body and out into the world. And they weren't light and fluffy emotions, either. These were the dark, something-is-weighing-you-down emotions.

I couldn't help it; I softened toward him. His painful look was how I felt. I got it. I did. Although I had shrieked like a crazy woman, he looked like he couldn't scream, even if he tried.

Just as I was about to keep going, he turned and our eyes met.

"I'm sorry," he said to me.

"Sorry for ... uh ... what?"

He sighed and shrugged. "Whatever it was that made you scream." He shoved his hands deeper in his pockets and his shoulders caved down. He started walking toward me, but stopped, not getting too close. It was like there was an invisible line he couldn't cross, unlike Stew, who always invaded my personal space.

"Yeah, well," I said. "I'm sorry, too." And I was. For screaming, and for my life as of yesterday.

"For what?" He attempted a little smile.

"For piercing your eardrums."

"It was a pretty good one." One side of his lip curled, but it wasn't a smirk, nor was he mocking me, laughing at me. Nothing like that. No, it was almost as if he understood my scream, even though he knew nothing about me.

"I tried my best," I said.

"Well, there's no reason to ever be sorry for trying your best," he said. "You screamed. So what? You must have had a reason."

"Maybe," I said.

He curled up both sides of his mouth in a semi-smile. "By the way, I wish I could scream like that."

I started to laugh, and it felt good. "Yeah, well, I've had practice. I'd like to say I went to school for it, was trained by a specialist, but that would be a lie."

He actually smiled, too, a full one, cheek to cheek. "You have a good sense of humor."

"Not everyone thinks that," I said.

"So? What does it matter what people think?"

"Good point," I said.

"Sometimes life just gives you something to scream about."

"That's for sure," I said. I sighed.

"And when the time is right, let it go."

"I did."

"You feel better."

"Kind of. Not sure it changed anything, though."

"Ain't that the truth." And just like that his smile was gone, and the vacant look returned to his eyes.

"I better get back to my run," I said.

He tilted his head. "Are you a rower?" he asked. "You look like one."

This time, it was my turn to just nod. No words. Was I? Still? Maybe not this summer, but I was. I nodded.

"Good for you," he said.

"It's a great sport," I said.

"The best and the worst." He ran his hands through his hair and sighed loudly.

Odd comment? But in a way, he was right. It was the best feeling to win after racing, but the training before the race was grueling. Like, hours and hours. And then there was the getting cut shit, after all that work. That wasn't exactly the best, and more like the worst. I glanced at the single again.

I pointed to the boat. "Why do you have the single on stretchers?"

"It needs to be rigged." He said this matter-of-factly.

"It is yours?"

"It is now."

"Owning a single would be a dream come true," I said. Kash and I had talked about one day rowing in singles. But you had to buy a boat, and they cost a lot of money. Money I didn't have. Money that would probably go to a top-end stroller.

"Yes, it can be a dream come true." He sighed, and ran his hands through his hair. "But ..." his words trailed off.

I waited for him to finish.

He looked at me and said, "Some dreams die." Then he started walking toward the boat bay. "I better get back to my *Lilybean*."

"Sure. Um ... nice chatting," I said.

Head down, he moved to where the boat was on the stretchers. Beside the boat, I saw a red toolbox on the ground, so he was probably rigging it.

"I'll let you get to work," I said.

"Until next time," he said, giving me a little one finger wave.

"Yeah, for sure—have a good day," I said.

"I'll try," he replied. "Not guaranteeing anything, though."

I started running, without even turning on my playlist. The entire way back, I thought about the man, and who he was, but also who he was rigging the boat for. Was he a coach? Or was it his boat and he rowed it? He didn't look like someone who would put on spandex and get in a boat and sweat it out. But looks can be deceiving.

Maybe he was going to be the club's summer coach. But did he think I was in the recreational program?

He did say *until next time*.

Did I look like a recreational rower? That made my stomach hurt. And my head. But most of all, my heart.

Balance

The tricky
part of being an
amateur athlete
is balance.
It's all about
combining
the highs and lows
winning and losing
determination and dedication
with family and friends
work and money.
Holly's balance
right now
is off.
She has to work,
manage this new
fam-jam,

and try
to carve out
a space in her life
for her goals
and dreams.
Every amateur
athlete needs
support.
 If she were on a teeter-totter
she would
be up in the air,
flailing,
struggling to get down
to the ground,
being bumped
until it hurt.
Her balancing
act
is going to
be a real
bitch
to figure out.

Chapter 7

When I got home, I showered, made myself a smoothie, and sat down at the kitchen table with my computer. The Bracebridge newspaper sat on the table, and I took a quick glance at it. Seriously, who reads a newspaper anymore? Stew did. He liked seeing his real-estate ads.

I picked it up quickly to toss it aside, and that's when I saw the headline for the sports section. My stomach heaved. They'd written an article about our high school four, and how all of us had been selected to try out for the Canadian Junior Team. It was a big deal in Bracebridge, us being local athletes and all. Of course, most of the article was about who had made it. Rah-rah for the Muskoka Rowing Club because three of the four made it! Everyone but me. Their names were the highlights. And, yes, there was my name, too, as the one who didn't make it. Great.

I read out loud. *"Holly Callahan is the only rower from*

the Canadian Secondary School Rowing Association's gold medalist coxed four who didn't make this Junior National Team, although she was the last one to be sent home. Still, quite an accomplishment for our small Muskoka Rowing Club."

I started ripping the paper. Rip. Rip. Rip. Paper flew everywhere.

I kept ripping. And shredding. Until the table and floor were covered with little pieces of newsprint. Exhausted again, I sat there amid torn paper, and thought about the last time I'd been in the newspaper, and how positive the article had been. Our crew had been featured on the front page of the sports section after our win, photo included. We were also honored at the final school Athletic Award Banquet. My mother had come to the banquet.

OMG. She'd been pregnant then.

I sat and sat. My body too heavy to move. Finally, I looked around at the mess I'd made with the torn newspaper. I couldn't leave it for Mom to pick up, even though I was mad at her. I slowly picked up every piece, tossing it all in the recycling bin. Then I sat back down and rebooted my computer.

Get over it, Holly.

I had to look for a job. Most of the job listings that came up were for fast food places. I guess I was going to have to work at McDonald's, and smell like grease for my entire summer. But it was money, and I could bike to work. I shut my computer, went to my bedroom, and got dressed into something more job-application appropriate. A pair of black pants and a summer blouse.

Then I headed to the garage and took out my bike, my only mode of transportation.

As I was riding, I cruised by Antonio's, the pizza restaurant Mom and I used to go to all the time, and quickly made a turn into the parking lot. It was definitely a step up from McDonald's.

The air-conditioning in the restaurant dried the little bit of sweat off me. Okay, how to do this? I'd never actually applied for anything before. I approached the desk and asked the girl working the front—who wore an Antonio's logo T-shirt and a name tag with *Amaya* — for the manager who accepted job applications.

She reached under the counter and pulled out a two-sided application form. "I'm the hostess. But fill this out," she said.

"Do I hand it back to you?" I asked.

"I guess so," she said.

Okay, this wasn't starting off so good. I took the form, which was on a clipboard, and sat down at a small table to fill it out. When I came to the experience part, I hesitated. I'd not really had any jobs to speak of, except babysitting, and tutoring my rowing friend in math, although she never paid me. But how did someone get experience without being able to get experience?

I sat there, thinking about what to write. I tapped my pencil. Nothing. This was useless. What was I thinking? I couldn't just walk into a restaurant and get a job. McDonald's might be easier. I put down the tutoring and babysitting in those work experience blocks, and took the form back to Amaya. She was staring at a sheet that looked like a table plan for the restaurant.

"Thanks," she said, hardly looking at me.

"Um ... should I wait for someone now, or do they call me?" I seriously was not trusting this Amaya to give my application to anyone. She was too busy.

"Usually they call." A group of people came in and she forced a smile.

I moved aside to watch what she had to do.

"Five?" she asked.

"Yes," said the man standing at the front of the group.

Amaya picked up menus and said, "Follow me."

As she was taking them to their table, more groups came in. They waited and when she returned, she started to question them, but then one person in the group asked her a question about gluten-free dishes, and she tried to answer, but didn't really know. I could tell, because Kash is celiac and always has to ask about food. Then, what looked like a server—he was wearing a button-down black shirt—came up and said, "You put that table of five in a section where there isn't a server. And told them yesterday's specials."

She looked down at the chart. And kept staring at it like she was engrossed in a novel. The line kept growing, as more people kept coming through the door. Obviously flustered, she seated another table. Could I even do this job? Did I want this job? I knew I could answer the gluten-free question, though.

A woman in a blue skirt suit came over, and she had a little name tag on that said *Manager*, but nothing else. That's who I had to talk to. She shook her head like she was pissed, took some menus, and guided three people to a table. Amaya came back and went to pick up more menus, when she knocked all the papers onto the floor.

"Nooooooo!" She bent down and started to pick them up.

That was all she needed. I felt for her. I went over and whispered, "I'll do that. You seat the tables."

"Ohmygod. Thank you," she said. She didn't even care that I didn't work there. She stood and told the next group to follow her.

Since no one else came in, I was left alone in an empty lobby. As I picked up the papers, I glanced at them, trying to figure out the floor plan. There were quite a few tables, as it was a good-sized family restaurant, but it seemed fairly straightforward. As I was putting the papers back, the manager returned.

"Who are you?" she asked. She squinted at me as if she was trying to place me. Did she think I was a new employee she couldn't remember?

"Sorry," I said. "I just filled out an application for a job, but then these fell, so I picked them up for Amaya."

"O-kay," she nodded. "Well, thank you," she said. She stared down at the seating chart. Then she said under her breath, "It's not that hard to figure out."

"No," I blurted out. "It's a grid. I'm sure you rotate, depending on servers."

She glanced up at me, and was about to say something, when the same server who had talked to Amaya earlier came up. "She keeps telling the wrong specials."

"I'll talk to her," said the manager.

I figured since they were under stress, I should leave. But with the way things were going, I was sure my application was going to be lost.

"My application is just under the counter," I said. I pointed and tried not to sound too pushy.

Then Amaya came back, and now she was almost crying. "He keeps yelling at me."

"You're telling the wrong specials," said the manager. She spoke quite nicely to her, which impressed me a little. Might be a decent place to work.

"You should hire this girl," said Amaya. She gestured to me. "We need another hostess."

The manager eyed me. "Where did you say your application was?"

"Under the counter." I pointed again to the shelf where I saw Amaya shove it.

The manager pulled out the clipboard and quickly

scanned it. "You don't have any experience." She didn't look up, and flipped the page over.

"No," I said. "But I'm a fast learner. And I tutor math, which means I'm good at math, and that table plan is just simple math." *Did I just say math three times?*

This made her glance up and look at me. Then she cracked a smile. "Let's go sit down and have a chat."

The "chat" was pretty basic, and the manager—who I learned was Bethany Collins—asked me how I would handle different situations, questions about seating people, and rhyming off specials, and what would I do if someone swore at me. I knew swearing back wasn't an option, although that would probably be my first choice. She also asked me about what I would do if someone grabbed my "buttocks." I wanted to say, slap the person and tell them not to grab my ass, but I didn't. I said I would find the manager. She liked that answer.

So ... I got the job, and was immediately put on the schedule. She gave me a menu and told me to memorize it for my first shift, because I had to do a test with the assistant manager. His name was Tim Turner.

As I was leaving, I saw Amaya in the front lobby. "I got the job," I said, holding up my thumb.

She clapped.

Since there were no customers in the lobby, I said, "I have to meet the assistant manager, Tim Turner, to do my oral menu test."

She raised an eyebrow. Then she looked around before she leaned toward me and said, "He's really hot. He's so buff and, apparently, an amazing track-and-field person." She tilted her head and looked at me. "You look fit, too."

"Good to know," I said. "About Tim Turner, that is."

Could it be that maybe I would be working with someone who was an athlete? Since I was also interested in what he was like as the assistant manager, the person I had to take a test for, I asked, "Is he nice or a jerk-face?"

She laughed. "He's a pushover. No worries. I screwed up so many and still got the job."

I nodded. "Thanks for the heads-up."

I had two weekend lunch shifts and three nights, which meant I could row. If I wanted to, that is. But after being at the Rowing Club today, and seeing the poster, I did.

I really did. In fact, more than wanting to, I needed to get back in a boat and grunt and grind, to pull through this shit of a life of mine.

Speak Up

I was amazon tall.
My mother was
only five feet
and weighed 110 pounds.
My dad said
I got his height
but my mother's
spunk.
She taught me to
speak up.
She said:
Be strong with
words and
actions.
That is great advice
until you go
beyond

being kind.
Words have such power and
once said,
they can't
be taken back.
Actions, too.
Both can cause
heartache
if not respected.
So ... my story is this ...
I would take that
day back
if I could.
That day where I said
and did
what
I wanted because
I wanted to,
and hurt
those
who loved
me
the most.

Chapter 8

I went straight from Antonio's back to Stew's house. And since I had time before my mom and the *many people* I lived with got home, I texted Kash, who immediately texted me, sending heart and flower emoji's.

can u talk

yeah

Next thing I knew, my phone was ringing.

"I got a job today," I said. Was I trying to make myself sound important?

"A job. Wow. That was record fast. Where?"

"Antonio's. I'm a hostess. I'll mostly work nights, I hope. So … I can row and train every morning. Gives me all day. I don't start until four on night shifts and eleven on day shifts." I was babbling.

"Any cute guys working there?"

"Didn't see any."

"Don't fight an epic summer," she asked.

"I'm not. I just don't want to be that girl who gave up. You know—her, the one who got cut, didn't make it, cried the blues, and quit. Athletes go through crap and don't give up. Whether it's you're-a-girl shit, or gay shit, or just hard-knocks shit, so many perservere. Many have a lot harder crap to deal with than me. Look at those who deal with racial shit. That's cruel- hard. I can't give in. And that means I don't have time for a boyfriend."

"Okay, okay," she said. "If it was me, I'd be on the hunt."

"Hey, I looked up a few good series to binge watch, so that could liven up my summer." Enough talk of guys.

She laughed. "Remember *Riverdale*? Your mom made killer chicken wings."

Kash used to come over to our "other" house and we'd hang on the sofa for hours. Mom even joined us sometimes. Kash had only been to Stew's house once. And it had been a disaster, because Stew talked ad nauseam that day about his walking on coals. Seriously. He'd just come back from some sales conference, and he'd had an "experience" he would never forget, and wanted to tell us all about it, every last boring detail. Afterwards, up in my room, Kash and I had howled, and pretended we were the ones walking on coals. That's when we nicknamed him Super-Stew.

"Why does everything have to be so complicated when you get older?" I blew out air.

"Holls, this summer is yours," she said. "Get out there and go for it. You make it next year, you're rowing every day, twice a day, and doing workouts. It's exhausting. No time for partying or sex. Let's face facts; we are known as the worst partiers in high school. Early to bed, early to rise, and all that. At the very least, meeting someone might get you away from the newly acquired family that you're being subjected to spending a summer with. How's Mom?"

"She's due in, like, December! Can you believe it? She's known for a month. A month!"

"Shit. Really?"

"I don't want to talk about her, though." And I didn't. I didn't want to talk about anything but our sport. "How's your boat?"

"Good." I heard the evasiveness in her voice, but we were friends. Best friends.

"It's okay," I said. "You can talk about it. I'm done crying."

"You sure?"

"Positive" I flopped down on my bed and stared at my white ceiling.

"Okay," she said quickly, "so, we had such a good workout today. But it was a killer. We had to run grandstands after." Her voice went to a different level, and I could hear the excitement, and I was happy for her, but the sinking feeling returned to my body.

My body stilled and I closed my eyes, and the room almost started to spin. Instead of training my butt off like Kash, I was going to be pulling shifts at an Italian family restaurant. I could feel the boat moving, hear the swooshing of blades entering and exiting the water.

"Grandstands on the first day?" I squeaked the words out. Grandstands were brutal. We didn't have them at our rowing club, like St. Catharines did down in Port Dalhousie, so our coach would make us go to the stairs near the park. We would have forty-five seconds to get to the top and down. Easy, first time, and we got to rest because we could complete in, like, thirty seconds. But by the tenth time, there was no rest. But I'd rather be running grandstands than working in a restaurant.

"So, listen to this," said Kash. "That girl Keira—the one who beat you out—puked. And the coach made her keep going anyway. *After* she puked, we had to dodge the puke. It was gross. But she's such a bitch, so it was funny that she was the one who puked."

"Why is she a bitch?" Yes, I was happy she was a bitch. I'm human. She beat me.

"She's always talking about her high school coach and how amazing he is, and how amazing her high school is, and how they have the best rowing program ever. La-di-da."

"I should have beat her," I said.

"What happened, anyway? We've never talked about that, the actual race."

"I dunno. Nerves? Too many tens and twenties thrown in? Or too much settle after the two-fifty-meter mark. It's hard to say."

"Yeah, maybe. Those hard tens and twenties are a balancing act. You still going out for the rec program?"

"Yeah. I saw the poster today, and they have a workout tomorrow morning." I paused. "It's worth a try, don't you think?" I kind of wanted her approval. Why?

"Oh, yeah, for sure."

"Okay, so tell me more about Keira being a bitch."

The conversation lasted for thirty minutes, and when

I hung up, I just lay on my bed. And stared at my white ceiling. Minutes ticked by. My chest throbbed, pain settling on top of it—that damn weight again. I wished the hurt would go away. Was I going to feel this pain all summer long? I liked hearing the inside scoop from Kash, but it was like I was putting rubbing alcohol in a cut that was still open. And it made me feel like I was on the outside, on the other side of the glass, hands pressed against it, looking in, watching, but not able to go through. I glanced at my hands, the calluses from rowing, knowing I'd done the work, too, but my work hadn't been good enough. They would soon disappear if I didn't row.

I heard my mother come home and I didn't move. The boys were yelling downstairs, obviously pushing and shoving. What did I do to deserve this? They sounded like rabid animals. And soon there would be a baby crying in this house. We were going from a family of two to a family of six.

Six!!!!!!

Okay, now the boys were clearly shouting.

I wanted to leave my mom to the torment of her *new family*, but I figured I should help her. Preggers and all.

I trudged downstairs. "Hi, Mom," I said.

Bags of groceries sat on the kitchen island. I started putting them away.

"How was your day?" she asked me.

So ... the softness in her voice softened me a little, too. "Okay. How was yours?" I put the lettuce and mayonnaise in the fridge. My mother was an emergency room nurse, and she had good, sometimes gory, stories.

"Good."

Nothing followed the *good*. No words about someone needing stitches, someone falling into a campfire, or treating some elderly person for wheezing, who farted with every wheeze. We always used to talk about her job. We had conversations—like, in-depth conversations— until we moved into Stew's house. But this was the worst it had ever been. We were like chess pieces, moving around and around the square board, avoiding each other.

"Do you need help with dinner?" I asked.

"Sure. I can always use an extra hand." She sounded tired. But then again, she was pregnant, and now a stepmother to two loud boys. But this was her choice. *Her choice.* What was that saying? Oh, yeah—you make your bed, now you lie in it. Well, she had lain in it, all right.

I got busy chopping vegetables for a salad, and the

sound of the knife hitting the cutting board was loud because the room was silent. I fiddled with my phone and put on an easy-listening playlist. When had Mom and I come to this? This horrible, awkward twosome that didn't know how to talk to each other, like we were a divorced couple?

I tossed the red peppers into the salad, then I proceeded to cut the cauliflower. "I had pizza at Kash's once," I said to make conversation, "made with a cauliflower crust."

Was I really talking about this? About pizza crust? When we had so much we could be talking about ... like a baby.

But there was this lump in my throat that wouldn't let me ask about the baby. She'd hidden her secret from me for a month, so why should I talk about it. It? Soon enough it would be my brother or sister!

"I've heard about that," she answered. "Good for those who are gluten free. How is Kash? I haven't seen her in a long time. You don't bring her by anymore."

"She won't be around this summer. Lucky her."

"I'm sorry, Holly. You two have always been inseparable."

"Not this year." I threw the cauliflower in the bowl. "I got a job today."

"Oh, my goodness. That was fast. Where?"

"Antonio's. I'm a hostess. I'll be working some nights."

"Nights?" She looked over at me.

"Yeah."

"You haven't done your drivers test yet."

"No time." I threw more cauliflower in the bowl. "I'll ride my bike and do the test in the fall. No biggie. Around the corner and back. I get paid minimum wage, but the manager said I'll also get some tips, because the servers give up a percentage of theirs, and that money gets split up between the bus people and hosts. I'm hoping to bank all my paychecks and save some of my tips, too. The hostess I met today said that sometimes you can even make extra tips if you do a good job."

"I don't know about this, Holly. Can't you get a day job somewhere?"

I put down the knife. I could feel the blood racing through my body. I'd got a job and it wasn't good enough.

"You know what, Mom," I snapped. Something inside me bubbled. Then the words just started flying out of my mouth. "Why don't you live your life, your *pregnant*, let's-be-a-happy-family life, and I'll live mine. You don't need to worry about me, because you have far bigger things to worry about. Like a baby. And making Super-Stew and his bratty boys all comfy-cozy happy."

She inhaled but didn't respond. I hated it when she did that.

"I'll be fine," I continued, since I wasn't getting the rise out of her that I wanted. "I need the money. Kash and I still want to go to Penn."

"Oh," she said.

Uh-oh. That didn't sound good. I glanced at her, and the look on her face was, well, let's just say it wasn't the look I expected or wanted from my comment about going to Penn. I eyed her, knowing something was up. "What?" I snapped again.

She shook her head.

"Don't do that," I said. "You need to tell me something. I can see it in your face."

"Not now, Holly. We have all summer. You've got enough on your plate right now."

"Yes, now," I said firmly.

She sighed. "Well, we were thinking the Orillia Lakehead campus might be an option."

"Lakehead?" Another blindside. "Like the *small* campus in Orillia?"

She nodded.

"You're kidding, right? And who is 'we'?" I used quotation marks for the word "we." As if I didn't know. But I wanted to make her say it.

"It might be an option," she said, ignoring my dig. "Even if just for the first year. You can get most of your basic first-year courses there."

"But they don't even have a rowing program."

"Holly, just look into the school. As an option. We could buy you a car and you could live at home."

"Why would you even want me to stick around?" I glared at her. "You're going to have a *baby* to occupy your time."

The air between us stilled, and she just looked at me, her eyes watering. "Why would you say that?" She put her hand on my shoulder. The touch seared my skin. "Of course, I want you around," she said. "This baby doesn't take away my love for you. And if you lived at home, you and your new little brother or sister could bond. I want that for both of you."

I had no idea how to respond. But then, I didn't have to, because Curtis came sliding in on sock feet, like he was a rock star.

"What's for dinner?" He pretended to play air guitar and was singing at the top of his lungs. And he wasn't a good singer, more of a screecher.

Something was really bugging me about our conversation. I had to speak. "Mom, if you love me so much, why are you discussing my university with Stew behind my back?" I had raised my voice to be heard over Curtis's horrible singing. "Did you put my university money into some sort of family money pot? I hope you didn't, because, FYI, my plans are to go to a university with a *rowing program*. I'm going out for the rec program tomorrow morning so I can keep rowing this summer."

"Holly, please. Let's discuss this another time." Curtis's screeching was increasing in intensity. I could see that she was trying hard not to say anything to him.

"You and *Stew* are making decisions for me." I knew I was being relentless, but I couldn't help myself. "The guy's known me for what ... like, a year. Where is the 'us' in all of this? Me and you?"

"We haven't made any decisions yet. You and I will talk. I promise."

"I sure hope so," I said. "But just know, if I get a scholarship, I'm going with Kash. I'll ask Grandma and Grandpa for the money, because they always support me."

"Holly, enough."

"I don't want Stew involved in this decision!" I had to hold my ground.

Curtis continued to play his air guitar, and the noise was bouncing off my brain. If he didn't stop, I was going to freak. The kid kept going, and when he jumped on the chair for some finale, I screamed, "Stop that!'

He sang at the top of his lungs anyway.

"Shut-up-you-little-fucking-twerp!"

"Holly!" said Mom. "Don't. He's only ten years old."

"So ... now I'm a bad example."

"I didn't say that."

I threw the knife I was using to cut the veggies into the sink and stomped up to my room. When I got up there, I paced back and forth, back and forth, the steam oozing from my skin. My mom and Stew had been talking about my life like I didn't exist, like I wasn't involved in the process. If I could pack a bag and leave, I would. What if I did run away? Where would I go? My grandparents were doing their "senior" road trip, so I couldn't even visit them.

I had nowhere to go.

Not even a dad's house.

Lorna Schultz Nicholson

The Settle

I rowed a lot of
races.
I loved racing,
had the bug
like Holly does.
Early in a
rowing race
after the intense
start
the boat has
to settle.
But if it settles
too much
it loses power.
There is a saying
that applies to
racing

but more to
life.
Don't settle
for anything less.

Chapter 9

My alarm went off at 5:15, and I got right out of bed. As much as I hated getting up in the morning, I also loved it. The initial alarm going off did make me groan, but once I was up, the morning gave me energy.

I was out of the house and on my bike in five minutes, and that included blending my shake. I'd put a bag full of the fruits and veggies together, and had it ready in the freezer to add to some almond milk. Good enough.

When I got to the rowing club, I immediately saw Madison and Tessa. When they saw me, they waved, so I waved back and walked over to them. I swore Tessa had makeup on.

"Hey," said Tessa. "What are you doing here?"

"Same as you," I said.

I saw Madison nudge her, trying to do it ever so discreetly, when it wasn't.

"Oh, right," said Tessa.

"I think there should be enough for a strong eight," said Madison.

Okay, there wasn't even enough for a strong four, let alone an eight. I glanced at the people who had arrived. I recognized a few from my high school, knowing none of them had rowed before, and some looked super young, were probably junior high, maybe from towns outside of Bracebridge, like Orillia or Gravenhurst.

"Do you know who our coach is?" I asked. I guess I hoped it was the older guy I'd met.

"Some guy from Huntsville," said Madison. "Apparently, he graduated from Western and isn't rowing anymore, so he wants to coach. The person who was supposed to coach can't now, because of personal problems. I guess this guy stepped up, so it's better than no coach."

"So ... someone who has never coached?" I thought about the coaches on the Junior National Team and how much experience they had. Then I had to tell myself that comparing wasn't going to help my mindset.

"Don't think so, but that's okay with *moi*." Madison shrugged. "I just want to do the Canada Day Regatta on Toronto Island. It might only be a thousand meters, so doable with a hangover. It's on the long weekend.

Party time, here we come. I guess it's like a shit show. Can't wait."

Really? That's why she wanted to row? That regatta was in just over a week's time. How good could the boat be by then? Okay, so I was different. I had to remember that, too. Kash and I talked about this all the time. We weren't recreational athletes, but others were. Each to their own. What was I doing here? Oh, right ... giving it a try.

A guy who looked to be in his twenties called all of us into the boat bay, where the eights and fours were stored. I followed and stood in the circle with the eight others. At least we had a coxswain. Being in the bay made me think about the single, and the man I'd met. I'd look later to see if it was still there. He had said the name was *Lilybean*, I think.

"Great to see you all out this morning, La-a-adies."

Bleached blond hair curled over his forehead, and he shook his head to move it. With his raccoon tan lines on his face, he looked more like a surfer than a rowing coach. "My name is Darryl and I'm going to be your coach. How many of you have rowed before?"

Three of us put up our hands. Madison, Tessa, me.

One girl put up her hand halfway and said, "I did 'Learn to Row' last year. Does that count?"

"Sure. Why not," said Darryl, shrugging, oh, so casually.

Learn to Row was like a weeklong camp. No racing, no training, no nothing.

"This will be a fun summer, and I'm ready to get started if you are," said Darryl. "I'll give the new *la-a-adies* a lesson on carrying the boat."

The way he said *ladies* made my blood start to speed up inside my body. I did not, and I mean *did not*, want a coach who was going to act coy and flirt.

"Why don't we take down the oars?" I said to Madison and Tessa.

"Oh, my God," whispered Tessa. "He's soooo cute."

"I love his hair," giggled Madison.

"You're joking, right?" I glared at both of them. "He's our coach."

"It's summer club," said Madison. "Relax."

"I'm going to take down the oars," I said. "So we can actually get on the water for a workout."

But there was no workout. I went for a row in a boat that wouldn't balance. Not even a little bit. The ninety minutes was unbelievably painful. Worse than being in a boat when I first learned. Instead of rowing all eight of us together, we rowed in pairs and fours. I sat a lot and just helped balance the boat. The one time we did try to row as an eight, the boat rocked side to side, and my hands smashed against the gunwales, making my knuckles scream in pain.

Finally, the row was over, and we headed to the dock. The coxswain was new and had no idea how to dock the boat. Darryl ran toward us as we were coming in (way too fast), and grabbed the bow ball, just in time—otherwise, we would have cracked right into the dock.

I didn't talk to anyone, as I slid my oar across and got out of the boat. I undid my oarlock and took my oar up to the boathouse. I'm sure they thought I was a super-bitch, but I didn't care. My summer was sliding further backward. My heart seriously ached.

We lifted the boat out of the water and carried it up on our shoulders. Once it was on its rack, we huddled around Mr. Surfer to be debriefed. There wasn't any reason for me to gather around, because I wasn't coming back, but I did anyway, to be polite. I would tell Darryl after, or maybe cop out and phone him, or worse, text. Yeah, that's what I would do. I couldn't settle and row on a bad crew. The row had been everything I thought it would be, but worse.

After Darryl had finished and had walked away, Madison said, "Woo hoo. This is going to be an epic summer."

I picked up my sweatshirt and started heading toward my bike, when I thought about the man again, and his single. I made a quick detour to the singles boat bay and walked to the back. I looked at the five singles that were in our boathouse. I spotted it.

The *Lilybean*. Funny name for a boat.

I ran my finger along the hull, feeling the smooth wood. I'd never rowed in a single and heard they were tippy, because of their narrow, sleek hulls. I had been told you had to balance, and never let go of your oars.

I sighed and left the boat bay. Dreaming. Just dreaming. To row a single, you had to have a boat, and to have a boat, you had to have support, because they weren't cheap. In my world, a boat was going to be replaced with some latest-and-greatest-baby-gear.

Turning Ten

I want to tell you
a story
and it relates,
I promise.
When I turned ten,
I begged my dad
to take me out
for a row.
I'd never rowed
before,
only watched.
 I was that kid. Strong. Independent.
Only child
who wanted
her way.
 A regret?
I was a pain in the butt.

Definitely.
Being ten meant
friends,
presents and balloons
at the bowling alley.
I won. Another regret.
Always, always,
wanting to win.
As you can see,
I have a few
regrets.
That bowling win
didn't mean
anything.
I only wanted
one thing
that day.
Daddy, pleeeeease.
You're too young, he replied.
Daddy, pleeeeease.
We went
out
in a double,

two sculling oars
each.
I floundered.
He patiently
taught
me.
At the end
of our row,
he praised me.
You're a natural, he said.
I'll never
forget
those words
on my birthday.

Chapter 10

I biked home, racing with myself to get some sort of workout. When I got to the house, the cars were gone. At first, I was happy to be alone, but then I got bored. I sent Kash a text, but it was unanswered, so she was probably still on the water, having a good hard row. Unlike mine. I'd hardly broken a sweat. I didn't start work until four o'clock. I paced. Since I had goals to accomplish, I needed to do some type of training. Time for a run.

Once again, I ran to the Rowing Club. Why? I don't know. I'm a sucker for punishment; I wanted to be morbid and sad and *not happy*. Maybe I just wanted to dream and tell myself I could do this. Reflect.

Or scream again. No. I didn't want to do that.

I would beat these stupid odds. When I was little, my mom would read to me every night. We would snuggle on my bed. Over and over, I would ask her to read *The Little*

Engine that Could. She would laugh because I knew the words by heart. She always told me I could do anything.

Big sigh. Next year, she'll have a new baby to read to.

I got to the park and headed to the boathouse. When I got close, I heard voices. I rounded the corner, and there was the man I'd seen the other day, and he had the single outside on stretchers again. He was talking to a woman with short gray hair, Gillian Storm, who had started the rowing club. I'd seen her on the water before, in a single, and she rowed in the adult program.

"See you around," said Gillian to the man. Then she left, going around the other side of the boathouse.

Neither of them had seen me, so I stood still for a second and stared at this man. Now he was deeply engrossed, with rowing rigging tools spread out in front of him. His head was lowered, and there was a look of ... of something almost possessive on his face. He went back and forth, fiddling with the rigger. I walked toward him. He still didn't look my way.

"He-llo," I said.

He turned and gave me a quick glance. "Oh, hello there. We meet again." Then he moved the level—that coaches used for rigging—to the middle of the boat and eyeballed it. I knew what a level was because of my high school coach. I looked at the little bubble in the middle of the level, as it floated back and forth, trying to settle in the middle between two black lines.

"Rigging?" I asked.

"Just tweaking a few things. Pitch is off a little." He bent over and put a pitch meter on the oarlock. He lifted his head to glance at me. "You know anything about rigging?"

I shrugged. "A little. My coach usually rigged our boat."

"How long have you been rowing?"

"Three years."

He went back to fiddling with the pitch meter, which kind of looked like a math protractor, but was a special rowing tool.

"High school program?" he asked without looking at me.

"Yeah. And last summer I rowed a pair with my friend. We didn't race, but rowed in the mornings to get better."

"That's a good start. How'd your high school crew do?"

"We won the Canadian Secondary School Regatta this year, in our coxed four," I said with pride.

Without glancing my way, he said, "Impressive."

Memories flooded my brain. When we crossed the line first, all of us flaked back for a nano-second, exhausted, trying to catch our breath, but then we sat up and screamed and splashed the water, laughing almost uncontrollably. What a moment! The biggest high I'd had in my life, by far. I'd been euphoric, and almost in an alternative state. Then, when I got out of our boat, in front of the grandstands in St. Catharines, for the medal presentation, my legs buckled, they were so spent. But I got on that podium and grinned huge. My mother was there, taking photos.

Had she been pregnant then?

I shook my head to get rid of *that* thought. In the boat on the way back to the dock, we sang the Queen song, "We Are the Champions." So hilarious—but we were giggling like we were five. Of course, we toned it down when we got to the dock—the same dock I'd come in on after losing just a few days ago. God, I craved that adrenalin rush, that high. I wanted it again and again.

"We won some small regattas, too," I said. "We were undefeated in our season."

"It's always fun to win," he said, with a little smile.

"Best feeling ever," I said.

"Did you like your coach?"

I nodded. "He was tough and worked us hard. But he was fair. I liked his commitment to us. It's not like we have a huge club or program, but he treated us like real athletes. He didn't baby us."

He stood up and did a little stretch, giving me some eye contact. "Do you row in an eight as well?"

"For the two years before, I did. We weren't very good the first year." I laughed a little, thinking about how we were all new to the sport, and how the sport was new to the school. Kash had begged me to go out with her for something to do, since basketball season was over. I fell in love with the sport from the first row. So did she. So much so, she was choosing it over basketball. Me, I was just so-so at basketball, anyway, so that choice was easy, especially after the high of winning.

"Everyone has to start somewhere," he said.

"We rowed in an eight my second year, too," I said, desperately wanting to keep this conversation alive, "and then some of us got selected to row in a four." I'm not sure why I was telling him all this, except Kash and my other crewmates were gone. I had no one to talk to.

"How'd you do?" he asked, fiddling with the rigger.

"We came second by only three feet," I answered. "So, last year we concentrated on just the four. We all liked working hard, so it helped us push each other."

He glanced up at me. "You got the bug. I can hear it in your voice."

I sighed, exhaling louder than I wanted to. "I love being out there. On the water."

Silence circled above us, and I watched as he focused on rigging his single. "Is every single different?" I asked.

"Every rower is different," he said. "The simple definition is that pitch is important, because it plays a big part in having the blade at the right depth. But four degrees usually works for most singles. It's all about the vertical on the oarlock."

He pointed to the oarlock. He was going over my head, but I wanted to learn. I knew it was like physics, another one of my strong subjects. He handed me the pitch meter, and although it did look like a protractor, it also had a level bubble.

"Put it on the gunwale," he said

I did. The arrow pointed to zero.

"Now, put it on the steel edge of the oarlock and look at the bubble, and make sure it's in the middle."

"It's not," I said.

"Okay, so move the arrow to get it there."

I did and the arrow went to four. "It's at four," I said.

"Okay, four is standard. This side is good now," he said. "Let's do the other side."

We went around and did the same thing on the other side. His hair flopped over his eyes, but there was no hair-flicking going on with him. He just let it hang like a limp noodle.

Then he stood up and fiddled around with the seat, running it up and down. Without looking at me, he asked, "Are you rowing this summer?"

"I'm ... uh ... not sure," I mumbled.

"If you want to get better, you should row in the summer months," he said matter-of-factly.

"I went through the seat races for the Junior Canadian team and ..." I sucked in a deep breath. He looked me right in the eyes.

"And now you're back home. I understand. If you're junior age, you're young," he said. "You have years ahead of you."

"I was the last cut," I said, wanting to make myself look okay. "I did try recreational rowing this morning, but the girls aren't very committed. So, I'm not sure what to do."

He nodded and started to put all his tools away. "Tough one. Don't give up if you love it. Find another way."

"I won't and I will. If that makes sense."

"It does." He gave me a little look, and I noticed that he'd cracked another smile.

Who was this guy? Who understood.

"What's your name?" I asked.

"Alan." He held out his hand.

"Holly Callahan." I shook his hand, and his grip was firm. I liked that. I hated the limp handshake, like I was a damsel in distress.

"Nice name." He sighed and pushed his hair back off his face. "Has a ring." Once again, he looked away from me, but I saw the dullness return to his face, just like I'd seen the other day. His eyes were almost back to being blank.

I stared at him for a second, just watching him pack his tools, methodically putting everything in a specific spot in his toolbox.

"Who'd you rig this boat for?" I asked.

He didn't answer. Did he hear me? Or was he too

focused? Should I ask again? I was pretty sure he'd heard me, but for some reason was avoiding answering my question. He looked as if he had shut down, closed the open door. Instead of answering me, he stood up, put his hand to the lower part of his back and said, "Getting old. Creaky joints."

Then he eyed me. "You ever rowed a single?"

"No," I said. "I've only ever done sweep rowing. I've never tried sculling rowing, even in a double or quad. Is it hard?"

"As hard as you make it."

"That's true for anything," I said.

"Holly, I like your attitude." He handed me both of the oars, which were so much lighter and shorter than the oars in an eight or a four. They had way smaller grips, too. Sculling used two oars and sweep rowing only used one.

"In sculling, the oars are called sculls. Do you want to take it out?" he asked.

"Take it out?" I stared at him.

Was he serious? He wanted me to go out in a single. My heart started beating like crazy, like someone was tapping fingers on my chest in this really excited way.

But nerves also sizzled inside of me. What if I was terrible? Okay, what if I sucked?

"Why not?" He shrugged. "This boat needs some movement." He paused before he said softly, "You asked who I was rigging it for. Maybe it was you."

"I'd love to!" I blurted this out. My entire body was tingling. I was being given an opportunity to do this. I couldn't pass it up.

"Let me show you how to carry it down to the dock."

After his careful instructions, I put it on my head and, holding onto the riggers, carried it down to the water.

"Now, roll the boat away from you and bring it to your waist," he said. I did. "Now, place it in the water gently. They are delicate boats."

Once I had it in the water, he told me how to get the oarlocks facing to the stern, and how to open up the water side oarlock by leaning over. The balancing part of getting in the boat was so different from an eight or a four, and I could feel how tippy it was. My heart now pounded, like someone was drumming with drumsticks instead of tapping, but I couldn't show him that, or he might not let me do this. And I wanted to, so badly. I took off my running shoes, got in the boat, and stuck my feet in the shoes attached to the foot stretchers. After doing up the Velcro, I adjusted the stretchers. Obviously, whoever rowed this before me, was inches taller than me.

"You ready?" he asked.

"I am." The oars, or sculls as Alan had called them, felt so much smaller in my hands. Like they fit better. I liked the dexterity of having one in each hand.

"Okay, I will give you a little push off. Just stay close," he said. "I don't have a motorboat. I'll coach you from the end of the dock. Just do a few strokes with arms only, first."

I sat at the back of the slide but didn't go up and down it. Instead, I just moved my arms, putting the sculls in the water and out. I cruised around in front of the dock, learning how to touch and back at the same time to turn the boat around. It spun around so fast, unlike the eight this morning, which had taken forever to turn around.

"Okay," he said, after I had gone back and forth a few times in front of the dock, using only my arms. "Go up to the top of the slide. Full compression. And let's try a full stroke."

I bent my knees, compressed my body, moving to the top of my slide. I angled the sculls in the water. It felt so strange to have one in each hand, instead of just one big oar. My chest opened up, and my arms were like wings. I buried the sculls in the water and felt the boat rocking back and forth.

"Move your hands up and down," he said.

I did what he said. The tiniest movement caused the boat to rock. It was so tippy. If I looked back, or even around, it would disrupt the balance, especially with my arms stretched so wide.

"Rowing is a push sport," he said. "Lock the blades of the sculls in the water, press your feet on the foot stretchers, getting those heels and legs right down, and drive your hips through. Does that make sense?" I knew the blade was the end of the oar, the part that was usually painted, the part that went into the water.

I nodded again. Some of this stuff I knew, but our coach hadn't explained it this way. Alan made sense.

"Take a stroke."

I inhaled. Pushed back. And exhaled. The boat glided on the water. What a rush!

"Once the sculls are out of the water," he said, "let your hands lead you out of the bow, then rock the hips forward, and move up the slide."

I did what he said. Since I wanted to keep moving, I slid up to the top of the slide again, sank the sculls in the water, and pushed back. I finished, and rolled the sculls around again, repeating the stroke all over again.

Whoosh. The boat cut through the water, moving like a sleek craft. My heart fluttered. I wanted to giggle, laugh out loud, I felt so giddy. This was incredible. But I didn't. I concentrated on what I was doing. I took another stroke and another. I rowed past the dock.

"Turn it around again," he called out. "One side touch, other side back. Just gentle strokes."

After quite a few more times back and forth in front of the dock, he said, "Bring it in."

I did what he said, even though I could have stayed out. I managed to dock it just fine, without his help. He stood there with a smile on his face.

"You're a natural," he said.

Realizations

Sometimes there are
moments
when you realize
something.
It's like a flash or
a bang
hits you,
then sneaks
inside you.
Suddenly, you have a
dream
which becomes a
goal.
Holly raced and won.
And craved more. More. More.
The burning so intense.
It was a realization

for her.

Mine came when I was eight.

Everyone is different.

Don't compare.

And if you live long

enough,

maybe

you'll have more

than one.

Here's my story.

My first overseas plane ride

was to Lucerne, Switzerland

to watch the rowing championships.

I ate Raclette. Melted cheese on potatoes.

I ohhed and ahhed,

said I was in heaven.

Press pause for a second ...

that is one effed-up saying.

Where is heaven, anyway?

I still don't know.

Everyone thinks that I do.

Sorry. I don't.

Back to the story.

Lorna Schultz Nicholson

From raclette to a regatta at Lake Rotsee.
Watching heats
from the grandstands,
sun beating down.
Every single race. Wrote down times.
Put on more sunscreen,
wear your hat,
said Mom.
Second day.
My dad and I pedaled bikes
to the start.
Me mesmerized
as the female singles
moved into position
touching it up to
stay straight.
Strong women.
Shoulder muscles.
Leg muscles.
But most of all
faces focused.
My entire body vibrated.
I wanted that.

To be alone,
just me and
a boat.
That was
my moment.

Chapter 11

Country playlist running through my head, I ran at full tilt all the way home, sprinting at the end, until I had to bend over at the waist to catch my breath. Tomorrow. I was going out again tomorrow.

Tomorrow. Tomorrow. Tomorrow.

And this Alan guy was going to bring a little dinghy motorboat, so that he could putt-putt beside me as I rowed down the river. He'd told me to tell my parents that I was rowing with him. I'd nodded but didn't say anything, so I wouldn't really be lying. I didn't want to tell my mother. What if she said no? And the way she was acting lately, keeping secrets, talking about my university behind my back, she just might. Plus, who knew where this would lead, anyway. It might just be one more row.

My heartrate back to normal, I stood up. Then I jumped as high as I could and punched the air, before

I leaped over two sidewalk blocks. What a morning. First, I had that awful, awful row. Then—boom!—I had the most amazing row ever! I needed to shower and get ready for work, though, come down to reality. I raced into the house, and the entire time in the shower, I sang. Sang! Instead of cried.

I was in my room, toweling off my hair, when my phone buzzed. I picked it up.

"Hey, Kash," I said, holding the phone under my chin with my shoulder.

"Just checking in between workouts," she said. "How was your row this morning?"

I stopped rubbing my wet hair and put my phone on speaker. How much should I tell *her*?

"Awful," I said. And I stopped there. For some reason, my new excitement was not something I wanted to share. Not yet, anyway. What if it went nowhere? I'd be a loser all over again.

"That blows," she said.

"Get this," I said. "The coach flirted with Madison and Tessa."

"Flirted? A coach? That's awkward. Where'd they get him from?"

"He's some university guy who used to row and now wants to coach. Oh, and Tessa had full makeup on."

"Shocker. She probably got up an hour early. What're you going to do?"

"Quit. But I don't want to talk about it. Tell me what's going on with you." I didn't want to lie. Not to Kash. Time to move this conversation along.

"You sure?"

"Positive."

Kash started talking about her workouts, Keira, the coach, the strength training they were doing at Brock University. She got to train in a university weight room. Yes, I was envious.

Then she said, "We're off to Europe in, like, three weeks. First, we're competing in a smaller regatta in Germany. Then we go to Lucerne for the World Championships. I'm soooo fricking pumped. I've heard the course in Lucerne is incredible. They ride bikes up and down to watch the races. And the food. Raclette is supposed to be to die for."

"Wow," I said. "Switzerland." Okay, I had been on a high, but this deflated me. I'd never been to Switzerland, and it was on my bucket list.

"I miss you," she said softly.

"Yeah, I miss you, too."

"Maybe you can suck it up and row and get to Henley. That'd be something."

The Royal Canadian Henley in St. Catharines was the one regatta we had talked about going to all spring, until we were recruited to try out for the Junior National Team. Now I was shit-out-of-luck for both.

"That rec boat won't be good enough," I said. "Only three of us had any experience. The set-up was the worst. They think going to Toronto Island for a fun regatta and partying is going to be the highlight. It's in just over a week, too. Can you imagine how awful the boat will be?"

"I had a feeling it was going to suck," said Kash. "But good on you for trying."

I started to shiver from my shower and now just wanted to get off the phone.

"You should be here," she said. "I'm serious. Our boat is missing something, and I'm convinced it's because you're not in it. I don't think it moves the same, and our times aren't as good."

That made me feel a little better. But I still couldn't

bring myself to tell her about my row in the single. "Thanks," was all I said back.

We talked a little longer before we hung up. I toweled my hair dry and got ready for work, putting on my black Antonio's T-shirt and a pair of black pants, just like what Amaya had worn the day I applied for the job. I needed to switch gears and learn how to be a hostess.

I arrived at work and was told to take a seat in the very back booth to wait for Tim Turner, the assistant manager. When he showed up, I tried to act cool, but Amaya was right, the guy was unbelievably good looking. He was buff, as Amaya had said, but what she didn't tell me was that he was Black and had this beautiful smile. He slipped into the booth, flashed his smile at me, dimples denting his dark cheeks, and I immediately relaxed. After we introduced ourselves, he got down to business and started asking questions about the menu. I answered every question and he kept nodding his head. As I rhymed off the menu, my brain was doing double duty, trying to figure out his age. I was thinking he was maybe eighteen or nineteen, so I wondered if he ran track at *university*? A part of me wanted him to be my age, still in high school, but I would have noticed him at our school, seeing he was a visible minority in Bracebridge.

I lowered my gaze—so I wouldn't stare at the muscles bulging out of his shirt—and finished answering the questions.

"Okay, we're done," he said, slapping the menu down on the desk. "You killed it."

"Thanks," I said.

He stood up and, for me, at five-feet-ten, his six-foot-three or six-foot four-inch frame was a perfect height. I didn't feel the need to slouch as I walked beside him.

"I'll take you out front," he said. "You and Amaya are going to work together tonight."

"Oh, good," I said.

Tim tilted his head and squinted a little as he looked at me. "You look really familiar."

"Doppelganger," I said, shrugging. "Could be a rock star, though." I used my hands to do some rap-style moves, trying to be cool. "Or ..." I stopped doing my silly movements, because I was just being awkward. "I have one of those faces."

He laughed and shook his head. "No, not one of

those faces. Not even close. But, yeah, idiot thing to say. Sorry about that. Let's get you to the front."

As we walked, I could tell he was giving me these sidelong glances. We were almost at the front when he snapped his fingers, the noise loud. "I got it. You're one of the rowers, in the four that won some national high school regatta."

And, just like that, my flippant comebacks were gone, and my cheeks burned. They were probably as red as the cherry tomatoes on the flatbread pizza on the menu I had just recited. "Um ... yeah, I was in that boat."

"I saw your picture in the newspaper," he said. "Only because my parents still get it delivered. I know. Backward. But my dad rowed in university for something like two years, so he was the one who showed me. Good on you."

"Um ... thanks," I said. Another one-word answer, if you don't count the um.

"Your win was so stellar for this city. Especially for a small club. Kind of unheard of."

"We had a great coach," I said.

Suddenly he had this look on his face and, bingo, I knew he had figured out that I was the one who was cut. Yesterday's paper.

"You ... um ... still rowing this summer?" he asked.

I lowered my head. This conversation was going downhill fast. "Not sure," I mumbled.

"I get it," he said.

I peered at him out of the corner of my eye. Did he get it? Or was he saving face for me? We'd been so pumped after all the accolades. Then, boom, I went from hero to zero. I wanted to get our conversation off me. "Amaya told me you ran track. What events do you do?"

"Four hundred is my specialty," he replied. "But I do two hundred as well, and sometimes eight hundred."

"Cool," I said. Thus, the Usain Bolt long legs. "University team?"

"Yeah," he said.

So, university, which meant older. And he was an athlete, so maybe he did "get it." Maybe I was going to work with someone I could relate to.

We reached the front desk, and Amaya was standing there, stacking menus.

"She aced it," said Tim to Amaya. Then he smiled at me.

He turned and walked away, and I couldn't help but sneak-a-peek.

"Um ... Holly," said Amaya, grinning. "I should show you this floor plan."

I turned my attention away from the track butt that was walking away from me, and did my best smile. "Sure," I said.

Everything she told me I absorbed in five minutes, and when I seated my first table, I easily rhymed off all the specials.

"You're good," she said, when I came back.

"It's just memory work."

"I always blow it," she said. "Although, last time you saw me, I was pretty hung, so I was one hundred percent worse."

I laughed. "That makes sense. Okay, so let's make a deal here," I said. "Let me take the people to the tables, and you organize all the menus and figure out the table situations. We'll work our strengths."

"Sounds good to me," she said.

Time seemed to fly by. A restaurant at its peak hour can be so busy, and I didn't even have time to pee. I seated tables, told specials, and walked a ton. If I'd had a Fitbit—my mother has one that Stew bought her for her birthday—it would have been dinging. By the end of the night, my feet were a mess of raw blisters. My usual shoes of choice were flip-flops, sneakers, and converse high-tops, but I'd pulled out a pair of low heels for the shift. Wrong move.

But there had been moments of fun, and the servers hadn't harassed me at all, or called me out because I made a mistake. There were a few servers, and one of the cooks, who looked familiar, and I figured they might have been a few grades up in my high school. Tim—and his cute butt and dimples—came out now and again to check on us, giving us the thumbs-up during the busiest time.

The restaurant closed at ten o'clock, and then it was time to clean up. I was given my orders: how to wash down menus, fill the salt and pepper shakers, clean the front area, and make sure everything was stacked and ready for the next day. Oh, and clean up the coloring books and crayons, since the restaurant was kid friendly. I remembered how my mom and I used to go to restaurants, and I'd color. It had been ages since she and I had gone anywhere together. Soon, she'd take her new kid to restaurants, and ask for the highchair. I shook my head to get rid of that thought.

"Hey," said Amaya. "A few of us are going over to Brendan's place. You want to come?"

"Um ... I probably shouldn't tonight," I said. Brendan was one of the servers. All I could think of was my row the next day, and how I wanted to be better in the single, go further, try harder, show Alan that I really was a natural.

"Okay," she said. "But it's fun. They have a pool, and his parents are super low-key. And since Tim and Brendan are best bros, he'll be there." She grinned at me.

Since I wanted to avoid the mention of Tim, I asked, "Does the staff go out a lot?"

Amaya shrugged. "It's summer."

"So it is," I said. "Everyone seems so nice, I'm sure the get-togethers are fun."

"Yeah. It's a good staff. Margo can be a bitch, but that's because she wanted Tim's job." She smiled at me. "Restaurant gossip."

"I should go home tonight," I said. Then I added, "But maybe next time."

"Sure," she said. "I'm sure there will be many more next times. Summer is just starting. Maybe we should organize a bonfire night."

"That'd be fun," I said.

"I'm on it," said Amaya.

Amaya might not be the best hostess, but I had to admit, she would probably win the staff social convenor award.

I rode my bike home, and when I got there, the lights were on in the house. Darn. Everyone was still up. I put my bike away and snuck quietly into the house. As I was getting a glass of water to take to my room, I heard someone on the stairs.

"I'm so glad you're home," said my mother, coming into the kitchen. "How was work?" She tightened the belt on her robe, but it sat a little above her usual stomach. I had to turn my head so I wouldn't stare.

"Good," I replied. "Busy. The people I work with seem nice. I recognized a few from school."

"That's good. Maybe you'll make some new friends. I do worry about this bike riding home."

"I'm fine, Mom."

She moved toward me. "How was your row this morning?"

I stiffened. Did she know I'd been in the single? But then I remembered about the recreational row. "Awful,"

I said. "I'm going to quit. I'll work out at the Sportsplex instead."

"Oh, Holly, I'm so sorry to hear that." She paused. "That must be disappointing."

Just then, Stew came into the kitchen, dressed in his Adidas sweatpant shorts, white socks, and slippers. Seriously. His fashion sense needed some work. I wanted to make a snarky comment about his outfit, but I held off. The less I said, the quicker I could get to my room.

"How was work?" he asked.

And now it was time for round two of the same questions. "Good," I replied. Same answer.

"You like the people you work with?"

"Yeah."

"Enjoying the workplace environment is important."

"For sure," I said. What else was I supposed to say? This was my first job. Plus, I wanted to get up to my room and shut my door.

"I heard you might look at the Lakehead campus in Orillia as an option for post secondary."

I gritted my teeth. God, he sounded like a robot. Words were sitting on the tip of my tongue, but I didn't reply. I was not going to that *campus*.

"Let's talk about this later in the summer," said Mom. "Next year, we'll be talking about this all the time. Now it's time to enjoy summer."

"Okay," he said. But then he glanced my way. "But just know, it's a great school. I got my undergrad at the campus in Thunder Bay. It would be a decent school for you." He turned and opened the fridge, taking out a package of ham and a block of cheese.

I glared at my mother. Maybe she didn't want to talk about this until the fall, but I sure did, especially after that comment. "If I get a scholarship," I stated, "I'm going to the University of Pennsylvania. Or I'm also looking at the University of Victoria."

Stew pulled out two slices of bread from the bag. "You do know that the University of Pennsylvania is an Ivy League School, so they don't give scholarships. You would have to apply for financial aid."

"Stew, Holly just got home from work," said my mother.

He turned to me. "Did you want me to make you a sandwich?" His voice was way too chipper for this late in the evening. "I'm making them for tomorrow's lunches."

"No, thanks," I said.

He turned back to his sandwich making. "There are good schools in Ontario. You don't need to go to the west coast. Flying back and forth is expensive."

"You know what, Stew," I said. "My grades are good. And I talked to the coach at Penn, and Mom is a single mom, so we'd hands-down qualify for some sort of financial aid."

Then it hit me. Maybe not anymore. Holy shit. That was a reality-check-and-a-half.

Fuming, I walked by my mother, and when she touched my arm, a jolt of something went through me, and I have to admit, it almost made me cave in, reach out, hug her, be hugged. Warm arms around me, comforting me, telling me I could be and do anything I wanted. I pulled my arm away from her.

I was out of the kitchen, away from sight, when I heard my mom. "Why did you have to bring up schools? She's going through a lot right now. You can't be so blunt with her."

"Mary, I was just making conversation. I didn't know I wasn't supposed to say anything. I have no idea how to handle a teenage girl. What to say? I'm trying here, but she bites my head off every time I say something."

"You have to be more sensitive to her moods. She just turned seventeen, and she's hormonal and dealing with a lot." There was a pause. "What if we have a little girl?"

Had she snuggled up to him? I wanted to vomit. I went to my room and shut my door. *Be sensitive to my moods? HORMONAL.* Thanks, Mom. She had basically just thrown me under the bus.

University

I had the college-slash-university
talks
with my parents.
They can be
stressful.
College is coming up soon
my mom had said.
Don't push me!!! I snapped back.
At sixteen,
all I wanted was
 to row for the
Olympic team
in a single.
I didn't think
I needed
balance.
Later, I heard her.

She has no friends. No fun. No balance. Teens
go out. To movies. On dates. To the prom.
Yada. Yada. Yada.
If she rowed in a
college eight
she would have friends
maybe eat pizza
cross-legged
on the floor.
At the time I thought
I was good.
Happy.
I thought there was
time later
for fun.
Maybe a boyfriend.

Later.

   University.

Later.

But then ... what happens ...
when Later
never
comes?

Chapter 12

"Lock the sculls in the water at entry," yelled Alan, from the little motorboat he'd brought down on a trailer. "And load them up with water. Then send your body back."

I went up the slide, put the sculls in the water, and pushed my legs down. I was still getting used to not calling them oars.

"Lock, load, and send!" he called out. "You have to say that over and over. Every single stroke."

I went up again. Loaded the sculls with water and pushed.

"Watch the speed of your hands around the finish!" The finish was when the blade of the sculls came out of the water, and you had to turn them, make them flat, so you could go back up the slide. Were they too fast? Too slow? I wanted to impress him. Do what he asked and make myself better, even though this was only my second time out in this single. Being on the water, in this single, gave me an energy I didn't have on land anymore.

"Let it run!" he shouted from the boat.

I stopped rowing, the boat skipping across the water for a few seconds before it slowed. Then I watched as he stood up in his small boat, making it rock side to side. He didn't seem to notice that any second, he could topple into the water.

"Do you like music?" he asked.

"Yeah," I replied. *Weird question.*

"What do you listen to?"

"Um ... country."

"You don't strike me as a country gal. But that's good. Me, I like jazz and classical."

"Okay," I said. "Well, I like pop, too. And some rap."

"Really. You like rap? Rap is just noise and a whole lot of swearing." He spoke with his hands, so his boat rocked, and I thought he was going to go face-first into the water.

Were we honestly talking about music? While on the water? While he was standing in a boat in the middle of the river, ready to fall in?

"Rowing is like music," he said. "The violinist can't play faster than the trumpeter. The country singer can't sing faster than the guitar. The drummer can't go faster than the rest of his band. It's the same in a boat. Nothing can be faster than the speed of the boat." He pretended to pull his arms in, roll them when they hit his stomach, and push them out like he was going around the finish of the rowing stroke. "If your hands are coming around the finish, faster than the boat is moving, you will disrupt the flow."

"O-kay," I said. His motorboat was swaying back and forth but he was oblivious. It was as if music was playing in his head.

"Do you understand that?"

"I think so."

"All movement in the boat is art; lines in songs, words in poetry, dancers leaping to the beat of the music. You pick what moves you. Whatever you choose, you must remember to think of the flow. Which means you must be patient. If you tried to read Shakespeare too fast, you would miss the beats, slur the words together. A dancer has to jump at the precise time. A singer has to work with the band." His hands moved like a musical conductor at the high part in the song. The boat swayed like *it* was the music and he was the artist.

I knew he wasn't finished, so I just sat there.

"When I rowed, years ago, we hammered away and didn't listen to the boat, or even watch the boat and its movement. That's not what I teach now. We're always trying to rush through everything, but don't. Move with your boat. Listen to the bubbles underneath. Feel them." Eyes closed, he clenched his fists and shook them. "Let them energize you."

Then he sat down and matter-of-factly said, "Let's try it again."

I moved up the slide. He revved the motor and it backfired before it putt-putted. I thought about his words. Lock. Load. Send.

I started rowing again, and I tried to feel the boat, its speed, and move with it, not against it or faster than it. I moved my hands around the finish, rocked my hips, moved up the slide, locked the sculls in the water, and pushed. Something clicked! I felt this weird flow. And I heard the best bubbles under the boat! They were effervescent, little pops of joy.

At least, for a few strokes.

"You're rushing!"

I slowed down my hands to get the feeling back.

"That's better!"

Again, I felt the boat almost float, and the water bubbles sounded underneath again. Pop. Pop. Pop. They were right underneath me. I went for longer, but then I lost the rhythm again.

"Too fast!" he shouted. "Patience with the movement."

Over and over. I worked on the speed. And the boat flowed better, the blades of the sculls did come out of the water more cleanly.

"Great job!" he called out. "You're getting it. Feeling it."

He putt-putted over to me. "To help with the speed, watch the puddles that the sculls make, as they move away from the boat."

I started up again. Over and over, he made me watch the puddles beside the boat. When the sculls entered the water, they made round puddles. I wanted to get the boat further and further from them with every stroke. I knew Alan was watching me with this eagle eye. The practice was like nothing I'd ever been through before. Alan was like some rowing manual, his brain wired with information and, to me, he made perfect sense.

"Let's take it in," he said. I had no idea how long we'd been on the water. My brain was exhausted.

I turned the boat around and started heading toward the dock.

"We've done a lot of technique today," Alan called out. "Let's try a couple of hard tens. Ten hard strokes, then ten easy. Get the boat moving. Just for fun. We always need to have fun out here. Try to push the puddles further and further."

I nodded and sucked in a big breath, as I slid to the top of my slide. Then I pushed back, locking the blades of the sculls in the water, sending them through the water, feeling the boat glide beneath me. This sudden rush of giddiness flowed through me, just like the bubbles that were flowing under my boat. I saw the puddles move past me. I could see the movement, hear the movement. Feel it. I could. I wanted to squeal but that would take energy, so I focused.

The boat picked up speed. I went to ten then slowed it down, trying to catch my breath. The water still gurgled. Wow, what a rush!

After ten easy strokes, I did another hard ten. I gave it my all, pressing my feet down to use every muscle in my thighs. On the seventh stroke, I felt the pull of the sculls and the boat tipped a little, crashing my knuckles together.

Lorna Schultz Nicholson

"You rushed it. That's why it's tipping. But overall, not bad," he said. "Take it in."

Once on the dock, I balanced and stepped out. It wasn't the hardest row physically, but it had been the best. By far. Something had shifted, changed. I felt the boat move, instead of just grunting through a workout.

It made me realize how I seriously had to grunt through my home life. The movement at home sucked big time. It didn't flow one little bit. I shook my head. Forget about that.

Alan putt-putted his boat into the boat launch area, shutting it off and jumping out, then pulling it in. He came to the dock where I was. "You have lots to learn but you listen well."

"Thanks," I said. "After I carry the boat up, I'll help you with your motorboat."

"Appreciate that," he said. "I'm heading home right away today. My wife wants me home to go to the Costco in Barrie. Plus, I've got some work to do on a deck I'm building for a new client."

"For sure." I lifted the boat out and carried it up to the boat bay.

That was the first time he'd mentioned anything

about his family or work. So, he had a wife? I knew nothing about him, really. Like, nothing. Except, he knew the president of the rowing club and he stored his boat at this club. The situation of me rowing in his boat was a bit weird but seemed right. He followed me as I carried the single up to the boathouse, guiding me, and it was obvious he was nervous that I might hit something.

I put the boat away without any problems. In other words, I didn't bang it against anything. Thank God. Another reason not to tell my mother about rowing in the single. She probably wouldn't let me row someone's personal boat, for fear of me wrecking it and having to pay for the damages. Especially now that she needed money for *other* things.

Both Alan and I headed back to the water to get his motorboat.

"Thanks, Alan," I said, as we hauled his boat out of the water.

"No problem."

"You sure know a lot."

He didn't reply and didn't even look at me. We hauled the boat out of the water and slid it onto his boat trailer, which we pulled up to his truck.

Once it was secure, he said, "See you tomorrow."

"Um ... sure," I said. He wanted to go out again?

He stared at me. "You don't want to?"

"No. No. I do," I said quickly. And I *so* did. "That was, that was the best row I've ever had. The best technical row, ever." My mouth spewed out words. "You ... um ... know what you're talking about. And, well, I'd love to come out again tomorrow, if you want to. I'd love to. Honest."

He nodded. "Same time. I'll lock the boat bay. Make sure your parents are okay with you getting a little coaching in a single. I'll talk to Gillian Storm, the president of the rowing club, and let her know you're rowing with me. You have a membership, right?"

I nodded. "I needed it to row for my high school. It's good until the end of the year."

"Good to know," he said. He gave his one-finger wave. "See you tomorrow. Same time." He walked away from me and, for a second, I just stood there, the adrenalin rushing through my body. I watched him get in his truck and drive away.

Then I realized, I didn't even know his last name.

Music

We lived in a three-bedroom house
with a den.
I walked into the den.
Dad listened to music
in his recliner
wearing headphones,
head moving side-to-side,
eyes closed,
smile on his face.
Who you listening to? I asked.
He turned, opened one eye.
Diana Krall.
I like rap, I said
to annoy him.
He turned his record player off.
Jazz vinyls
were his hobby.

Lorna Schultz Nicholson

Okay, he said,
let's have a listen.
On my phone
I picked a
Jay-Z song
with a lot of
F-bombs.

Chapter 13

After Alan drove away, I got on my bike and rode home, thinking about his analogies: comparing rowing to music, poetry, dance. He had almost looked possessed when he was talking to me. Strange dude. But so full of knowledge. Although I wondered who he was, in a way, I didn't care. I wanted to learn as much as I could from him, and I wanted to keep him a secret. From *everyone*. Even Kash.

Why didn't I want to tell her?

What if she said I was being an idiot? Trusting a man, who was obviously a coach, but also someone I didn't know? I didn't want to hear that, because I was going back. No one could stop me. Something was compelling me to do this and there was just no hesitation.

I thought I would be alone when I got home, so I dropped my bike on the front lawn. I went to unlock the front door, but it was open. Could there be a burglar in the house? First step in, I heard the voices. Curtis and Stew. I sighed in relief, glad I wasn't in danger, but after that initial sigh, I groaned. Stew was here.

"I'm fine, Dad," said Curtis. "Go back to work. I can stay here by myself."

"Where is Holly?" Stew asked.

"I'm right here," I said, walking into the family room. Curtis was lying on the sofa with a cloth on his head.

"Where were you?" Stew stared at me.

"Um ... out with friends." The lie just came out. My summer was amounting to zero friends, but Stew sure didn't need to know that. He was already way too involved in my life.

"Curtis isn't feeling well, and your mother can't be here with him." Stew ran his hand through his hair like he was flustered. Stew? Flustered? I hid my smile. I was enjoying this new look. Was he actually human? Had the bloody coals he'd walked on burned his feet? Wait until I told Kash about this.

"The camp tried her at work," he said quickly, "but they couldn't get her, so they got me."

"You are his father," I said.

"Yes, I know that." He blew out a rush of air. I'd yet

to see Stew in any sort of panic and it was a good look on him, made him a little like the rest of us.

A petty part of me liked that my mother had always been available for me when I was sick in the infirmary at school. She would leave work to pick me up. But ... I knew my mother, and she must have honestly been busy.

Stew glanced at his watch. "I have to get going here. I'd like you to stay with him."

"Okay," I said. "I can stay until 3:30. Then I have to go to work."

"I have a really important meeting this afternoon." Stew sold commercial real estate—sometimes even in Barrie and Toronto—warehouses, and big office buildings. He was always in meetings, important meetings, according to him. Any sale amounted to a "solid financial commission." He was also always at sales conferences, and he won awards for his sales, and was the guy-of-the-month, and did presentations for other real estate agents on the positive side of selling and how to make a positive deal, and how to stay positive throughout the deal, blah, blah, blah. And—this was the worst of it—he had his picture on the city buses. The first time I saw it, I almost died of embarrassment.

Lorna Schultz Nicholson

Right now, he sounded rushed and not-in-control at all. I was loving it.

"I'm sorry," I said. "I just started this new job."

He stood up and tapped his fingers together, as if he was thinking. I stared at him. I wasn't giving in to him, not a chance. Let Stew stew.

"I can stay by myself for a few hours," piped up Curtis from his prone position on the sofa.

Stew turned to him. "No. That won't work." Then he looked back at me and he had this pinched look on his face, like his tie was tied way too tight, and was digging into his neck.

"Holly, are you sure you can't go in a little later?"

"I *can* stay," I said. "But *only* until 3:30. Call my mom again. She might be off around 3."

He exhaled and ran his hand through his hair. "Good idea. This meeting has been on my calendar for a long time. And I'm so close to sealing a big deal, which would be great for the summer. We can do a family holiday."

Okay, now I really wasn't going to budge. A family holiday? No, thanks. I smiled at Curtis. "How about we watch television," I said. "And I'll make you some lunch."

Stew exhaled, ran his hand through his hair, and

walked over to Curtis. Then I watched, as he sat down beside him and kissed his forehead. Gently, too. Like a real dad. I'd never in my life had a dad touch me like that. I stood there, staring, wondering what it would be like. How different was a father's touch to a mother's touch?

"I have to go back to work, okay, Bud?" he said to Curtis. His voice was so soft and tender, and I felt this emptiness inside me. Like a hole. I'd never had that part of me filled up.

"I hope you're feeling better soon." He put the cloth back on Curtis's forehead.

Curtis stared up at Stew, with these big brown eyes, and said in a really whiny voice, "Can you come home at 3:30, pleeeease, Daddy? Or Mary? Please."

"I'll see what I can do."

Curtis nodded his head.

Stew pushed a strand of Curtis's hair off his face and said, "Okay. I'll figure this out. Someone will be here at 3:30. Just for you, kiddo." He touched his son's cheek with his finger.

"Thanks, Dad."

Stew gave Curtis a kiss on the cheek, and I had to turn away. The moment had such power. Was it this gentle side of Stew that had swayed my mother? Even I had to admit he treated my mom with respect, and they had their tender moments.

"How about I get that lunch?" I said.

Stew stood, rattled his keys, and didn't even look at me before he left. As soon as the door had shut, Curtis sat up and grinned. "Let's make ham and cheese sandwiches."

"You little turd."

"I hate that camp. It's, like, the most boring thing in the world. All summer I have to go to camps, and some of them suck so bad. Let's play video games."

I picked up a cushion and threw it at him. "After my shower."

"Hey!" He ducked and the pillow flopped to the floor. "You could say thanks, you know. You get to go to your job, plus you miss the sharing stuff at dinner."

I eyed him. "Do you like that sharing stuff?"

"Like it? I hate it. Or as the Grinch would say, I loooooath it."

I laughed.

I showered, then made grilled cheese sandwiches and a salad for lunch, although Curtis opted for potato chips instead of the salad. Whatever. I sure wasn't going to be the nutrition police with the kid. Then Curtis and I sat in front of the television and played video games. More skilled than me, he beat me almost every time. Once, and only once, I nailed his butt to the wall. He almost looked pleased that I had won, like he'd taught me something.

After my win, I got up and did a little victory dance.

This time he threw a pillow at me. Then he said, "Sometimes you're okay, you know."

"Is that so," I said. "Same goes for you."

"My dad's okay, too, sometimes."

"I'm sure he is." I had to say something nice. Stew was his father.

"When my mom left," said Curtis, "he took over and didn't send us away somewhere, even when she didn't come back. Kids at school told me I was going to get sent away, to people who would be really mean to me."

I plopped down on the sofa beside him. "Kids at school can be jerks. I'm sorry about your mom." I glanced at him. "My dad did the same thing to me, only I was a baby. I don't have memories."

"I was six," said Curtis, "so I remember her. Sometimes

she was really nice. And she smelled good, better than dad, like flowers or something. They fought all the time, and she took a lot of pills. I used to find empty bottles all around the house. I guess that's why she left. My dad said she had to go away to get better, but then she never came back."

"That's tough," I said. Our legs were stretched out, thighs touching, feet on the coffee table.

"When she wasn't on the pills, she was good," said Curtis. He picked at the lint on the cushion. "She sometimes made cookies, and we went for ice cream before dinner. My dad *hated* that."

"Yeah, I can see that bugging him," I said. "He does like his rules."

"She read us stories, too, and did all these crazy voices. She loved reading *Winnie the Pooh*. It wasn't my favorite, but I didn't say anything, because I liked her reading to us. She said she related to Eeyore. He's always moping around." He paused, and I didn't say anything, hoping he would talk some more.

Finally, I said, "I always liked Tigger."

"He's so bouncy," said Curtis. "My mom had lots of days where she moped around like Eeyore, sometimes in her pajamas all day. Those days we didn't get any breakfast or lunch, and Dad would have to get us takeout for dinner. Kevin tried to make stuff but, yuk, it was awful. Maybe she'll come back one day and I'll get to see her."

That was the most Curtis had ever talked to me. I thought about what he said about his mother. What would happen if this other woman, the mother of Stew's kids, cruised back into their world? According to my mother, one of the reasons she "fell" for Stew was that he had fought for full custody of his boys and was so dedicated to them. He made their lunches, took them to school, attended all the parent-teacher meetings, and kissed them goodnight. The mother had gone through some sort of depression and did pop pills, and apparently, when she was released from the hospital/rehab facility, she just decided not to come back. Which is pretty shitty, if you ask me.

"What do you think would happen if she did come back?" I asked.

"I dunno. My dad is with your mom now." He paused and picked some lint off his sweat shorts. "Which kind of sucks for my mom, if she did want to live with us again. But I think she has a boyfriend, just like my dad has a girlfriend."

"Interesting," I said.

He shrugged. "It's okay, though. Your mom is nice. Is she my stepmother?"

My mom and Stew weren't married, unless they'd done that in secret, too. Wouldn't surprise me. Or was it coming next? My mother had gone the back route by getting knocked-up first.

"Sort of," I said. "How do you feel about the baby? You're going to have a new brother or sister."

"I hope it's a boy."

"Hey." I nudged him with my shoulder. "Maybe it will be a girl."

Did I honestly just say that? I'd never actually thought about this baby being anything but an it.

Ego

I had a big ego.
I know that now.
I was a protégée,
a star,
the one who
early on
had it all.
But I didn't
have it
all.
I know that now, too.
I never experienced
first
love,
those tingles that
happen
with a simple

Lorna Schultz Nicholson

touch.
I refused any of that
because I was
swayed by
newspaper write-ups,
television interviews,
twitter likes,
talking about
how good I was,
how I was going to be
a star.
I was supposed to be
the one
to medal for my country.
Maybe it's okay that
Holly
has to
fight and battle for
her spot
on the water
and off.
She has
to work,

meet new people,
save money.
All her struggles
will keep
her ego
in check.
And maybe
help her
give in to
tingles?

Chapter 14

"Here's your tips," said Tim. I got an envelope with cash after my shift. The servers had to give a percentage of their tips, and it was spilt between the hosts and bus people. I wasn't old enough to serve but wished I was, because I knew the servers went home with major cash every night. I opened the envelope and counted nineteen dollars. This money I would stash in a jar, along with the fifteen I had made last night.

I shoved the envelope in my pocket when the server, Brendan, came up to me. He was Tim's best friend.

"Holly," he said, handing me a ten-dollar bill, "you were a force tonight. I want you to have this as extra."

"Um ... thanks," I said. This was a bonus, for sure. I put the bill in the envelope with my other tips.

Then Margo, another server, came up to me and did the same thing—only she gave me a five-dollar bill and she mumbled, "Good job tonight." I was actually surprised, because she was a bit of a bitch, and liked to make snarky comments about Amaya and Tim.

But I had just made an extra fifteen because ... I'd seated tables properly, rhymed off a few specials, and quickly cleaned tables so I could seat more. Sweet deal.

Across the room, Amaya was smiling at me, giving me the thunbs-up. We'd done a good job, working as a team. She walked over to me.

"Some of us are going out again tonight," she said. "Just to the park to hang out for a couple of hours. You wanna come?"

How many times could a girl turn down the offers before they dried up? I thought about my row with Alan. That's what I wanted to do more than anything, more than going out to a park with people I barely knew.

"Um ..." I said.

"Just come for an hour."

One hour would mean everyone would, hopefully, be in bed when I got home. I wouldn't have to participate in some awkward family kitchen conversation. "Okay," I said. "An hour."

The chosen park was located about a ten-minute walk from the restaurant, and was by the river but not by the rowing club. I walked my bike beside Amaya. By the time we got there, it was already eleven o'clock, so kids on swings were non-existent. We found a table and sat down. I felt uncomfortable, like, not sure what I was doing, hanging out in a park when it was dark out, doing nothing, really. This was not my style. I wanted to go home to my house with my mother, where I could sit on our ratty sofa and watch television, knowing I had a hard workout in the morning.

More people from work showed up. I saw the plastic cups coming out of Amaya's backpack and the bottle of alcohol. I guess I did know that this was going to happen, as soon as I agreed to the park social. My non-existent drinking nights were because alcohol could hurt my training, and not because I was a prude or religious, or anything like that. Amaya handed me a cup and I took it. I didn't even know what was in it, but I didn't want to ask and sound like a complete loser. I guessed since it was dark, I could fake it and get out of here in less than an hour. What if Alan made me do a power workout instead of just technique?

"Thanks," I mumbled. "I owe you."

I looked around the group. Brendan and Margo

now sat on the grass and, by the red ember glowing in the dark and the skunk smell, I knew they had lit a joint. Amaya sauntered over to them, leaving me alone, feeling awkward. I watched the joint being passed around, cheeks sucking in, paper burning as it went from hand to hand.

"Weed and me don't agree," said Tim.

Where had he come from? I turned to him and he smiled at me. I shrugged, not knowing what to say. I'd tried it once.

"Want to go on a swing?" he asked.

I looked over at the swings, sitting there, barely moving as there was no breeze. Stars shone in the clear sky, and the air was hot and humid. Summer had arrived. "Sure," I said.

We took our cups and headed to the kids play area. The swings were modern ones with plastic seats and chain links that were also covered in plastic. Side-by-side, we swung back and forth, holding plastic cups in our hands. Tim took a sip of his, so I did, too. It burned like someone had lit a fire in my throat. I started to cough.

"Tequila will do that," he said.

I wiped my mouth. "Tequila?" I managed to squeak out.

He laughed. "Oh, yeah."

I shook my head, trying to get rid of the vile taste in my mouth. "I can feel it hitting the bottom of my stomach."

"Better with lime and salt." He was still laughing. "My first shot was in first year university," he said. "I was boring in high school."

I tried to swish the taste out of my mouth. "What university are you at?" I asked.

"University of Arizona in Tucson. Good tequila down there. And weather. Desert life has its perks. We can run outside all year."

"That part sounds good."

"For sure."

"Did you ... um ... get a scholarship?"

"Yeah."

"Like, full ride?"

"Yeah. Needed it, too."

"I get that. Decent track program?" I used my feet to help me swing back and forth.

"My first year was tough," he said. "I didn't compete much. At Christmas, I wanted to quit, which, of course, was nuts. I'd worked so hard to get there, so I couldn't just give up after a few months. But last year I did okay, until I hurt my knee. Such a drag. I'm rehabbing it now—that's why I'm in Bracebridge, working. I need to get it ready for fall."

I computed his age in my brain. He could be nineteen if he was in his second year. "How'd you hurt it?"

"Goofing off. After practice, screwing around on the hurdles for fun. Hit one and hit the track."

"Ewww. That sounds painful." I paused. "You're an assistant manager, already. At the restaurant."

"Less walking. I've worked there every summer since I was fourteen. Bethany was cool to give me a manager job this summer, where I wasn't on my feet. They're good to me. I can't complain."

He'd just made my age, a just-turned-seventeen, sound so young. I was going to keep my mouth shut about how old I was. But, then again, he'd probably seen my application.

"What high school did you go to?" I asked. "I don't recognize you."

He laughed. "And in this city, I can't hide very well."

I glanced at him. I thought about Kash being called names for being tall, but this was different. His situation wouldn't just be teasing and rude, this would be getting called names because of race.

"Have you always lived in Bracebridge?"

"We came from Toronto when I was around ten. We vacationed here all the time, and then an adminstrator position came up for my dad at the hospital, and he applied and got it. My mom is a hairdresser, so she can work anywhere. My parents wanted to get out of the city, so we moved. Bracebridge was a bit of a shock, because my elementary school in Toronto was definitely more diverse." He glanced over at me and gave me a lopsided smile. "You ask a lot of questions. How about we play a game? You ask a question, then I ask one."

I shrugged. "Okay."

"I'll answer your question about high school," he said. "You wouldn't recognize me, because I went back to Toronto for high school to run track in a competitive program. I lived with my grandparents. So, you're right, you didn't see me wandering the halls here." He swung in the swing and glanced at me. "My turn for a question." He paused for a brief second before he said, "Don't quit rowing. Just because you didn't make a team."

"Um ... that's not a question." I kicked dirt.

"Okay. Are you looking for a scholarship?" He stretched his long legs out. I could hear the others, laughing hysterically about something. Figures I'd be the one in the serious conversation, but this was where I was happiest, talking about anything to do with being an athlete. I'd sort of met a kindred spirit here.

"Beep. Time's up," he said. "Two points for me because you didn't answer."

"I didn't know we had rules to this game. Or points."

"We do now that you're not answering."

I blew out air. "Okay, here's the skinny. I was sort of recruited by Penn last year. Their coach called my coach to talk about our whole four. And we met with him. But they do financial aid and not scholarships, so I don't know how it all works."

"Coaches put in recommendations."

"I didn't make the Canadian Junior Team, though. Now I need to get on their radar again next year."

"It's a process," said Tim. "Recruiters came to my track meets."

"What sucks is my mom and her boyfriend are ganging up against me to go to the Lakehead campus in Orillia—not even Thunder Bay—and live at home." There was no way I was going to tell someone I barely knew about my mother being pregnant. She was forty-five!

"Do they have a rowing program there?" he asked.

"Nope. And for me, that's a problem."

"Penn has a great sports program and pretty cool campus."

I looked at him and, even though it was dark outside, I saw something honest in his face, like he understood. "You've been there?" I asked.

"Okay, that's your question." He gave me an impish smile. "The answer is: yeah. We had a track meet there this year. I actually watched the rowers on the Schuylkill River."

"Ohmygod. You did? We're supposed to take a trip this year if we're recruited." I paused. "My friend and me." *Would that happen now?*

"Boathouse row is pretty rad," he said.

Something in my heart exploded into tiny pieces, all floating with no direction. I'd looked at photos of the boathouses and wanted it so badly. I shuffled my feet, creating a little dust beneath me.

"Keep at it," he said softly.

I had to get off this topic. "You asked if Lakehead had

a rowing program. That's your question. My turn now. Did you run up the steps like Rocky Balboa?" Time to lighten this conversation. I had also looked at a photo of those steps in Philadelphia, and wanted to run up them just once.

"Ye-ah." He flexed his muscles. "A-dri-ane!"

Amaya yelled out, "What's going on over there?"

"We're talking about Sly," he answered. "You know, as in Rocky Bal-bo-a." He tried to do the Sylvester Stallone voice, but he wasn't very successful.

I laughed. He laughed. And the gang smoking the joint laughed.

But then Margo piped up and said, "Come on, Mr. Manager, you of all people can do a better thug voice than that."

I blinked in shock. Had she just said what I thought she said? The laughter subsided a bit and was replaced with a weird embarrassed, awkward kind of laughter. Since I had a great-uncle in my family, (my grandpa's brother), who married a Black woman, and I knew that my grandpa supported him when the rest of his family wouldn't, I couldn't stand what she had said. I blurted out, "That's a racist thing to say."

"Relax, new girl," said Margo. "It's not racist. Anyway, he knows I'm joking."

"It's a totally racist comment," said Amaya. "You should apologize."

"Okay, little *hostesses*, chill out. Mr. Assistant Manager knows I'm kidding. He knows I love him."

"Margo," said Tim, "Shut the hell up."

"It's just a joke," said Margo. "You know that, right, Tim?" She blew him a kiss.

"You know as well as I do, that's not really a joke," said Tim. "Quit while you're ahead."

"Yeah, and it's not the least bit funny," said Brendan. "Turner's right. Shut. The. Hell. Up."

I turned to Tim, who just shook his head and rolled his eyes. Then he said quietly, "I hate that kind of crap."

Margo stood and grabbed her bag. "God, you guys. I was just trying to be funny. You don't have to jump down my back. I didn't mean anything by it." She left in a huff.

"You cool, Turner?" Brendan asked.

"I'm cool," answered Tim.

I swung back and forth, moving my feet in the dirt, thinking about what had just happened. Then I heard him ask, "Do you live close to here?"

He gave me a little smile. Since he was moving on, that was my cue to as well. "I didn't know it was your turn to ask a question," I said. I took a beat before I answered him. "It's Bracebridge. Don't we all live close to everything? My turn. Are your parents supportive? Of your track?" I'm not sure why I asked that, except that the conversation with my mother was still bugging me.

"Yeah, they're great," he answered. "I'm lucky that way."

"That's cool," I said. What else could I say? His answer was positive.

"My track has cost them," he continued. "No doubt about that. The scholarship has helped. Without it, I'd be driving back and forth to Orillia, too. My little sister is an unbelievable hockey goalie, wants to make the Olympic team. Those pads of hers cost huge dough. Between the two of us, we drain them. They travel so much for both of us."

"My mom used to be like that. Supportive, that is."

Just thinking of my relationship with Mom made me sigh. Now that there was a baby on the way, would she spend her money on it? I still couldn't fathom that, come December, I was going to have a baby brother or sister. We were so far apart in age. If I did get to go away to school, I wouldn't be around to watch "it" take its first step. But who knew if I would even get to go away now? I felt as if my mother was spreading out her love, and I was on the bottom of her list. She was obsessed with having this baby, and she was giving up my future for it.

"Hey, you okay?" Tim put his hand on my shoulder.

I sat up tall. "I should be asking you that question."

"I'm fine," he said. "Thanks for your comment, by the way. Not sure it will help you at work, though. Margo might stop with the extra tips."

"I don't care about that," I said.

My phone pinged. How long had we been talking? I pulled my phone out of my pants pocket and saw that it was midnight already. My mother had sent three text messages asking where I was. I kind of liked that she *might be* worried. I fired a text back, telling her I had to work late but was on my way home.

"I've got to go," I said. I dumped the rest of the tequila on the ground and stood.

"Don't let the gang see you do that."

"Do what?"

He bumped me with his shoulder. "Dump good tequila," he whispered in my ear.

I turned and his face was so close to mine. He smelled like wintergreen and trees, or bark, or something woodsy and masculine. The combination was intoxicating, minus the tequila. "Okay," I whispered back. "Thanks for the heads-up."

"You want me to ride you home? I've got my bike here, too."

I shrugged. "You can stay. I'm fine."

"Nah, I'm ready to go, too."

We said goodbye to the group and hopped on our bikes. We didn't talk much, but the company was nice.

"Nice house," he said when we were in front of Stew's place.

"Not mine," I said. "My mom's boyfriend's place. We moved from a small house to this. I liked our house better, but she doesn't." After I said that, something booted me inside, like I'd said something I shouldn't have, like I was trash-talking her. I might get a little kick for talking smack against Stew, but I got a big steel-toe for talking smack against my mother.

We were standing under streetlights and I could see

his face. Was he going to kiss me? In ninth grade, I'd had a boyfriend for two months, and we'd gone at it a few times. But since then, I'd been too focused on sports. Last year, we'd been so dedicated to our four, and doing well in St. Catharines, that I lived for my workouts. All I wanted was the medal, and we got it. *Nothing in life is free.* That's one of Stew's sayings that I believed.

"I should go in," I said.

"You working tomorrow night?" he asked.

"Yeah," I said. "But then I'm off for a day. Does the schedule change every week?"

"It can. If you put in the days you need off, we try to accommodate. I don't work the lunches. I need the time for my physio appointments."

I nodded, thinking that I needed zero lunch shifts during the week, too, so I could row with Alan. That is, if he wanted to keep going with me. "Yeah, nights are better for me, too, during the week. But I like lunch shifts on the weekend."

He nodded. Then grinned.

"What are you smiling about?"

"Nothing. But FYI, I do the scheduling." He put his foot on his pedal and moved closer.

"Is Margo always like that?" I looked into his eyes.

"She wanted my job. She's doing some restaurant management course and thought she should have it. Bethany gave it to me because of my injury, so she's mad."

"That doesn't give her the right to say what she did."

"No, it doesn't. But I need the job, so I'll ignore her at work. She's not worth my energy." He kissed his peace fingers then pressed them to my cheek. "I gotta get going," he said. "Early physio."

I leaned into his fingers, and my body heated unexpectedly. Tingles spread through my entire body, and it shocked the crap out of me. And I didn't want to break away. I could seriously feel the pulsing of his fingertips.

The moment only ended because he pulled his hand away.

"See you tomorrow," he said.

I nodded, unable to speak. He took off, pedaling away from me, and I watched him until he was out of sight. What was I doing? I didn't have time for a boyfriend.

But, damn, he'd felt good.

Ups and Downs

The Olympics are
the ultimate dream
for an amateur
athlete.
But training for them
is brutally
hard.
Holly will figure
that one out.
Some athletes get injured.
Some get tired of training.
Others give up
for family reasons
or because they
want to party
or they realize
they don't have

what it takes
or they get
involved with
someone
who isn't
supportive.
Like the Olympics
life is
hard work,
full of ups
and downs,
circumstances you can't
control,
people who
want to
control.
Sometimes you just
gotta
sit tall,
not collapse,
look at your
outside world
and stay

calm inside.
Keep that
chin up,
dig deep,
and work
through
the
shit.

Chapter 15

"Let's try some pyramid rowing," said Alan.

I nodded. I'd already been on the water for an hour. I'd worn a watch today—for my heart rate and to see the time. We'd been doing technique, and he'd had me working on hand speed, moving with the boat.

"Ten hard strokes, then ten easy strokes, followed by twenty on, twenty off, thirty on, thirty off, forty on, then back down to ten. I'd like you to do at least five sets. Maybe seven for added bonus. Or ten, if you've got the energy. This training is all about going up and down."

Again, I nodded. Five sets I could do. But ten would be a killer. Was he testing me?

"Turn around at the end and we'll get started."

I let the boat run and spun it around. Then I started. One set felt good, and I powered through all the times, even the forty-stroke one.

The second set, I had to dig deeper, especially with

Lorna Schultz Nicholson

the forty strokes. The breather in between sets was three to five minutes of steady rowing. I slowed down and tried to catch my breath, just rolling up and down the slide, putting the sculls in the water, and doing easy pushes.

"Ready!" he called out.

Ten strokes was easy. Twenty a little harder. Thirty seemed like forever. I had to seriously grind through it to keep up the pace. Then came the forty. I powered through the first twenty strokes, then I felt myself dying. Alan never said anything when I finished that set, so I assumed he wasn't happy with me. I had to do better. In between, I focused on breathing and getting my heart rate down. Two more sets for five. Two more. I could do it.

By the time I finished the next two sets, my legs were like rubber, and I was shaking and wobbling in the boat. My hands kept crashing together as well, and my knuckles were getting raw.

"Easy row for five minutes." He putt-putted beside me.

"I noticed a lot of collapsing in your body, especially in the forty strokes," he said. "You can't let that happen.

Think of sitting tall, keeping your chest up and off your rib cage, and lift those ribs so your belly button is open."

I tried to do that, even though I was tired.

"Holly, keep your eyes up and your chin horizontal to the water."

His boat chugged beside me. I didn't dare look at him.

"Look off the stern of your boat. Look at the world in front of you, while keeping your focus inside your boat. It's magic, even when you're pushing beyond your limits."

I blew out oxygen, sat tall, lifted my chin, and looked in the distance. Far in the distance. Was he right? Sitting tall did make me see more. But how did I look outside but stay inside? And could I hold this during the tough stuff? The minutes of rest went by way too fast.

He said, "Turn around and let's do the sets again."

I sucked in a deep breath. Okay. I could do this. It was like running grandstands. Only harder. Up. Down. Up. Down. *But. I. Could. Do. It.*

I started up on his command, and pushed as hard as I could, desperately trying to sit tall. The wind had picked up a little and that, put together with my fatigue, made my balance iffy. A little wave tilted the boat.

"Chin up," he yelled.

I righted the boat, but not before my knuckles smacked against the side. Sharp pain seeped through me. I kept going. Sitting tall. Staring ahead. Pushing. *Keep breathing.* Focus. I talked in my head. The hard strokes became harder and harder. Was I going in a straight line? I felt like I was. I pushed through, then I got to the forty strokes and, when I started to die around twenty strokes, I heard him.

"Exhale on the drive. But stay lifted," he yelled through the wind.

I grimaced and pushed, blowing out air with each stroke.

"You're at thirty-two strokes per minute," he yelled. "Take it to thirty-four!"

I tried to increase my stroke rate. I did. Or I hoped I did.

"You're still at thirty-two. Crank it up!"

Guess not. I had to get there. But my reserves were gone. I was rowing on fumes.

Just five more strokes and I would get a break. I pushed and went up the slide. Faster. The boat was moving faster, so I had to go with it. Four more. Three more. Two more. One more. My heart was racing. I could hardly breathe. I wanted to collapse and let the boat run. But I had to finish the workout.

How much more was he going to make me do?

Two more sets. Then another. Then another. I'd smacked my knuckles twice more and could see that they were bleeding. But I held on and finished all ten.

"Not bad," he said when I'd finished the last set. "I wasn't sure you could do ten."

I was so glad it was over.

"Now we're going to do it one more time," he said.

Again? "You said we would do max ten," I gasped.

"So, I lied," he laughed. "One more for luck."

Luck? I swallowed, my throat dry, and grabbed a sip of water. Then I turned the boat around. Was he seriously laughing? I managed to push through another set, but my muscles were screaming when I was done. I'd barely kept my head up.

"Take it in," he said.

As I rowed easy, my limbs felt like cement that wasn't setting properly. I made it to the dock, and when I got out, my knees almost buckled. I undid my oarlocks, while Alan putt-putted in. He didn't say anything, and I wanted him to tell me I had done a good job.

Lorna Schultz Nicholson

Maybe I'd disappointed him.

Was I always disappointing people? Even myself?

I took the boat up and put it on the rack. Then I went down to help take the motorboat out of the water. We worked in silence, pulling the boat onto the boat trailer. Was this my last row with Alan? Maybe I didn't go hard enough for him.

He broke through my thoughts and said, "What did your parents say about you rowing the single?"

"Um ..." I stammered. I hadn't talked to Mom, and Stew didn't count. What to say? Avoidance was the best way to handle this question. "My dad isn't in the picture."

"Sorry to hear that," he said. He sounded so sincere.

I shrugged. "Not a big deal."

"That would be to me," he said. Then he gave off this heavy sigh, and briefly closed his eyes. When he opened them, he blew out air and said, "If I was your dad, it would be a huge deal."

He shook his head as if to get rid of whatever he was thinking about. Then he said, "I talked to Gillian, the president of the club, and she's completely fine with us working together."

He wasn't giving up on me. This made my heart skip a beat. "Thank you for doing that."

"If I'm coaching you," he said, "we need five water workouts a week."

Five?! "O-kay," I replied, stunned. Five was a full training program. I wanted to shriek, I was so happy to hear this. Every morning I would be on the water.

"You should also be doing some strength training. I can give you a program that my ..."

He stopped mid-sentence and fiddled with the boat trailer.

Although I was thrilled with this news, I couldn't help wonder ... what exactly was going on here? Five days? Weights? What was I training for? I was afraid to ask, in case he snapped at me, and I had the feeling he could do that to his rowers. *His rowers. Who did he coach? Why did his words trail off?*

Just thinking this made me blurt out, "Where did you coach?" I couldn't help it.

"Right now, for your progress, that's not important," he said. "I want you to focus on being in the boat. The purity of the sport."

He didn't make eye contact, and I could tell he was

getting ready to get in his truck and just drive away. Again. I thought I deserved to know something about him, anything, if I was going to do this training program, which I wanted to do, even though I had no idea where I was going with it.

"I think if we're going to do this, I should know something about you," I said.

"I used to coach. You're right on that one."

"O-kay." I stared at him, hoping he would look at me.

"What difference does it make who I am?" He tied up his boat. "I'm here now. Coaching you—and that's all you need to know. At this point in your training, the less you know about me, the more you will learn."

"Five days a week is a full program," I said. "Why do you want to continue with me?"

He kept his head bowed for a moment. Then, finally, he lifted it and glanced my way. "You have something." He stared me right in the eyes. "When you sat tall," he said, "and opened up your body, stared ahead, you moved the boat. I saw the focus. I saw you almost leave your body and move toward that feeling of being one with the boat. That's a gift."

It had happened. He was right. I'd felt it.

I didn't have a response.

"I like what I see in you," he said softly. "I like coaching athletes like you."

"Thank you," I whispered.

Then he put up his hand. "I said I see something, but you have a long way to go. Don't let your ego get to you. Don't rush through everything just to have it now. It will be the end. I can promise you that."

That statement just plummeted me right back to earth. "Thank you for that," I said.

A voice spoke in my head, like a ping-pong ball. He wants to see what you're made of. *This is a chance. Don't throw in the twenty yet. Like you did in the seat race and bombed. Just chill. Let the race unfold.*

"I'm willing to work," I stated.

He stopped moving and just stood still for a moment, staring, and I was reminded of the first day I met him. That sadness behind his eyes made me step back, move away from him. It was like it oozed out of his body and swirled in the air around him. I didn't want it touching me. I didn't want to be in his bubble, in case it just burst all over me, toxic pieces of sadness. I'd enjoyed the row, felt satisfied with the hard work, wanted to improve, and during my entire time out there, had only thought about the moment. I didn't think about being cut, about my mother, moving, Stew, the boys, the baby. I needed this badly to survive my summer. I couldn't screw it up by asking too many questions.

He continued to just stand there. I didn't move either, and just watched him. Finally, he exhaled and straightened his shoulders a bit. He turned to me and ran his hand through his graying hair. "This training might help you reach your goal of making National Team next year. I want to help you try. I hope that's a good enough answer to why."

He wanted to help me. Someone wanted to do something *for me*. "It is," I said.

"Good," he said. "Let's leave it at that, then. As long as your mom is good with these extra workouts. That's important."

"She'll be fine," I said. "Thanks for helping me."

"I'm enjoying being out here, too. So, thank you." He gave me one of his little silly smirks. "I wouldn't waste my time out here if you weren't willing to work." He pointed to my hands. "Make sure you put some antibiotic cream on those knuckles."

A phone rang. I'd never seen him on his phone, not even once to check for a text message. He pulled it out of the pocket of his cargo shorts. And he stared at it, looking confused.

"This is a new phone," he mumbled. "I don't know what button to press."

It continued ringing. I stepped forward and pointed to the green button. "Press this," I said. I also looked at the name on the screen. Bella Coleman.

He answered, "Hello." With his phone to his ear, he walked away from me so I couldn't hear. His head was lowered as he talked.

The call didn't last long, and when he was off, he came back to me and said, "I can only go on the water, Monday to Friday. Weekends are for family."

"I'm good with that."

"Family is important," he said. He sucked in a deep breath, and there was that dullness again. "The most important part of our lives. Family should be above everything."

I didn't answer. I didn't want to talk about family, because I wasn't sure I agreed with him. I mean, my mother: sure—but what about this new little sibling I was going to have? Would that little person become the *most important part of my life*? And was I to believe that Stew and his kids were now my family? Wasn't buying this. Didn't want to talk about it. Nope.

He glanced at me and made eye contact. "It's also important to balance your interests off the water. Get away from the boat, the training, and have other hobbies and interests. Friends, that kind of stuff."

I almost laughed out loud. *Friends and that kind of stuff?* Alan was getting all-psychology on me this morning. I made eye contact back, just to try and see what his reasons were for this talk. The phone call had done something.

"Um ... you mentioned something about a training program," I said. I had to shut down this family talk.

"Strength training is critical to success," he said.

"You could email it to me."

"I don't email anymore," he said.

"You don't email?" Who didn't email? Weird.

He shook his head. "I will bring a paper version on Monday. I'm not going to monitor or coach your weight workouts. That will be up to you to be honest and do the work. Tomorrow, go for a long run, at least an hour, and do some sort of weight workout that includes bench pulls. Forty pounds, ten sets of twenty. Sunday, take the day off, or go for a nice easy run or bike ride, or even just a yoga class or a good stretch class. Monday, I will give you the strength training plan."

This was a lot of work for him. I was so confused, but I wanted to do this, and the internal pull I felt to show up, work hard, was powerful.

"Um ... how much do you charge?"

He shook his head. "Nothing. We both need this."

For the second day in a row, Alan got in his truck and drove away without saying goodbye, just giving me his little one-finger wave.

I rode my bike home, thinking about everything that had just happened. There was no end result to this, no regatta to race in, just a whole lot of training.

Then I thought about his phone call. So weird and secretive. Who was *Bella Coleman?*

When I got home, both boys were now faking sick. They could be alone because Kevin was older, and I was supposed to be there for some of the time. I went into the family room where they were playing video games. Kevin glanced over at me.

"Hey," he said.

"I'm going to take a shower. Then I'll make you lunch."

"I'm hungry now," he said.

"I need to shower."

"Make it before you shower. Dad said you would make us lunch and it's noon already. I'm starving."

I stared at the little shit. "Here's the thing, Kevin," I said. "I'm taking a shower now, then I'm making you lunch. And if you're that hungry, go to the kitchen and make something yourself."

Curtis didn't look up from the video screen. He moved his shoulders like he was really racing a car. "Come on, Kevin," he said. "I'm beating you."

Kevin went back to his controller.

I went to my room and, even before showering, I went on my computer. Was Bella Alan's wife? Did they share the last name? I had to give it a try. I googled *Alan Coleman rowing coach.*

A list of sites popped up on my screen. I read the date on the first one. February 1, 2013. Over eight years ago. Weird it was first. I immediately opened it.

As I read, my heart just sank, like, down through my entire body to the soles of my feet. My skin went cold, and my throat dried up, making me gasp.

Boat
With No Name

It was my 15th birthday.
I asked for
my own single.
To win an Olympic
gold medal,
I needed my own boat.
Brand new, shiny and sleek,
 I washed it,
rigged it, too. Yes, I learned how to rig.
It was my baby.
Name it,
said Dad.
Couldn't think of a name.
It can be the Anonymous,
said Mom,
always the funny one
the lightness,

Lorna Schultz Nicholson

the air we breathed.
One whole year,
never lost:
Canadian High School Championships,
American High School Championships,
Royal Canadian Henley.
I won in
my boat
with no name.
I rowed every
race of my career
in that
nameless boat.
One night at dinner
we thought of names.
What about MoDa?
(Get it, Mom and Dad. Lol. So silly.)
Or Mada. Or Dama. Or Damo!
Even Mr. Serious laughed
until he cried.
My parents don't
laugh
anymore.

Sometimes they
try,
it's a trickle
of a laugh
but neither
of them
laughs
until they cry.
Mostly,
     they just
     cry.

Lorna Schultz Nicholson

Chapter 16

I stared at my computer. My stomach heaved, and I put my hand to my mouth.

A photo of Alan stared at me. The article accompanying the photo was titled, "Swells Capsize Rowing Single." He stood on the end of the dock, looking way younger, wind blowing his hair, helicopter overhead, searchlight shining on the water. A motorboat was dragging a single. I leaned forward to read the article. My heart sank further and further with every word.

Wicked Winds cause Despair and Damage in Victoria, British Columbia.

"Daughter of Olympic Rowing Coach Missing."

An unexpected storm hit Victoria, around 5 PM on February 1st, with wind gusts of 110 km/hr wreaking havoc across the city. Sixteen-year-old Lily Coleman, daughter of Olympic rowing coach Alan Coleman, was out on Elk Lake in her rowing single when the wind picked up. Her boat capsized in the storm. Emergency helicopters were flown in to try and locate Ms. Coleman, but the winds were even too severe for them to fly close to the water. When the winds eased to 60 km/hr, around midnight, Ms. Coleman's boat was found floating upside down in the middle of the lake. The search for the body is still ongoing.

"Ohmygod," I whispered to myself. Every word in the article stabbed my heart for this man, whom I had just met, who had been an Olympic coach, a National Team coach, and also the head coach for the men's team at the University of Victoria, which was a powerhouse during his time. Silken Laumann had even gone there. I looked at my poster. Did he coach her, too? Maybe he coached her in the single, like he coached this daughter, Lily.

Obsessed with getting to the bottom of this horrible tragedy, I kept searching, and came up with another article, posted the next day, from the Victoria *Times Colonist*. Victoria was a way bigger city than Bracebridge, and this had been a big story, one that captured the front page of the paper. The photo accompanying the article was of divers going into the lake, and there was also a side photo of Alan in his motorboat, coaching his Olympic crew. He looked so intense and focused. He'd coached in the Olympics!

Search for Missing Rower Ongoing
Sixteen-year-old Lily Coleman, daughter of Olympic rowing coach, Alan Coleman, is still missing, after an unexpected storm hit Victoria on the evening of February 1. The winds escalated to 110 km an hour within the span of 30 minutes. The city was taken by surprise by the storm, and trees and hydro wires were knocked down all over the area. Ms. Coleman's single rowing boat was found capsized in the middle of the Elk Lake. Divers are now searching the water for her body. Ms. Coleman appears to have gone out for a row on her own, even though there was a Cold Water Rule in effect.

She went out alone? Wow. Even I knew about the Cold Water Rule. No one was supposed to row when the rule was in effect. No one. What would have possessed her to go out? Beside the article were two photos of her. One looked like a standard school photo, probably her most recent, Grade 11, maybe. She was pretty, blonde hair, and it looked like she had brown eyes like her dad's. I shook my head. This was Alan's daughter staring back at me. No doubt about it. Then there was a photo of her standing on the dock, holding sculling oars in her hands, and Alan was beside her. She was almost as tall as Alan, which meant she was probably six feet, if not more. I enlarged the photo and leaned forward to get a good look. I blew out a rush of air. Alan looked happy, like, genuinely happy. I'd seen him smile before, but I'd never seen him look that happy. There was something in his eyes, a spark, pride for this daughter.

I kept scrolling, searching for more information.

The date of the next article I opened was exactly a week after the day Lily disappeared.

Rower Still Missing
Hypothermia Can Cause Disorientation

An unseasonably cold winter has plunged the temperature of the water in Elk Lake. The month of January saw parts of the lake frozen, which hasn't happened since 1952. Although the air temperature has risen in the past few weeks, melting the ice on the lake, the temperature of the water remains below zero. On February 1, Lily Coleman, daughter of Olympic coach Alan Coleman, went on the water for a row in her single rowing boat. A sudden storm took Victoria by surprise, and Ms. Coleman's boat capsized. It is possible that she was able to exit the water, and is suffering from hypothermia, which could make her disoriented and mentally fragile. If you know the whereabouts of Lily Coleman, please call the Victoria Police Department at 1-800-768-4411.

Had she succumbed to hypothermia, as the article was suggesting? They had still been searching for her body in the lake a week later. That would have been excruciating for Alan. Every day, searching the streets, but every day, nothing. No body.

I googled Elk Lake and a photo popped up. It wasn't that big a lake. How could they have not found her body? Did she end up on the streets, wandering around? Is that where they had found her? Then it hit me. Was she still alive today, maybe brain damaged? Maybe they had to care for her at home. Or maybe she was in an institution? Here in Bracebridge, though? Our city was small, more like a town, and we didn't have that kind of place, just the seniors centers. How did Alan end up in Bracebridge? All it was famous for was Santa's Village.

After reading that article, I had to search some more to find answers.

"Still Searching for Missing Rower!"

This one was another week later! She still hadn't been found. I found a YouTube video, where Alan and his wife, Bella, had stood in front of the television camera and begged for news of their daughter. They showed the photos that had been in that first article. This was heartbreaking. Lily had been their only child.

I kept going. And found another small article.

One Month Later, Body Still Not Found.

Underneath the heading was the subtitle, *Parents Search the Streets.*

I read the article, every single word. Tears pressed against the back of my eyes. Alan and his wife Bella had gone to the streets and put up signs, asking if anyone had seen their daughter. They'd even checked all the homeless shelters in case she'd suffered a trauma and couldn't remember who she was. There was a photo of them standing in front of a soup kitchen. They both had vacant eyes, blank stares, hollow cheeks, and red-rimmed eyes. I couldn't imagine what that must have been like, walking up and down streets, showing a photo of Lily, only to hear, "I've never seen her."

It made me feel sick to think of Alan doing that. Such desperation. I continued searching for that last bit of information. I knew I had to make lunch and get ready for work soon, but I had to do one last look to find out what happened.

One more scroll and I found it.

Jogger Finds Body.

I put my hand to my mouth and moaned. Lily's bloated body had been found by a jogger *in June*. I couldn't imagine finding a body while out running. I would freak out and scream. The jogger would have been the one to call the cops. Once they identified the body, the news would have been delivered to Alan and his wife.

A knock sounded on my door and I jumped, putting my hand to my heart. How long had I been at this? Oh, crap. I'd been an hour already.

"Yeah," I said.

Curtis pushed open the door. He squished his eyebrows together. "You haven't showered yet?"

I closed my laptop. "I'll be quick," I said.

"I made lunch," he said.

"You did? Wow. Thanks, Dude." I pretended to punch his shoulder.

He laughed and stared at my hands. "Did you get in a fight?"

I'd forgotten about my shredded knuckles. I clasped my hands together. "Fell off my bike."

"Looks like a fight to me." He grinned. "Did you?"

I tried to smile and pretend like I hadn't just discovered news that had sent me spiraling. "Yeah, just like this." I did a few jabs in the air and he rolled his eyes.

"You'd lose for sure if you punched like that."

I wanted to laugh, but my brain was on overload with what I had just found out. This was Alan's daughter I had been reading about. My body was seriously sweating with this news. But the kid had made lunch. How sweet.

"Let's go eat this lunch you made," I said, trying to sound normal.

"It's just sandwiches. You can shower first. They won't go bad."

"Sounds amazing. I'll be quick," I said.

Curtis turned and left, and I shut my door and leaned against it, closing my eyes. No wonder Alan had such sadness oozing from him. What a horrible way to die. How was I going to deal with him now that I knew about this? How would I talk to him? Did I let him know that I knew? I had no idea what to do with any of this information.

And there was one really big question that kept circling around my brain. I'd looked at that photo of them pulling the boat out of the water, tried to zoom in on the side of it to see if it had a name, but couldn't get a good closeup.

Was the *Lilybean* his daughter's boat?

Was I rowing in a dead girl's boat?

Missing

Lights twinkling
on the
Christmas tree.
Early. Pitch black outside.
Presents under a tree.
One was
soft and cuddly
a bow around
its neck,
a little jumping
ball of
fluff.
Santa brought me what I asked for!!!!!
I squealed. I was seven.
You name him, said Mom.
He licked my face and
I laughed and

Lorna Schultz Nicholson

he jumped
and an angel ornament
fell.
Angel, I said.
Angel wasn't an angel.
He chewed my Barbie,
peed in my room,
dug up the back yard.
But Angel slept on my bed,
curled up
at the end.
One day,
I came home from school
and saw the open gate
in the backyard.
I called and called.
Up and down the streets,
Dad and I went in his car.
Angel, come! Angel, come!
We made posters. Angel's best photo.
We put them on telephone poles,
mailboxes,
store windows.

I didn't sleep all night.
My bed felt
empty.
Someone phoned
in the morning,
because they saw
the poster
and they had Angel.
He was alive!
My parents had experience with
posters.
Sadly, they only worked
           for Angel.

Chapter 17

Work was a struggle.

I managed to rhyme off all the specials, but it took concentration. All I could think of was Alan. Alan Coleman. The rowing coach who had lost his daughter. The man who had been coaching me.

Tim talked to me, and I answered in one-word sentences. I know he was confused, maybe even hurt that I was being so distracted, but I just couldn't speak, and needed energy for the specials, to remember, to smile. Amaya was off and I had to handle the front desk by myself. I buried myself in getting the customers seated, not having time to go searching for information on my phone.

At the end of my shift, Tim came over and said, "The new schedule is out."

I almost groaned out loud. I had wanted to talk to him about my shifts and I'd forgotten. I needed all nights during the week and days on the weekend, if I wanted to row five days.

Was I rowing in a dead girl's boat?

I straightened the menus, trying not to think about what I had found out.

"I managed to give you all nights next week," said Tim. "Tuesday and Friday off."

I stopped my shuffling of the menus, all now perfectly straight, and looked at him. "You're the best. Thank you so much."

"No probs," he replied. I swear he was looking at me funny. Was I acting as weird as I felt?

I wanted to say sorry for being so distant all night, but the words wouldn't come out. "I really appreciate it."

"Are you okay?" he asked.

"I'm fine," I said. "I wanted to do a good job with Amaya gone tonight."

"You did." He nodded.

"Um ... you want to do something now?" he asked. "I'll be done in fifteen. We could go for a walk by the river."

Yes. No. Yes. No. With everything swirling in my head, I did want to escape, but then I didn't. Stupid, I know. But what if I was forced to sit up and talk to Super-Stew and Mom? Maybe I needed to get out of my head, even if just for a short time.

"Okay," I said. "For a bit. I work the day shift tomorrow."

"Understand," he said.

I finished filling the salt and pepper shakers, and for the second night in a row was given extra tips, except from Margo, who had basically ignored me all night. I didn't care. I wasn't going to suck up to her, not after what she'd said to Tim. All my extra money would go into a jar I kept in my closet. I texted Mom to tell her I would be a little later, but not to worry. She texted back and said Stew would pick me up. I said no, go to bed. Both of them. *Please, both of them.*

Tim and I got on our bikes and rode to the park where I rowed every day, but we stopped closer to the falls, away from the boathouse. We found a secluded bench to sit down on, and for the first few minutes, we were like two lumps, just sitting and not talking. I had so much going on inside my head, small talk just didn't seem possible. Did he call her *Lilybean*? Was that her nickname? I should have gone straight home. I was so zoned out.

"Your boathouse is near here, right?" Tim finally asked.

"Yeah." I pointed to the area where the boathouse was. There were no lights on at this time of night. "Ours is so small, unlike the St. Catharines Club. They have something like nine boat bays."

He nudged me with his shoulder. "Yeah, but look how good your team did for such a little club. That's impressive."

"Thanks," I mumbled.

"I told you about boathouse row in Philly," he said, "but I also just so happened to be in Victoria for a high school track meet, when the crews were rowing on Elk Lake. They have a pretty sweet boathouse, too."

Elk Lake!

Why did he have to mention that lake tonight? Lily Coleman died in Elk Lake. The same question ran through my mind, and it had been there all night. Elk Lake wasn't huge, so why couldn't they find her that night? I looked out at our river. There had been summer swimmers die in the river because they got caught and couldn't swim. Anything was possible with water. What would it be like for Lily, in the cold water and wind, all alone? Even the emergency helicopters couldn't find her that night. I shuddered, just thinking about what had happened.

"You cold?" Tim asked. He pressed his shoulder against mine.

"Not too bad," I said. I let my skin touch his, and my body tingled. I let us stay like that. It was like there was glue on our arms, keeping us together. I liked his skin on mine. I did. It felt comfortable, and it seemed to help me relax from my keyed-up state.

"Um ..." I said to make conversation, "the University of Victoria used to be such a rowing powerhouse. They won everything." Alan coached them. The guy who was coaching me. And he coached in the Olympics. It still seemed unbelievable that I had met him. I now understood why he didn't want me to know who he was. He'd said he wanted to keep the workouts pure, and he was right—now that I knew he'd coached the Olympics, I thought about him differently. Not only had he coached, but he'd won Olympic gold medals!

"Maybe you could go there instead of Penn." Tim's voice broke through my thoughts.

"I've been thinking about that," I said. "I'm not sure about my financial situation anymore, though."

"Gotcha," he said. "University is expensive." He paused before he asked, "What kind of training are you doing if you're not rowing? Must be tough to keep the intensity up without being in a boat."

"Running, weights, ergometer work to simulate."

Liar, liar, pants on fire. Lies just spewed out of my mouth. My rowing with Alan was a secret I was keeping, even from Kash, because ... I had no idea where it was going, or if it was going anywhere. Why was Alan coaching *me*? Any crew at our club would want him to coach. He could have his pick. *How did he end up in Bracebridge?*

"Good for you," said Tim. His voice penetrating my thoughts. Again.

"Must be tough for you, too," I said. I had to get the conversation off me. "Having to rehab."

"It's brutal." He shook his head. "I hate it. There are so many track meets going on right now, and I'm not in any. It's knocking me. All my friends are racing and I'm not, and I just think I'm losing so much."

"I'm sorry," I said.

"Yeah, it just so sucks. I need to make some decisions soon."

"About what?"

"I dunno." He shoved his hands in his pockets and slouched on the seat, stretching his long legs out in front of him. Now our thighs touched, too. "Like, what am I running track for?"

"Do you love it?"

"I do, but I'm also going into my third year at college. This injury just bites big time and has set me back."

"Must make you feel out of control."

"You got that right." He turned to look at me. Our faces were close. "You know, thanks for saying that."

"I understand," I said.

"How about you?" he asked.

"Ah. Unlike you, I had control. I just had to win a seat race, which I blew."

"So, a coach once drilled me with this one. You learn more from losing than you do from winning," he said.

I laughed. "If my mom's boyfriend said that, I would roll my eyes. But you made it sound right, because you get it and it's sincere. Our coach gave us that one, too."

"It's an athlete's mantra. Kicker is, you have to analyze the losses to get the victories."

"That's so true." I paused, then I said, "I've lost two goals this summer. I got cut from National Team, and now I won't go to Henley. Two big bombs."

"Henley is a big regatta, right?"

I nodded. "Yeah, it's huge. I quit the club team, but they weren't going anyway. I lasted one row because the boat had no commitment. Like, I mean, nothing."

"Hey," he said, "now it's my turn to say I'm sorry." He put his arm around me.

It felt good, I guess. His arm, that is. Like someone cared. And someone understood. Someone who was an athlete and treated me like an athlete, and not like some child who had a little hobby that needed to stop right now, because a baby was more important.

As we sat on the bench, not talking, his arm around me, my head leaning into his shoulder, the wind started blowing, shaking the branches above our heads, and making the water slap up against the shore. Slap. Slap. Slap. Almost a rhythmic sequence. Over and over. Little river waves coming in, little river waves going out. Had Lily been lulled to sleep out in the boat, as her body temperature dropped? The wind continued and seemed to pick up speed and, suddenly, leaves were being shredded off branches right above us. I started shivering.

"Where did that wind come from?" Tim stared above us.

I stared out at the water again. I could see it cresting.

The paper had said that about the water when Lily had died, but it said there were *huge* whitecaps. No one rowed in whitecaps. Our boats couldn't handle rough water, especially a single. I wondered if she saw the helicopter, or heard it? Looked up, tried to call out? When she capsized, did she hold onto the boat? Or did she get thrown and lose her boat?

"I have to go," I said. I was suddenly really shivering. "It's late, and I might have to buck this wind on the way home."

"I'll ride you home again," he said.

"You don't have to."

He leaned closer to me. "I know," he whispered. "But I want to."

His warm minty breath circled me, and I didn't draw away from him, even ... when his lips touched my neck. His lips, gentle and sweet on my skin, made my body instantly tremble and want more. I felt sucked into him. Like he was a raft of some sort. Something, someone, I could hold onto in the midst of my storm, my shitty so-called life. Lily had been in a storm and needed a real raft, but maybe I needed this raft.

I moved my head just a little, slowly and deliberately,

so it wasn't my neck his lips touched. Despite everything my brain was saying—that this wasn't the answer—my body wanted him to kiss me. By the trembling going on, it really did.

My head manouver worked. And he kissed me. And I let him.

I really meant for it to be one short sweet little kiss, but then something took me over, and I got into it, and I kissed him back with way more energy than I think either of us expected. And instead of allowing it to be over, I slid my arms around his torso, pulling him close so I could stay locked to him. His reponse was to pull me closer as well. The kiss was soft, tender, perfect, and much longer than anticipated. His lips felt perfect on mine. After our sweet, tender kiss, we pulled back and our noses touched.

"Wow," he whispered.

"I should probably get home," I whispered back.

"Me, too," he said.

Our breath swirled around us, creating a mist of quietness that only allowed the sounds of the wind and the water moving to be heard. And our breathing. Neither of us got up to go, and instead, we just sat, bodies touching. Skin against skin. Summer skin. Hot skin. The wind picked up and died down. Lily was alone on the water. Did she ever have a boyfriend?

I'm not sure how long we sat there, seconds, minutes, but there was too much energy sizzling between us to just get up and go home, no matter what the time. Neither of us wanted to break apart. It couldn't be helped when our lips locked again, and this time we opted out of the sweetness, and went for the frenzied kiss, the one you see in movies. Movement, shudders, moans. Pushes. Presses.

He had one hand on the back of my neck and the other one on my thigh. I had one hand on his chest, and the other on his back. My body tingled and ached all at the same time. We kept kissing and kissing, our heads moving. God, he felt so good. So amazingly good. I just couldn't stop kissing him. Then, in a bold move, I got up and straddled him, pressing my chest against his. He moaned and I could feel his hardness through his pants.

He moaned again and ground into me. I pressed back on him, as I undid a button on his shirt. Then he pulled my T-shirt up and I let him. *I let his hands caress my stomach, my ribs.* Soon he would touch my lacy bra.

Suddenly, he groaned and said, "We need to slow

down. This is crazy. I can't do this here." He gently pulled back from me.

And it hit me, too. What was I doing? What were we doing? This could go no further, not here in a *public park*. I pulled back and he held his hands up.

"Whoa," he said. "It's not that I want to stop, but—"

"—I agree," I replied. My breath was coming out in gasps. This was so unlike me to be the instigator, the aggressor. I untangled myself from him, crawling back off his lap, and sat back down on the bench. My entire body was shaking and still on fire, hot and sweaty. Would I have done it right here if he had kept going? I swear I would have.

"What just happened?" he asked.

"I have no idea," I gasped "This is ... not like me." The fire inside was being put out by a wash of shame.

"I'm okay with it." He laughed a little, then he touched my cheek. "But it's not safe to do it in a park."

"A public park at that." I started to laugh. "We could get charged with indecent exposure. Can you imagine a cop shining a light in our faces?"

He shuddered beside me.

I stopped laughing. "What is it?"

Lorna Schultz Nicholson

"Some cops are cool with me, but there's a few on the force here that I stay clear of. They don't like me too much."

I touched his cheek. "That's just shitty. That must be so hard to navigate." I paused. "I started it," I said. "I would have fessed up."

"Yeah, like they would believe that."

I leaned my cheek against his shoulder, and he put his arm around me. "You could have been blamed for something I did," I said.

Silence took over again. The wind still blew around us.

Finally, Tim said, "It felt right, you know." He took my hand in his.

"Yeah," I said. "It did." I squeezed his fingers.

And then my phone pinged. "Bad timing," I said. I pulled it out and glanced at it. Another text from my mother. "I gotta get home," I said.

"I'll ride with you." He leaned in and kissed my cheek before he stood.

We rode our bikes, not saying much. He knew the way to Stew's house, so I didn't even have to give the directions. What was there to say after something like that?

We parked under a streetlight at first, but then I moved, preferring the dark.

"Thanks for riding with me *again*," I said. Now, I was back to being Holly, instead of the mystery girl in the park, and I was feeling awkward, shy, and completely weirded-out for acting so out of character. And for possibly putting someone at risk. I might have recent crap going on at home, but Tim had been dealing with shit his entire life.

"No problem." he answered.

It's kind of hard to kiss with both of us on bikes, and I guess I was thankful, because I needed time to process what had just happened. *We'd never even dated.* Why did I kiss him? Without that first kiss, there wouldn't have been the temptation for sex in the park. *Sex in the park.*

But the truth was—it had felt good. Made me forget about my home life, and Lily. Poor Lily. Had she ever had a boyfriend?

After saying goodbye—where Tim simply kissed his fingers and put them on my cheek—I went in the house, and this time, my mother didn't come out of her bedroom to see me. Good thing. I didn't want her asking questions. What would I tell her?

I'd almost had sex in the park; go back to sleep.

Too Much, Too Soon

At the five-hundred-meter mark
in a rowing race,
throwing in a hard
twenty
can be dangerous
to the race plan.
The hard strokes
can tire you out,
cause lactic acid build-up,
make the rest of the race
fall flat.
Here's another saying.
Too much, too soon.
I had too much, too soon
in my rowing career.
But you know that already.
Then there's Holly.

What was she
doing
in that
PARK?
That was a little
TOO MUCH, TOO SOON
if you ask me. Lol.
But good on her.
Wish I'd done
something
like
that.

Chapter 18

The next day, I got up early and went for my run, then went to the Sportsplex to do a workout before my lunch shift. Every year for my birthday, my mom bought us a year-long pass. When I was little, we used the pool, and now I used the gym facilities. My body ached, but I powered through. Then I powered through a busy noon-hour lunch crowd. As I seated tables, I replayed what had happened with Tim. He wasn't on the schedule, which was such a relief, but then I was disappointed, too.

Granted, now that I'd had a night to sleep on what had happened, I had no idea what I was going to say to him next time I saw him. The guy was in university and probably had his share of sophisticated girls. Not a high school girl who acted all horny, and would have taken off her clothes in a PARK.

He had texted me to tell me he had a "great time."

Me too. At work!! See you soon

I hoped that was okay. What else was I supposed to say? *Hey, I had a great time, too. Sorry for acting like a horny high schooler.* Obviously, my inexperience with guys was showing.

Talk about being confused.

After my lunch shift was over, I went straight from work to Stew's house. I was exhausted physically from rowing all week, and emotionally from finding out about Lily, and then acting so inappropriately with Tim.

My mother was in the kitchen, chopping vegetables. For a second ... I just stared at her. Even though her hair was casually knotted, and she wore an oversized top over shorts, her face had this pretty pink blush. Her skin looked so fresh and clean. I wondered if she looked that good when she was pregnant with me.

I just wanted to talk to her.

I wanted to tell her about Alan and Lily, but I couldn't.

I wanted to tell her about Tim, but I couldn't.

Well, I didn't actually want to tell her *all* the park details about Tim, but I would have liked to share that I met a cute guy, and I kind of, maybe, liked him, just a little.

She turned and glanced at me. "Hi, Honey. I've hardly seen you this week."

"Work is busy," I said.

She tilted her head and eyed me. "You look tired."

"I'm fine," I said, getting a glass for a drink of water. "Aren't you the one who should be tired?"

"I'm in my second trimester now, so I've got this weird energy. How's work?"

"It's actually kind of fun." *Why, oh why, can't I just ask her about her pregnancy?*

Oh, right, because she lied to me for a MONTH.

"Why don't you sit down for a minute? Talk to me. Are you hungry?"

My mom's favorite line to get me to talk was, "Are you hungry?" I went to the pantry to get a snack of something. When I came out with a bag of Tostitas and a jar of hot salsa, I asked, "How are you?" I sat down at the kitchen counter and ripped open the bag.

"I'm good," she said. Then she pointed to the chips. "I've got jalapeños."

"Sounds good," I said. While she rummaged through the fridge, looking for the jar of jalapeños, I asked, "Any good stories from work?"

Some of her stories were broken legs and arms, but then other stories were serious car accidents, where parents cried and paced and wrung their hands, families arriving in the middle of the night.

It made me think.

Alan didn't get the chance to sit in a hospital with his daughter. For four months, there had been no closure. Being in the hospital made an illness real. Just disappearing would be horrible for parents. I stared at my mother. Would she look for me for six months? Walk the streets with my photo? Or would she give up and carry on with Stew and her new ready-made family, including new baby? I shook my head. How could I even think like that about her?

Mom put the jar of jalepeños beside me on the counter. "It's summer," she said, answering my question. "Lots of people in and out, especially tourists wanting to see Santa in the summer. Everything from poison ivy to broken arms to swelled bee stings."

"Drownings, too, I bet."

She shrugged. "With a drowning, a person is usually revived by the water, or gone by the time they are pulled out. Then it's a police matter."

"Yeah, I guess that's true."

She went back to chopping vegetables.

"Have you ever seen anyone with hypothermia?" I asked.

She looked over at me with raised eyebrows. "That's not something that happens in the summer. Not here, anyway. The water's too warm."

"I read about it happening—in a book," I lied. I dipped a corn chip in salsa and topped it with a jalapeño. "But of course, it was in the winter."

Mom chopped and I crunched. I waited for her to talk but she didn't.

"So," I said. "I'm curious. You ever encountered it?"

"I've had a few brought in during ice fishing season," she said. "If the body is heated before the organs shut down, the person can survive. Hypothermia really depends on how low the core temperature goes and for how long. But one time, a young woman jumped in the river, and we just couldn't get her temperature back up." She shook her head sadly.

I loved this side of my mother, when she talked so clinically and passionately about her work. "That would have been awful, Mom." I paused. "In the book,"

I said, "someone just went right under the water, and it was February, and the winter had been cold and ... um ... he died. They found *his* body later."

"That's possible." Mom nodded. "If the body shuts down, the person could slip under the water, and then drowning would take place." She paused and waved her hands. "This is not summer mom-daughter talk."

Suddenly, it hit me that the rest of the house was quiet. "Where is everyone?" I asked.

"Stew took the boys golfing. Nine holes, or something like that. I'm not up on my golf, but they are. I don't think they'll be back for another couple of hours." She paused, smiled, put down her knife, then walked over to me and started to massage my shoulders. Something she used to do for me all the time.

"Did you want to do something? We could go for a walk. Walking's good for me."

After finishing a shift at a restaurant, the thought of walking was enough to make me cringe. "Not really," I said. "I just walked for hours at the job."

"Oh. Okay. Totally understand." She kept kneading my muscles. "You're tense."

"What happened to your hands?" She stopped

massaging me and picked up my hand, running her fingers over my shredded knuckles. In the light streaming through the kitchen, they did look pretty bad.

"I bashed them up against a stone fence," I lied.

"How?"

"I wasn't watching where I was going, and my tire hit the wall and my hands went forward."

"Were you on your phone?"

"Something like that," I said.

"There's something called distracted driving on a bike as well as a car, you know."

I swiveled and stared at her, wondering if she was making a joke. She had a little smirk on her face, so I guessed she was, sort of, but not really. I wasn't in the mood for little jokes, so I didn't laugh like I might have before. Before when? Before Stew and baby news, or before finding out about Lily Coleman?

"Have you put antibiotic cream on them?" she asked, touching my knuckles gently, as only my mom can. She'd cleaned up every scrape I'd ever had.

I nodded but didn't look at her. "They'll be fine," I said.

"You sure you don't want to do something? We could go for ice cream."

Ice cream did sound good. We'd always gone for ice cream. It was a summer thing, and we'd get our cones and sit down on a bench and indulge. And we'd always get different flavors, so we could try each other's and have four flavors instead of two. Sometimes we sat on the bench and found something that made us laugh until we cried.

"Okay," I said. "Let me change out of this gross T-shirt."

I quickly put on shorts and a tank top and ran back downstairs.

Mom was outside already, weeding her flower beds while she waited for me. For a second, I stared at her again, as she pulled a weed. All the time we were living in our small house, with the small yard, she dreamed of having a garden, and instead, she grew herbs on our small deck. Now she had an amazing water-pond garden in the backyard, and this flower garden out front. She had a way of bringing her plants to life, nurturing a seed into a flower.

"I'm ready," I said.

Just as we were heading to her car, Stew drove in with the boys. As soon as the car stopped, the boys jumped

Lorna Schultz Nicholson

out and were bouncing like tennis balls, excited about something.

"Dad got a hole-in-one!" Curtis called out to us.

Stew got out of the car all smiles, threw his ballcap in the air, and then gave my mom a kiss. "Where are you ladies heading off to?"

"Ice cream," I said.

"Ice cream!" Both boys jumped up and down. Curtis turned to his father. "Can we get ice cream, too?"

"How about we go after dinner?" said Stew. "We can all go. I'm cooking, by the way."

"We were going to go now," I said. "Just Mom and me."

"Okay," said Stew. I saw the crushed look on his face.

"I want to go to Licks after dinner," said Kevin. "I'm getting Cotton Candy."

"Tiger Tail rules," said Curtis.

"Dad's hole-in-one rules!" said Kevin.

I looked at Mom. She was smiling, and basically leaning into Stew. Our moment, our time, whatever we'd had, was gone. Over. Here I was again, coming in last. Getting cut.

She looked over at me. "Are you okay with going after dinner, Holly? We can still go now if you want. I'm game for before or after. Or both." She laughed. "I'm eating for two. I can always do ice cream."

"It's okay," I said. She looked so happy with Stew. "We can go after."

"Oh, that's great," said Stew, in his annoying-happy voice. "Thanks, Holly. Let's go in and celebrate my hole-in-one. I'll pour you a nice glass of sparkling water with lemon. Ice cream it is, after dinner!"

I blew out a rush of air. This was not the time to rock the boat, not when I was rowing every day and not telling anyone. And I was going to keep it that way, too. Her life was hers. And mine was mine. That's just the way it was.

I turned and walked back to the house.

My Dad,
My Coach

My dad was also
my
hard-ass coach.
He rarely hugged
after a race
but I always knew
his pride
by the shine
in his eyes.
But, holy hell,
he made me work.
Holly is getting a taste
of what he's
like.
Yeah, I feel for her.
He putt-putted in
his motorboat,

speaking through

his megaphone.

Keep it up. Don't stop.

 Damn it. DON'T LET UP!!

            Sometimes he threw

his megaphone

when I didn't do it right,

when I thought I did.

At least he hasn't

thrown his megaphone

at Holly yet.

One day

after practice

Mom asked, what's wrong?

Dad's a jerk.

My dad. My coach.

My coach. My dad.

He was both. Good idea?

Not so sure now.

Pig-headed, the both of you, Mom had said.

Mules digging your heels in the dirt.

Stubborn, obstinate, head-strong, self-

willed. Say sorry.

Lorna Schultz Nicholson

So we did.
Always.
Well, almost always.
There's that
one
fight
Dad and I had
        on the day
I died.

Chapter 19

On Monday morning, I rode my bike to the rowing course. Alan was already there when I arrived. He smiled at me, and I was a bit shocked because the guy rarely smiled, *unless he was standing with Lily.*

I knew about her, but he didn't know that I knew. How was I to pretend?

"We need to get on the water right away," he said.

In Lily's boat?

I had to get that out of my head! Maybe it was a different boat.

If it was her boat, it would have been shipped or driven to Bracebridge. We were at least a five-hour flight from Victoria to Toronto, and then there's the drive north from the Toronto airport to Bracebridge. Or ... if driving by car, it's at least a five-day drive. Victoria was on an island on the west coast, other side of the country. How did he end up *here*, anyway? Why didn't he go to St. Catharines?

Or even somewhere like Princeton, or Boston, or even Europe, to get completely away. Did he just disappear from everything after the accident? Give up his entire life? Did he get to Bracebridge and just decide to stay?

Too many thoughts; not enough answers.

All weekend, I'd thought about how I might open up the conversation about the boat, about Lily. No words would come out of my mouth. I took the boat down and, without hesitation, got in it and pushed off. The water was flat, the air still, humid, and sticky like a sucker that had been licked by a little kid.

For the first forty-five minutes we did technical work, and I worked on hand speed around the finish. I kept my focus on the sculls going in and out of the water with the speed of the boat, and nothing else.

As I was turning the boat around at the end of the course, he said, "We're going to do some timed sprints."

Perfect. I was happy to move on from technique.

"Remember, we talked about the puddles. I want to work on your boat speed, getting out past the puddles. We'll start with a minute on, a minute off, and I want you to keep your stroke rate above thirty-two."

I nodded.

He called out the start of the first minute, and I picked up my pace. Up the slide. Push.

"Thirty strokes per minute. Not good enough!"

I sped things up. My lungs burning. A minute could be ages during speed work. I kept pulling; he kept yelling.

"Don't just pick it up with your arms. Get the boat moving past your puddles!"

Finally he said, "Bring it down."

Then, "You look like a bloody old lady out there."

I kept my gaze ahead. There was no way I was going to look at him. Not after that comment.

"Ready!"

I swallowed to get some saliva happening.

"Go!"

I started pushing. Trying to get my speed up. But trying also to work on the synchronization of hands and boat.

"More! You're sitting at thirty. Push!"

With every stroke, I did exactly as he said. I pushed.

"Is that all you can give? Push harder!!"

I gasped for breath but kept pushing. Finally, he told me to take it down. I refused to look at him. The minutes ticked by.

Then we went to forty-five second intervals. Less time, higher stroke rate.

Then thirty. Less time and even higher stroke rate. My breathing was in gulps and gasps, as I tried to get oxygen to my beating heart.

After thirty minutes of hard rowing, he had me slow it down. I rowed for another full two thousand meters. Just a paddle, he said, but then he talked to me all the way down about my technique, and added in some hard twenties. So much for the easy paddle.

When I got to the end, I bent over my sculls to try to get my heart rate down a little, and to rest. Pure exhaustion settled into my entire body. I so hoped I was done.

"Take it in," he said.

I turned the boat around and rowed slowly back in, trying to focus on everything he had taught me.

At the dock, as I was stepping out of the boat, he said, "You work hard. I like that."

"Thanks," I said. Compliment? After all that nastiness about me looking like an old lady? I was a bit shocked. Plus, he rarely gave compliments.

I lifted the boat out of the water, walked it up, and carefully, ever so carefully, put it on its rack. There was no way I wanted to bang this boat against anything. That would be a definite no-no. Especially if it was her boat.

As we were bringing in his motorboat, I worked up my nerve. As nonchalantly as possible, I asked, "Where did you get the name for your boat?"

He didn't answer.

"Sounds like jellybean," I said, trying to be funny, but sounding like I was five. Because I was embarrassed, feeling awkward, and like a complete fool, I blurted out, "Jellybeans are my favorite candy."

Seriously, Holly? What a ridiculous thing to say. And jellybeans weren't my favorite candy—sours were.

"I have your training program," he said, ignoring my question completely, and the fact that I was saying the stupidest things. I was grateful for the ignore.

"Okay," I said.

"How are your knuckles?"

"Better."

We yanked the motorboat onto his boat trailer, and he made sure it was securely fastened, without saying a word to me.

"I'll get that program," he said, jiggling the boat for

the last time, making sure he would be able to drive away without it falling off.

I waited. Watched him walk to his truck. He returned to me with a *stack* of papers, enough to fill a one-inch binder.

"Wow," I said. I was expecting one sheet.

"All the exercises are laid out, and I've given examples of how to do them properly," he stated. He pointed to one of the exercises and I stared at it. "See the angle of the back here. It's straight. I don't want you going any lower than forty-five degrees when you're picking up the weight."

Standing beside Alan, I was closer to him than I'd ever been. Usually, we were at a distance. I wondered what his relationship with Lily had been like. His *other* relationship with her. Not the father/coach one. But the father/daughter one. Did he push her hair off her face? Did he tickle her? Did he wipe her skinned knees? Did he tuck her in at night? Read her stories?

No dad ever wiped my skinned knees. Or read to me. My mother did that. Beside me, he felt like a coach, but also a dad, someone who cared about me. I shook my head. I needed to focus on what he was telling me.

Page after page, Alan went through the exercises I was to do, and I tried to concentrate. I kept glancing at him, seeing the intensity in the lines etched across his forehead and around his eyes. He didn't even notice me looking at him, he was so engrossed in what he was explaining, teaching.

Finally, he stacked the papers back together, and handed them to me. "You need to do a weight workout today. Since you're working on your own, I didn't put anything in there that would need a spotter." He glanced at me. "You do have a place to work out?"

I nodded. "I can go to the Sportsplex. But I'm not sure I can do this today."

He looked at me and frowned. "What? Did I work you too hard? You can't handle a weight workout? That wasn't a hard workout."

"That's not it," I muttered, shaking my head. "I have to work today," I said. "A full eight-hour shift. I have tomorrow off. Could I switch up?"

He stared at me with this stunned look on his face, the frown gone and replaced with disbelief of some sort. "You have a job? You haven't graduated high school. I never made—" He just stopped talking mid-sentence.

Now that I knew his story, I knew what he was going to say. *I never made Lily work.*

"I need to work," I mumbled.

He nodded thoughtfully. I guess I expected him to say I had to do it, make the time, but he surprised me and said, "I understand. Switch up to suit your schedule. Family is everything, you know."

"Um ... I appreciate that." I couldn't make eye contact.

"Okay, well, until tomorrow." He gave me his little one-finger wave that meant he was done talking.

"How much do singles cost?" I asked. I was trying to play this light, look for another way around getting answers, even opening him up a little.

"They're expensive," he said. "Are you trying to save for one?"

I shook my head. "No ... no. That's not why I'm working. I need my money for university."

Again, he did his thoughtful nod. "In that case, just keep rowing the ..." Again, his words just trailed off. And he stared off into space. Was he remembering her? I wondered if he saw her as a young girl or a teen, or even a baby, in these moments of silence. Or did all of the stages just pop up whenever?

"The *Lilybean*," I said, finishing his sentence. "I like the name. It has a nice ring."

"Me, too," he said. His shoulders caved a bit and his eyes, they went to that faraway place. "Me, too," he repeated.

He ran his hand through his hair and sighed. "I should get going."

He was in his truck and driving away in mere seconds. And I was left standing with a pile of notes.

I was trying to make room for my notes in my backpack, when I heard voices. I looked up and saw Madison and Tessa running on the trail behind the boathouse. If only I could hide. No go. They saw me.

"Hiya, Holly," said Madison. "What are you doing down here?"

"I ... um ... was just out for a run," I said without thinking. Had they seen me with Alan? I didn't want any rumors floating around about me rowing. As far as I knew, the only person who knew I was rowing with Alan was the president of the club.

"You always run with notes?" Tessa pointed to my hands, then started laughing.

"I rode my bike here, then I ran. Reading material

by the water," I said. *Get the conversation off you.* "How's the boat going?"

"Good. We recruited another girl to fill your seat," said Madison. "She's not as good, for sure, but it's a body."

"It's fun," said Tessa. "Our coach is dope. Like, such a cool guy."

"Good to hear," I said. "I wish I could have stuck with you guys, but my mom is making me work."

Why did I feel the need to lie to Madison and Tessa? It was as if I lied to everyone. They were "those" friends who were school friends only, people I might say hi to in the hallway, or work on a project with if I had to, but never saw them outside of school. It's not that I disliked them, we just didn't connect.

I thought about Alan. Right from day one, I'd connected with him. Not my age. Not exactly a barrel of laughs. But there was something that drew us together.

"Seriously?" Madison made a face, and I nodded my head.

"Yeah," I said. Simply to be polite and make conversation, when all I wanted to do was ride away. Bracebridge was such a small place, and my mother worked at the one hospital. If she found out I was doing something behind her back, I was done, especially because of all the lies.

"That blows. Like full-time? I've got a part-time job but that's it."

"Full-time," I said.

"So ... you're not rowing at all?" Madison gave Tessa a look, and I couldn't figure it out. What was going on? Did they see me on the water when they were running? Were they happy to be in on some secret about me?

I put my helmet on and picked up my backpack, papers sticking out. "I should get going." I got on my bike, my back to them.

"Yeah, we should, too," said Tessa. "We have to put in extra runs for our coach. Too bad you're going to miss rowing in St. Catharines."

I turned sharply. "You're going to the Henley?"

"Oh, yeah." Tessa moved her hands in a circle to do the classic oh-yeah dance.

Suddenly, I felt like I couldn't breathe. Henley? They were going to Henley? The greenness of envy reared its ugly head inside of me, and started gnawing at the lining in my gut.

"Highlight of summer, for sure," said Tessa.

"Good for you. I better go," I said. I got on my bike and started to pedal. I wanted to cry. Instead, I gritted my teeth, and clenched my handlebars, digging my nails into my palms.

Water

Human beings need
water
to live,
that's a fact.
Some people
like Holly and me
need it for the
 soul.
But water
has two sides.
 Serene and gentle.
Tough and mean.
Early mornings are often
thoughtful flat water
where
reflections happen.
Sunrises spread like

Lorna Schultz Nicholson

smooth butter.
Birds land with skids
creating
perfect ripples.
Those are the
just breathe moments.
But water
can be angered
if not treated
with respect.
Can scream
like cymbals crashing
Go out of tune.
　　　Do damage.
I know.

Chapter 20

After hearing the recreational crew was going to Henley, I kept asking myself why I was training so hard. I wasn't going to Henley. They were. It hurt, stung so badly, but I kept training for no reason. Monday and Tuesday, I got on my bike and went to rowing club. And Tuesday afternoon, I did the workout at the Sportsplex that Alan had given me.

I was pushing myself for what? There was no end result. And I was lying to everyone around me to get "there," when I didn't even know where or what "there" was. Huge lies that just seemed to spew out of my mouth. The workouts taxed my body: the lies taxed my brain cells. But I kept doing both.

The first time I had to see Tim after "our night" was on Wednesday, and I almost called in sick to work. Tim had a three-day weekend for some trip to Toronto, so didn't work Saturday, Sunday, or Monday, and Tuesday

Lorna Schultz Nicholson

was my day off. We texted back and forth, but neither of us mentioned getting together.

Dressed in my black work T-shirt, I sat on my bed and rocked back and forth. I had straddled the guy. Big groan. In a park, an outdoor venue. My embarrassment barometer was off-the-charts red. How was I going to face him? What if he was one of those guys who went around telling everyone about the girls he had? My intuition said he wasn't, but what did I know? It wasn't like I was experienced with guys.

It was all I could do to get on my bike and ride to work.

I snuck into the restaurant and tried to be discreet, quiet, just go to the front desk. Amaya didn't say a word to me about him, nor did she even give me any silly, I-know-what-happened smile. Then Tim waltzed by the front desk and grinned at me. I wanted to die of embarrassment. But my heart fluttered instead. He came up beside me. Stood close, too. Tingles ran up and down my entire body.

The restaurant was busy, so we didn't have time to talk until the end of the shift. I'd just finished wiping down all the menus, when he came up to me. "Do you want to go out for ice cream?" he asked softly.

"Would anything be open?" It was already eleven. I was so exhausted from all my workouts and, yes, those damn lies.

"Dairy Queen *might* be," he said.

The thought of riding my bike to the Dairy Queen seemed like such a feat. Tim stood so close to me, and his presence was causing flutters inside me that were flapping like hummingbird wings. I seriously didn't know what to do about him. Since I'd started rowing, I'd told myself I didn't have time for a guy in my life. I had one goal and one goal only, to make National Team. Any kind of relationship would take too much of my energy.

But ... now I wasn't going to Henley.

And ... where would this with Tim even lead? There was no end result. Just like my rowing. Come fall, he'd be back at university, and I'd be back in high school. Everything I was doing this summer had no direction, and it was like I was floating aimlessly.

"Maybe on the weekend," I said. "I just started weight training again, and I'm done for the night."

"Sure," he said. "I totally understand." He smiled at me and raised one eyebrow in a funny gesture. "I'll hold you to the weekend."

I laughed at his funny face, and held up my hand for a high-five. He gave it a little tap, but then he held it and squeezed my fingers for a second longer, his touch making my heart race, in that good way. I smiled at him before I drew my hand away.

Although the news about the recreational boat going to Henley stung me all week, it also made me push harder. It made no sense. Everything Alan asked me to do, I did. He had this way of just being awful, incredibly mean, and brilliant. I wondered if he had been hard on Lily, too. He still didn't know that I knew about her, and I had no idea how to let him know.

When Friday morning rolled around, my day off work, I could barely walk. My muscles were stiff and sore. I still had this last row left before the weekend. I slowly rode my bike to the rowing club. All I could think of was Saturday being just one workout, and Sunday a rest day. All I wanted to do was melt in a bath of Epsom salts.

I beat Alan to the club, and after parking my bike, I went down to the dock, sat down, and stretched. My muscles were tight, so I eased into the stretches. The sun was hot today, like scorching, and it beat down on my skin like a flatiron sizzling hair. Every day during the week had been hotter than the day before. No wonder everyone rowed early, not like I did, from eight-thirty to after ten. Alan liked to row at this time to "avoid the crowds." I guess now that I knew he used to be an Olympic coach, I understood that. Everyone would want his advice.

I heard Alan's truck and stood up, shaking my legs. I went up to the boat bay as Alan was unlocking it.

"Hi," I said.

"How are you feeling?"

"Good."

He eyed me. "Tired?"

How did I answer this? Did I give in and say yes, or pretend I was all good? "Not really," I said, hoping I was running somewhere in the middle.

"Then you didn't work hard enough."

Oh, crap, now I'd gone and done it. I wasn't honest ... again.

"Let's get the boat out."

"Okay," I said. "I'll go get the *Lilybean*."

"Just call it a boat," he snapped at me. "Don't use the name."

"O-kay," I said. "I'm sorry." And I was sorry, now that I knew about Lily. Was today some sort of anniversary? Her birthday? A day where she did something spectacular?

He swallowed and his Adam's apple moved up and down. Then he ran his hand through his hair. "Yeah, me, too." He waved his hand in front of his face. "Today is going to be a short row. I know you're tired, even if you won't admit it."

True to his word, the row only lasted an hour, but it was a grueling hour. Short sprints, over and over. But I was shocked when he told me to row to the dock. I did as he asked, grateful beyond words. I docked, got out, and carried the *Lilybean* up. We didn't talk. No words. Same thing when we went to put his motorboat on the trailer. We worked in silence.

Had I done something wrong? The guy was impossible to read.

When his boat was loaded on the trailer, and everything was okay for him to drive away, he said, "Good work this week."

"Thanks," I muttered. All this work for what? I wanted to ask that but didn't.

He eyed me. "Have you ever raced in a single?"

"Um ... no," I answered.

"Right. Of course, I knew that." He shook his head. Then he said, "You could enter the under nineteen Junior single category at the Royal Canadian Henley. I think you'd do well. I talked to Gillian Storm, president of the club, and you can go under the Muskoka Rowing Club name."

What? Had I heard him right? Race? Oh, God, I'd love to race. But ... "I ... don't have a boat," I blurted out.

"Row the ..." he paused for a second and broke our eye contact, "... the *Lilybean*." After he said *Lilybean*, he exhaled, air slipping through his jaw and teeth, eyes closing. Then he immediately inhaled and opened his eyes. That's when I saw the pain that I'd seen the first time I met him.

He was going to allow me to race in her boat. If it even was her boat. I still didn't know. Was he trying to move past her death, push through something that was holding him back? I stood stiff, like a metal pole, unable to move. This was so unexpected. Yes, I wanted to be happy, jump up and down, as this was a dream come true, but I was so shocked and completely unprepared. Plus, there was the reality of such a suggestion. Logistics hit my brain instead of happiness.

"How would I get the boat there?" I asked.

He shrugged. "I'd go with you. I'd drive. It's under three hours."

"Do I enter myself?

"I can enter you."

"As my coach?"

He nodded.

"You would do that?"

He looked away, out to the water. "I haven't coached in years, you know. Years. I ... um ... quit quite a while ago. But being on the water these past few weeks has been ..." he stopped talking. I didn't speak, hoping he would finish.

After an uncomfortable silence, I was about to speak, but he beat me to it. "It's been ... not what I expected." He ran his hand through his hair. "Not what I expected at all."

"Has it been okay?" I asked.

He made eye contact with me, and I saw a little glimmer shining through his pain. Or was I just wishing, being hopeful, that I was the one to bring him into the future, and out of the past. I wasn't a therapist, but he looked like he had more life in his eyes.

"It has," he said.

"Have you told your wife? Bella?" After all my

research, my hours of scouring for newspaper articles, I just blurted out her name. How stupid of me.

He tilted his head and frowned at me, like a realization had hit him about something. "You know. Don't you? Who I am?"

I nodded, unable to speak.

"Of course, you do." He shook his head. "You're a teenager and you know the Internet. Why would I think you wouldn't know?"

"I'm sorry," I whispered. "For what happened."

"Me, too," he said, shaking his head. He ran his hand through his hair again and sighed. A huge-long-sad sigh. "But this boat—her boat—it needs to be rowed."

So now I knew. It was her boat.

"I didn't want to tell you who I was," he said, "because I didn't want you to start trying to impress me or get nervous around me. I wanted our workouts to be about you and the boat, about the feel of the water. About you making the boat move through fluid movement. About the artistry of the sport."

"It has been," I said.

"Yes," he said. "That's why I think you're ready to race. And why I'll coach you."

"It would be a dream for me to race in Henley," I said.

"Great." He nodded. Then he did his key jingling. "I should get going," he said.

I wanted him to talk about what had happened, but it was like he'd clamped his lips shut. Or even just talk more to me. Maybe his pain was too deep to continue talking.

"Do you think I can do this?" I asked instead. Just to keep him from leaving.

"I do," he said. He turned to face me. "You have determination. And inner drive. You want to prove something. But most of all, you have a feeling for the boat." He paused. "In that way ..." he said softly, "you remind me of ... her."

He exhaled. Again. Then, much to my surprise, he continued and said, "The boat had no name the entire time she rowed it. I named it after she was gone. I ... just ... couldn't sell it or even give it away." His voice broke. "That's ... what I used to call her. She was my Lilybean."

His eyes watered up. A tear slid down his cheek. He shook his head and swiped at it. Then he put up his one finger, waved it, and walked to his truck.

Regrets

Holly and I
are similar in
a lot
of ways.
Hard work and
all that.
But we'll both
have regrets.
I didn't have
patience and
was impulsive
on that
last night.
Was so stubborn.
Holly is, too.
Stubbornness is good
on the water

Lorna Schultz Nicholson

but not so good
on land.
I regret the
awful things
I said,
on my last
night
on earth.
Holly might
regret her
lies.
Just saying.

Chapter 21

My bike ride home was slow. I could barely get the pedals around, because everything was swirling inside of me, and it wasn't as if I was in a rowing race, going forward. No, it was like the boat inside me was being pushed with the wind, sideways and back and forward, and I was floundering to get it straight. I thought about my conversation with Alan and this Henley suggestion, and it was so exciting. I wanted to race so badly. Alan was a former National Team coach—no, a former *Olympic coach*—and he thought I could do it.

But racing in Henley came with major complications. Of epic proportions. Family kind of got in my way of being happy.

But ... I had to try.

I had to. For him and for me. Of course, I couldn't stop thinking about our conversation about Lily. I arrived home to a quiet house, and I did what I wanted to do all week, fill the tub up with water and Epsom salts. I slithered into the hot water. My muscles were ready to chill, but my brain was still a mess of screaming thoughts. He would enter me in the race. Drive the boat on a trailer. I would go to St. Catharines. The trick would be telling my mom and Stew. What if they wouldn't let me go because I'd lied to them?

What if I didn't tell them?

I splashed water on my face.

Mom hadn't told me about her pregnancy. She wasn't the only one who could keep a secret. I could use my own money to pay for my entry. I could make up some story about going to someone's cottage for the weekend, some new friend from work. I did have new friends.

Like Tim. What was I going to do about him? I slid further into the tub. The warm water now covered my limbs, the salt absorbing into my skin, and hopefully into my aching muscles. I liked him. A lot. But if I was going to Henley, I didn't have time for a boyfriend now.

Twenty minutes later it had cooled and was gross, so I got out and toweled off. In my room, I looked at my phone and saw that Kash had called. Three times. Three times meant something.

She answered after the first ring. "Where are you? I've been trying to get you."

"What's up?" I asked. "How's training?"

"Are you dating some older guy?"

I flopped down on my bed. "What are you talking about?"

"I heard something."

"From who?"

"Some friend of Chandra's. So, are you?"

"There's a guy at work I rode my bike home with a couple of nights, but we're not *dating*."

Had Tim said something about our kiss, kisses, park fiasco—to someone who knew someone who knew someone? Oh, God, what had he said? I'd crawled onto his lap. Let him lift my shirt. This is how really bad rumors started. It had only been one ... one what? Certainly not just one kiss. But one night of something weird, but we didn't do it.

"Is he older?" Kash asked.

"Like just a year and a half or so. Nothing huge."

"Why didn't you tell me?" She moaned. "I need exciting news like this. Training is so hard, and I do nothing else. Eat, sleep, train. Repeat."

"Because, like I said, it's not a big deal."

"Good for you—you're making something of your summer."

Yeah, I was rowing. That was how I was making something of my summer. I didn't say anything.

"Is he hot?" she asked.

Something about this conversation was seriously irritating me, and I wasn't sure why. I snapped back, "Um ... sure, if you want him to be."

After I snapped, I felt bad. But this conversation was almost condescending. She just assumed that I was having a shitty summer, and that "some older guy" was making it all better.

What was making it better was rowing and Alan, so I guess an older guy was making it better. But for sure, *now*, I wasn't going to tell her that. And, for sure, I was going to do everything in my power to get to Henley, to prove to people that I had a summer happening, and wasn't just a big loser who crawled on a guy's lap to feel better.

"Hey, what's going on with you?" she asked softly.

Now she was back to sounding like Kash, my best friend, and that made my anger dissolve pretty quickly.

"Nothing," I said. I stared up at that white ceiling.

"You sound like something's up and you're not telling me." She paused, but then she squealed, "Oh, my God! You didn't have sex, did you?"

"Nooooo." The blandness of the ceiling was comforting. *I might have, if he hadn't stopped us.*

"Okay. Because remember, we have to tell each other when we do. Have you been partying a lot, then? Are you out getting shit-faced?"

"No! I don't know what you want me to tell you. I'm working, and there's a sort of cute guy, and we hung out at the park. Not like a date or anything. Maybe we kissed."

"You kissed! Why didn't you tell me?"

"Once." *What a big fat lie.*

"Let go, girl. Go for the hot and heavy sex all summer long. I would if I were you."

"What the hell, Kash? If I were you? You mean if you were the one who got cut, you'd figure out how to have fun, anyway? That's just insulting."

"Soooorry. I didn't mean it to be. But you're so intense all the time, and maybe this is the one summer where you could have some fun. Next summer, you're going to be with me, rowing, working out every day. We can be intense together. It's grueling."

Grueling. I knew all about that, too. I yawned, thinking about how I'd love to sleep all afternoon. "Is your strength training hard?" I asked.

"So hard. Our water workouts are killers, too. I've never been so tired in my life."

"Me, either."

"Is that a joke? If you're not starting work until, like, four, you must get to sleep in all day. God, I would do anything to sleep in."

"I'm working out, you know." I almost wanted to throw something at my white ceiling to make a mark. Kash and I hardly ever fought. Was it her being a bitch? Or me?

"Sorry again," she moaned. "You're right. I'm just tired. Our coach keeps telling us we're in the middle of the race right now in our training. The part where it's so hard you can't even breathe. My body feels like it weighs a million pounds. My legs are sore all the time. All of us lie down and rest in the afternoon to keep up our strength. You should see how much I'm eating."

I understood what she was saying, because I was tired, too, but I couldn't admit it, so I said, "Think of the outcome. You could win gold in Lucerne at World Championships. You'll push through the next thousand meters."

And me ... I could race at Henley! I had something, too.

"God, I wish you were here," she said.

I wanted to tell her about the single, so we could be on equal ground again, talk without me having a huge secret. She might be hurt that I hadn't told her, but maybe it was time. "I have something to tell you," I said.

In the background I heard the voice. "Kash, we gotta go. Bus is waiting."

"Call me later," she said. "I'll have time to really talk."

"Yeah, okay." I pressed END on my phone and sank deep into my pillow. My moment of truth had passed. The heaviness of my limbs extended to my eyelids, and I couldn't do a thing to keep them open.

First Funeral

I want to tell
you
a story.
My grandma died
when I was
eight.
I remember asking,
What's a funeral, Mommy?
When people say goodbye, she answered.
We dressed up and
went to a church.
We never went to church.
Photos of my grandma
sat on a table.
A big wooden box
sat up front.
I'd never seen a dead person.

Daddy cried a little.
Mommy cried a lot.
After the church, people
came to our house
including
my younger cousins
Shyla and Jerrod.
We played in my room
but they
touched my things.
I said, Don't touch. Don't touch.
Then I yelled
DON'T TOUCH
I wasn't a kid who
didn't share so
what was the deal?
Death was the deal.
I was taking my
grief out
in weird ways.
My mom came up.
Grandma would be happy
if you shared, she said.

I ran to Mommy,
hugged her
and cried
because I missed
my
grandmother.
The hole
of death.

Chapter 22

When I woke up from my nap, it was 4 PM, and I could hear noises downstairs. I was lying on my bed with a soggy towel wrapped around me. So gross. I got up and shook my damp hair. After throwing on some shorts and a T-shirt, and running a brush through my tangles, I went downstairs. Groceries covered every inch of the island. Mom was unpacking. This grocery thing was a new deal for her, way more to buy now. A video game blasted from the family room.

"I thought you were working," she said to me.

"Day off." I went to put this massive block of old cheddar cheese in the fridge. We never used to buy bulk cheese like this. My stomach rumbled. I needed food. I got the scissors and snipped open the package, cutting off a slice.

"If you had the day off, what'd you do?" She smiled at me, as if she was interested in my day.

I shrugged. "Not much." A big part of me wanted to tell my mother my good news about Henley. My great news, actually.

But what if I just broke down and told her? How would I explain the lies?

"Did you run?" she asked.

"Yeah." Lie.

"Have you ever thought of running some sort of race? A woman at work runs these ten-kilometer ones. Or you could even do a half-marathon. That might be something good for you to do this summer."

"Are you trying to deflect my lack of rowing onto something else?" *Which, of course, wasn't true, because I was rowing.* I still had to go to the Sportsplex today. If I timed it right, I could miss the dinner-sharing-time.

"I just thought, since you like to run, entering a race might be fun for you. I know you like competing. And I know you like to be active. And exercise is good for you."

Exercise? So, my athletic endeavors were to be taken over by *exercise*, like I was some middle-aged woman with a gut and ten pounds to lose. Every time I wanted to tell her about rowing in the single, she said something that made me not want to.

"It's not what I want. Anyway, I've been going to the Sportsplex a lot. Doing strength training. I'm going there around five today."

"You could still give the running a try. Maybe you'll find you love running races as much as you like rowing."

"It's not what I want."

She put her hand on my shoulder. "I'm sorry you didn't make it, Holly. I know this is hard on you. I hate seeing you up in your room all day, especially when it's sunny. I'm worried about you. There are other sports you can do, too. Even recreational volleyball down at the park might be fun."

"What are you trying to say here? Are you telling me to quit rowing completely? Just because I quit the rec program doesn't mean I'm quitting the sport."

"I don't think quit is the right word. Maybe just take this summer to think about your future. You get such good grades that you could be and do anything. It doesn't hurt to have alternative options."

"Don't worry about me, Mom," I said. "I'll figure it out. Just don't get Stew involved in *my* life. *I'll* figure it out."

"I do worry, Holly. Being up in your room for so many hours isn't good for you. Why don't you invite some friends over? We've got a big backyard now."

I really wanted to give her a snarky comment about the "having someone over" deal. Like that was going to happen, with Stew and the boys. But ... I had to keep the peace, so I could go to Henley. Now more than ever, I wanted that. Someone believed in me and it wasn't her.

"I had Kash over once," I said. "And just for the record, I'm having a great summer." I gave her the best fake smile I could. "I love my job. I'm making money and I have some new friends. And I am taking time to think about things. Everything is all good."

"I'm so happy you're making new friends. Invite some home this weekend, let me get to know them." She smiled at me. "Stew was also thinking we could go on a family holiday in a few weeks. He's got a line on a nice cottage. Might be fun to get by a lake and relax."

Uh-oh. "Um ... I'm working." There was no way I could go in a *few weeks*. Not a chance. Stew must have closed his deal to organize this little vacation. "But you guys go. I can stay home and work."

"Could you take a few days off?" Mom asked.

"Doubt it. I kind of just started, and I'm low on the totem pole." *Plus, I had to train, be on the water. Especially now. This wasn't an option. I was going to Henley to race.* I quickly glanced at my mom's face and saw that she wanted to do this.

"I could go late August," I said. The Royal Canadian Henley was in early August. If I could get through the training and race, I could patch everything up with her for lying and go on some stupid family holiday.

"August might not work for Stew," she said.

"July won't work for me," I retorted.

On Saturday night, when the talk at work started about going out after closing, I said yes. I had promised Tim. Plus, I needed my mother to think I really did have some new friends. The party was at Brendan's house, some house with a pool. I went up to Tim and asked, "Did you bike to work today?"

He nodded.

"I'll ride with you to Brendan's."

"Yeah, sure." His smile was genuine. "I was hoping you'd want to go."

Before leaving the restaurant, I texted my mom.

Going out with new friends from work. Don't wait up

She texted back.

Have fun. If you need a ride, call

I sent her a few happy-face emojis. Okay, she was taking the bait.

Tim and I rode our bikes to Brendan's house, and our conversation was a bit awkward, or at least, I thought it was. This was the first time we were going out anywhere after our park incident, and I was still feeling a bit weirded-out by what I'd done. We talked mainly about work. When we got to Brendan's, we were led to a patio with a pool and a firepit. We sat down by the firepit.

"You want something to drink?" Tim asked.

I lifted a water bottle. "I didn't bring any alcohol."

"I can share."

"You don't have to," I said.

"You have a workout tomorrow?" he asked.

"Day off. I'm sleeping."

"Then you should go for it tonight. Why not? It's summer."

"Yeah, so it is." I managed a fake laugh.

He wrapped his arm around me and I leaned into him, allowing his body to be against mine. Was I being unfair to him, knowing he wasn't my summer goal? Yes,

I liked him, but since Alan had given me the news about Henley, it was all I could think about. Rowing in Henley ruled everything. I wanted to race. Nothing, not even a guy I liked, was going to stand in my way.

Tim poured vodka into red plastic cups and handed me one. I took it and pretended to sip. He took a big swig.

"Doesn't drinking affect your performance?" I asked.

He did his one shrug thing. "It does. But, hey, I'm not going to the show. Not now, with this injury. I'm not making the Olympics. Who am I kidding? I just want to finish college and get a real job."

"Is this what you want?"

"Not really."

"Is there any way?"

He sighed. "I read this article that said athletes always know when it's time to quit, hang up the cleats, the skates—the oar, in your case."

Lily's death crashed through my brain. Her choice had been taken away before she had the time to finish her pursuits. From all I'd read about her, she'd had the potential to medal at the Olympics. My chance was still in front of me. I was still *alive*. And not injured, either.

"You think it's time to quit?" I asked him.

"This summer has been brutal." He sighed. "The show is getting further and further away."

I thought about this. I still wanted to go to the "show." I wanted to push through, and one day make the National Team, despite my mother and her odd conversation today. And maybe I still had a chance. Why was I even at this party?

"Do you know where the washroom is?" I asked.

I was given directions and, surprise, surprise, it was locked. I waited outside the door, hoping whoever was in there was just going to the can, and not in there for other reasons that involved sticking things like tongues and genitals in other places. Finally, the door flung open and out stumbled Tessa. She looked at me with glassy eyes.

"What are you doing here?" she asked, slurring her words.

"I work with Brendan." She weaved from side to side. "Are you all right?" I asked.

"I'm fiiiine. Where's your boyfriend?" She giggled, which was followed by a hiccup.

Oh, yeah ... this was the source of the rumor that Kash had heard. "He's not my boyfriend," I said.

"I wish you wouldn't have quit our ssssummer crew," she slurred.

"You do?"

"Uh ... yeah. You would have helped so much. Ashley hit the dock." She started laughing.

"Shocker," I said.

"I bettttter go," she said. "I need another drink." She made the peace sign with her fingers.

I allowed her to go by me before I went into the washroom. As soon as I had the door shut, I locked it and poured the vodka down the toilet, which was followed by filling it up with water to the exact level where the vodka had been.

Lifting my head, I saw myself. My eyes looked back at me and searched my face.

Would the baby look anything like me? Have my nose? My eyes? I sure hoped it wouldn't have my ears or my mouth, two parts of my face that I just hated. The baby. I still couldn't wrap my head around having a new sibling. My mom's so-called dream.

Forget about the baby, I had to get ready for Henley, hide the fact that I was rowing. That was my goal now, *my dream.*

I unlocked the door and went back out to the party. Tim was where I had left him, by the firepit. I sat down beside him, leaned into him, and whispered, "I'm going to go soon, if that's okay. I'm not feeling so hot."

"Sure," he said. "I can ride you home."

I stood up. "No. No. You stay." I kissed my fingers and put them to his cheek. Then I left.

What I Want

When Holly said
IT'S NOT what I want,
it sounded like
something
I had once said.
On that night,
I went into my
dad's office.
I want to go
on the water
this aft, I had said.
No, Lily. It's not part of the
training program.
I don't care,
it's what I want.
He turned,
his chair squeaking.

Lorna Schultz Nicholson

Dad, the water is like glass!

Look outside!!!!

Lily, no.

IT'S WHAT I WANT.

You're exasperating me, he said.

You're exasperating me, too!

Lily, the water is

cold

and my rowers are

doing a

weight workout.

I crossed my arms

and scowled.

I'm not everyone, you know.

My program! My rules! He yelled.

Stop fighting,

said Mom

from the kitchen.

Dad turned his

back on me,

became silent.

I stood

and waited,

hating his silence.

I got my coat.

Where are you going? Mom asked.

To the DAMN *gym,*

She hated my swearing.

I did it for effect

that night.

Then ...

I said some other things

to her.

Mean, awful things.

Hurt, she turned

her back

to me.

That's when

I saw the brass key

to the boat house.

I took it

and left.

Lorna Schultz Nicholson

Chapter 23

"I've prepared a mini training schedule for you," said Alan on Monday morning. "Four weeks, minus two days. We will need time for tapering and travel as well."

After a day off on Sunday, I was feeling a little refreshed, and excited about the next weeks, but my stomach was doing somersaults. This was it. I was going for it. First step to getting a seat in the Canadian boat next summer was racing *this summer*. Even without my mother's approval.

He handed me a sheet of paper that was a calendar. Every day was marked with exactly what I had to do, and it was pretty specific, including projected times. How long did it take him to write this up? No wonder he'd been an Olympic coach.

"Because we don't have a lot of time, and we can only be on the water once a day," he said, breaking into my thoughts, "the next two weeks are going to be hard, and you better be tired. When I used to coach, we were always on the water twice a day. You need to strength train three times a week and run twice a week. Your runs should be at least forty minutes. Work with that schedule of yours."

I nodded.

He continued, "Although, over the years, I've learned that more is not always best. In life, we do need balance, and I want the weekend set aside for light work, and even friends and family." He looked at me. "You need to have some fun. But balance doesn't mean late nights … if you get my drift."

"Okay. I understand." *Get my drift?* My mom said that. Too funny.

"The third week will be your toughest. You're going to have to dig deep, especially near the end. That will be the week where you will want to call me all kinds of names, and you might even think of quitting."

I nodded. I wouldn't quit.

"Then the fourth week, I will start to taper, so workouts will be shorter, a little less intense. We're on a crunch schedule, and I would taper more if I had the chance, but one week is going to have to be enough."

I just stared at the paper, trying to absorb the workouts.

"You good?" he asked.

"Yes," I said.

"Let's get started, then. Today is five-hundred-meter sprints. I will be timing every one."

I got on the water, and every five hundred I did was at full tilt. Rest in between for five hundred meters. Then full speed again. And again. And Again.

I think I was on about number eight, about halfway through, when he yelled, "Lily, you're slowing down! Keep the pace up!"

Lily?! Had I heard right? I grunted through the last hundred meters of the five hundred, and then slowed down to catch my breath, rowing easy strokes, trying not to puke over the side of the boat. This was the hardest I'd ever worked, and I was pushing myself beyond what I'd ever done before.

Alan stood up in the motorboat. "I want more effort on the next one, Lily!"

Okay, so he seriously was calling me Lily. Was he just back in time? Reliving something? I didn't have the energy to correct him. Was he remembering her? I just kept my sculls moving, slowly, in and out. Before I could get completely rested, though, he was yelling at me to go again.

"I want that stroke rate higher! Chin up. Chest open."

Oh, God. Oh, God. Oh, God. I grunted and gritted my teeth and pushed. And pushed. And pushed.

"Good job, Lily! Keep it moving! You're clearing those puddles."

Stars swam in front of my face. How much further? I tried to count in my head but couldn't make my brain work. Finally, I heard him tell me to take it down, row in. I swear he called me Lily again, but maybe I was delusional.

At the dock, he said, "Good job, Holly. I'm proud of your work today."

"Thanks." My appreciation was barely audible. I got out of the boat and almost collapsed. But at least he had called me Holly and not Lily.

I put the *Lilybean* away, and we got his boat on the trailer and the bay locked up. I was actually on my bike before he was in his truck.

As I was pedaling my bike through the parking lot, I passed a little red car with a woman driving. The woman looked familiar as she passed me. I did a double take.

Was that Bella? Lily's mother?

I stopped pedaling and pretended to fix something on my bike, glancing back to see if she had parked by the boathouse. She had, and I could see her back as she headed toward it. When she disappeared around the corner, I got on my bike and rode back, thinking maybe I could pretend that I had forgotten something. She'd never come down before.

I heard their voices as I got off my bike, and it didn't sound good. The conversation seeped through the wood of the boathouse, sounding more like a fight. *Were they standing by the Lilybean?*

"You can't bring her back by coaching someone else." Bella's voice.

"That's not what I'm doing."

"Then what are you doing?"

"The girl is good, Bella. She works hard."

That made me feel good.

"Like Lily did? Is she like Lily? Are you trying to bring Lily back? Because you can't, you know. She's never coming back."

"Yes, she works hard like Lily. But she's not Lily. What's wrong with wanting to help her? I don't think she has much family support. No one has ever come down to watch her."

Uh-oh. That's because no one knows I'm rowing.

"You're becoming obsessed again," she said.

"We're only out once a day. How can that be an obsession?"

"You were up all last night, creating a program."

"I don't sleep at night, anyway."

"And you're letting her row Lily's boat!"

"Things have been changed in the boat, so it's almost a different boat."

"You named it after her! After she died! That didn't change a damn thing about that damn boat. I wish we had left it in Victoria. But oh, no, you had to pull it behind us. All the way across the country."

"I'm sorry," he said. "I'm sorry I did that. But she was ... *Lilybean*. Bella, our *Lilybean*."

"I never called her that," she said. "You did!"

The voices stopped. I heard murmurings but no words. I stood still. I had to leave, get out of here before they realized I was listening. They were having a moment that I didn't belong in.

"I miss her so much." I heard Bella, and by the change

in her voice, the strangled sound, I knew she was crying. I got on my bike and rested one foot on the pedal and one on the ground.

"I do, too," said Alan, his voice also cracking.

"Don't make this girl Lily. Please. No one can be Lily. She's gone." Sobbing now.

"She's not Lily. No one will ever be our daughter, Bella."

"I think the summers are the hardest," said Bella. Her words warbled. "The fucking hardest," she said louder. "They're so fucking hard, I want to scream every day. I want her here, with me, eating dinner at our house. Maybe she'd have a boyfriend, friends. I'm so sick of hearing about summer weddings. Next it will be babies. We got robbed, Alan. Robbed of life with her."

"Come to St. Catharines. It'll be good for you to get away."

"I can't believe you just asked me that! What is wrong with you? I will never watch another rowing race again. Do you hear me? Never! And I wish you hadn't started up again. We came here to never be around this sport again. But you … oh, no, you had to tinker with the boat, bring it back to life."

"It's making me feel alive again. After eight years."

Again, the voices stopped. Were they leaving? Was she leaving? Storming out? I really needed to get out of here. I hopped on my bike and took off, riding as fast as I could, no stopping.

All the way home, I thought about the conversation I'd eavesdropped on, and it made me think of my own dad. He'd just dumped me like a green bag of stinking garbage and never looked back, never grieved once for his little girl, or tried to find me. He'd probably never cried for me like Alan did for Lily. If my dad loved me that much, was that proud of me, I'd be so happy.

As soon as I got home, I went straight to my room and booted up my laptop. I googled Lily Coleman and looked through all the articles, wanting to find one that had a bit of information on her mother. Finally, I found a buried YouTube video that I hadn't watched yet, some television show about parents grieving, and how to deal with death. Bella was the featured guest, and it was a year after Lily's death, six months after the body had been found.

The interviewer sat across from Bella and said, *"Bella, thank you so much for being here today. I'm sure this can't be easy. Grief is a topic that is hard for all of us to* handle, but perhaps today, with you sitting here with me, you can help somebody going through a similar situation." She smiled at Bella.

Bella. Did not. Smile back.

"Bella, it's been a year for you, and I'm wondering if you feel there is any truth to the statement: time heals." The interviewer spoke softly, in gentle tones.

"Your grief is your own," said Bella robotically. "People will try to tell you how to act, how to feel, but they can't understand. Your grief is yours alone, and everyone needs the time they need."

I thought that was good advice, but she sure was acting unemotional, like she was reading this from a textbook.

"Maybe you could walk us through your emotions after it happened," said the host. "It might help people understand their own emotions."

Bella clasped her hands and sat tall. She looked so stiff, sitting on the studio sofa, wearing a dress and heels. "At first it was shock. I didn't want to believe it." Her voice trailed off, and now she just looked uncomfortable, awkward, like she shouldn't be there. Then it was like her body just collapsed. I watched, mesmerized by her sudden slouch and sagging energy.

"I think that is normal," said the host, trying to carry the conversation.

Bella just sat there, staring at her clasped hands. Then she spoke softly. *"People were kind. They brought food. Some of it is still in the freezer. But ..."*

Bella sat up tall, again, now looking a bit possessed. *"Some I just threw out, screaming as I did. I yelled at God and whoever else I could yell at. Water. The sport of rowing. Her boat."* She shook her head. *"I lost it that day, which was weeks later, and just crumpled to a heap on the floor. Not my finest moment."*

The host nodded her head and said, *"So, for you, shock and anger were both part of your grieving."*

Bella looked dazed, and wasn't staring at the host, or listening. *"I should have seen that she'd taken the key. Why didn't I see that the key was missing? I could have followed her."*

Bella stood. *"I can't do this."* Then she ran off the stage, leaving the host by herself. I wiped tears off my face, not even knowing that I had started crying.

I shut down my computer, thinking of Bella and how she'd spoken earlier today. She hadn't come much further, seven years after this interview. The shock had maybe left, but the anger was still there. Her grief hadn't quit.

The relationship, when Lily was alive, sounded so perfect. I thought about my relationship with my mom, and how we used to have something like that. Once, we went to Disneyland, and we'd had the three-day pass. We were up at the crack of dawn every day, and I begged to go to the breakfast, so I could get autographs from the characters. We hadn't been anywhere together in a long time.

Not even for ice cream.

What I Said

Are you ready to
hear
the nasty words
I said
to my mother
that night?
Dad runs you, Mom.
You're under his control.
You need to stand up to him.
Stop
being such a
FUCKING DOORMAT.
Yes, I said that.
Her eyes
showed hurt.
No comeback words
came from

Lorna Schultz Nicholson

her mouth.
She turned her back
and
walked away.
Last thing
I ever said
to my mother.
I wished I had
one more minute,
one bloody minute
to take
that back
and
say something else.
Like ... you're pretty special, Mom.

> *Like ... you're funny, my rock, my*
> *inspiration.*

> *Like ... you're the strongest*
> *woman I know.*

Or even something simple,

> *like ...*

> *I love you, Mom.*

Chapter 24

"Come on, you have to give me more than that!"

Alan yelled from the motorboat. It was a good thing we were far enough down the river, so no one could hear his voice. Any closer, and all of Bracebridge would have heard him yelling at me. Right now, I hated him. Like he said I would. Tears welled behind my eyes. I wouldn't let him get to me. I grimaced and pushed my hips and legs back, my leg muscles ready to burst and explode into tiny pieces in the atmosphere.

"More!"

Oh, God. I couldn't do anymore. I could barely breathe fast enough to get oxygen to my lungs, my muscles. But I did. Because there was no way I would give him the satisfaction of seeing me give up.

"Okay, that's good," he called out.

I slowed down, my breathing rapid-firing, and rowed one slow stroke after another, while he sat in his stupid

Lorna Schultz Nicholson

motorboat with his damn stopwatch. Always timing. Always wanting more time shaved off. The guy thought he was a king or something, lazing around in a boat with a *motor*, calling out orders. Some days, I just wanted to tell him where to go.

But, of course, I wouldn't. He was helping me.

When the workout was over, I got out of the boat and we didn't speak. I often didn't know if he thought I did okay, was pleased, liked my progress. Today, I figured he was disappointed. Had Lily disappointed him, too? Had he yelled at her?

I was about to get on my bike when he said, "Good work today."

The comment sank to the back of my throat and stayed there. Shocked, I turned to look at him. "Thanks," I barely got the word out.

"Do you hate me?" He had a silly smirk on his face.

"Maybe." I tried to smile back. Just a little. He was infuriating. Annoying. Frustrating. Mean. And kind, when he wanted to be.

"Are you going to watch the Junior women's races?" he asked. "You can livestream them."

"Of course," I replied.

Kash had left for Europe, and they had a preliminary regatta in Hamburg, Germany, before the World Rowing Championships in August, in Lucerne. I wondered if, by the time the Henley came around, Kash would know I was rowing, too. Her first heat in this preliminary regatta in Germany was tomorrow morning at four, my time. I would have to set my alarm.

"Are you going to watch?" I asked him.

"I just bought a new little iPad. Haven't had much technology for years." He paused. He had this super thoughtful expression on his face. Then he said, "First race I will have watched in eight years. But the female singles race will be important for me to watch—for your race. I need to get up to speed on times and names."

Crazy. He was going to watch races because of me? No one had ever taken an interest in me like that. This was that kind side.

"Is there anything I should watch for?" I asked.

"Watch the stroke rates through the race. Especially in the last half. It's important to keep up a pace, but not fatigue through the twelve-fifty and fifteen hundred marks. You want to be able to row that last five hundred with everything you have. Does that make sense?"

"I think so."

"My Lily had a bit of a setback in her first international race," he said.

I'm not sure if I'd ever heard him say her name like that before, in a sentence that wasn't filled with heavy sorrow.

"What happened?" I asked.

"It's such a fine line. You can't race thinking you need to save energy, but on the other hand, you need enough energy to finish strong."

"Did she follow the race plan?"

"She sailed through the first half, then cranked it up, but used up all her energy by the fifteen hundred. She learned that time, though." He shook his head. "She was so young."

"And so good," I said.

"Yes. She was. That was the only race she lost."

He looked over at me. "She was more than rowing, though. She had a strong will, and she could be really funny."

I nodded. This was new. This chit-chat about Lily. "She had to have a strong will to be so successful," I said.

"She never had a boyfriend." He sighed a little.

"Sometimes I wish she could have experienced something like that, too. Not just the rowing."

"She was pretty young when she passed," I said. For some reason, using the word "died" seemed harsh.

"Sweet sixteen." He looked away. "And never been kissed." He looked back at me and attempted to smile. "Isn't that how the saying goes?"

"You don't know that," I said. "We don't tell our parents everything."

He nodded and smiled. "Thanks. I needed that today. Maybe I'll just believe she had that experience." He paused. "Make notes," he said. "On the races. Bring them to me."

"Okay," I said. And that was Alan. Just change the subject and get back to business.

"We'll talk next week."

I nodded. Homework. I thought about what he'd said about not watching a race since Lily had passed. "Did you seriously not even watch the *Olympics*?"

He shook his head. "My Lily would have been there. I would have been there. I couldn't. It hurt too much." He knocked his chest with his fist.

"I understand," I said. "But you've missed watching two Olympics now."

He ran his hand through his hair and exhaled, the pain back, etched on his face. "She would have been rowing in both of them," he said. "She had a long career ahead of her. Could have rowed into her thirties. Maybe medaled three times. Who knows?" He shrugged. "She never had the chance to find out. But what hurts even more is she never had a chance to maybe marry, have her own family, have a career other than rowing."

"I've read a lot about her," I said softly.

He made eye contact with me. "She didn't have a lot of friends because of her schedule, but I'd like to believe you two might have hit it off. Been friends. I asked her once if she wanted to get married one day. She almost clubbed me over the head. But I took that as a yes."

I laughed. "I don't blame her for wanting to club you."

"But then she told me she did, and she wanted to have four kids, because she didn't have any brothers or sisters." He shook his head.

"I'm an only child, too," I said, without thinking. The title I'd had for all these years would be stripped from me—by a baby. I was not going to be an only child anymore, and I would have to stop saying that to people. I was going to have a real blood sibling.

He inhaled deeply, then exhaled. His lips were drawn into straight lines, and I knew he was thinking about something. Then he said, "When Lily was alive, she was always enough for us. But now, my wife might have coped better with another child. But then ... maybe not." He shook his head. "I can't think about that because it's not reality. Lily will always be our one and only—and that's just the way it is."

His eyes took on the vacant look, as he stared out to the water, and I knew I'd lost him to memories. But then he said, "She was such a fireball, and had me wrapped around her little finger."

"She sounds like someone I would have liked."

He turned back to me. "I'd do anything to have one day, even just twenty-four hours, back."

I had no response.

I rode my bike home, going slower than a country love ballad. It didn't help that the July heat beat down on me. But I was also thinking of Alan talking about Lily today. The regrets he had for her. Maybe she had been kissed. We certainly didn't tell our parents everything.

At least, I didn't.

When I got home, my mother's car was in the driveway. Weird. With our schedules, my mom and I didn't cross paths a whole lot. She left for work in the morning, and I was still sleeping. I rowed, came home, ate, slept for an hour, got up, and by two, was out the door for either my strength workout or my run. From the gym, I went straight to work. She was never home during the day. She used to work nights, but now she was on straight days. As soon as I entered the house, I heard her voice and Curtis's. I groaned.

"Hey," I said.

Curtis was lying down on the sofa in the family room, with a cloth on his head. Mom was hovering over him with a smoothie of some sort.

"Hi, honey," was all she said.

"Sick again?" I eyed Curtis and he gave me the don't-tell look.

"Were you out for a run?" my mother asked, staring at me. Obviously, my clothing gave away that I was doing something active.

"Bike ride," I lied.

"I have to get back to work. The camp called me at work because they couldn't reach Stew."

"Go," I said. "I'm good until two-thirty."

She frowned. "I thought you started work at 4:30?" She'd asked for my schedule and I'd given it to her.

"I have something I have to do before work."

"Oh. New friends?"

I shrugged. "Yup."

"Why don't you bring them by for a barbecue? I'm sure Stew would love that. He loves entertaining."

"Go back to work. I can make Curtis a sandwich, or whatever his little belly wants."

"If his stomach is sick, maybe just make him something like soup," said my mother. "Would that be okay?" my mother asked Curtis, pushing the hair out of his lying eyes.

"Sure," he whimpered. It was all I could do not to burst out laughing. Good actor, I'd give him that much. We were a family of liars.

"Remember," said my mother on the way out, "invite your friends over this weekend. Maybe tomorrow night, since you're off."

Mom left and I playfully punched Curtis on the arm. "You are such a faker."

"Grilled cheese," he said. "With potato chips!"

"What camp do you hate this week?"

"I looooved the band camp. This one is like a *science camp*. Who wants to go to a stupid science camp?"

"Not you, obviously. Why don't you just tell your dad you hate it?"

"That would be like committing murder."

"That's a bit dramatic, Bud."

He grinned at me. "Let's eat!"

I made sandwiches and put a ton of potato chips on his plate. I was trying to eat healthy, so I avoided the chips and made myself a turkey sandwich, piled high with lettuce and tomato.

"You're not going to be able to bite that sandwich," said Curtis. We were both at the kitchen table.

"Watch me," I said. I took a big bite and half the good stuff fell on my plate.

He howled. "Told you."

About halfway through eating my sandwich, Curtis asked, "You really going to invite friends over, like your mother wants you to?"

"Probably not."

"I don't think you have any friends."

I laughed and threw my paper serviette at him. He caught it with one hand and threw it back. "Why would you say I have no friends?" I asked.

"You never have anyone over."

"Um ... my friend Kash has been here. Remember?"

"That was ages ago. Like, when you first moved in. I hated you then."

"I hated you, too." I stuck my tongue out at him.

"You can have friends over now."

"It's not really my house," I said.

"You live here, too. You even have your own room."

"True. But it's still white."

"That's your fault."

"True again."

At work, after arriving fifteen minutes before my shift, I went to the manager's office and knocked on the door. When I heard Bethany's voice telling me to come in, my throat dried. Here goes another lie. I walked through the door.

"Hi, Holly, what can I do for you?" she asked.

"I want to request some days off in August," I said, crossing my fingers behind my back.

"What days?"

"August fifth to twelfth." The regatta was only five

days, but I needed time before to travel. Alan said we needed to leave early, so I could row the course and get acclimatized. He'd already secured a billet for me, because I told him my mother couldn't come.

"That's quite a few days," said Bethany. "I told you when you first started that holidays were kept to a minimum during the summer months. You agreed."

"It's a family holiday. I have to go." Family holiday—yeah, right. *And the lies keep piling up, like mounds of trash.*

Bethany glanced back at a big white board that hung on the wall behind her desk. She was still staring at it when Tim came in.

"Hey," he said. "What's shakin'?"

Bethany swiveled in her chair, facing forward again. "Holly needs some time off for a family holiday. From August fifth to the twelfth."

Oh, God. Now Tim was involved in my "family holiday" lie. I hadn't seen Tim all week, because I'd had Tuesday off and he'd had Monday and Wednesday. We'd texted a lot, and he'd wanted to go for a daytime bike ride, but I said I was on babysitting detail, which was true. I promised a night out on the weekend again. My heart raced every time I was close to him.

But here I was, building up my mound of lies to him, too.

"You want me to deal with the time off?" he asked Bethany.

"Sure," said Bethany. "If you think the floor can handle it, I don't see it as a problem."

Nooooo. I didn't want Tim handling it.

"We'll be fine," he replied. He smiled at me. "I hope you're going someplace fun."

"Thanks so much," I said. "I appreciate you making this work." A jab jolted me inside. I was most definitely putting Tim in an awkward position as a manager. He was my boss and I'd lied to him.

But ... it was like I was a ball rolling down a steep hill. I couldn't stop myself.

I stepped out of the office and headed to the front lobby to start my shift. Margo passed by me and gave me a little smirk. "Sucking up to the manager, I see."

"No," I replied. "I just needed to ask for some time off."

"Right. I'm sure your request was granted, too." She rolled her eyes. "While the rest of us wait in line."

Oh, God. What had I done now? Knowing her, she would make trouble for Tim.

Sweet Sixteen

Here's a saying,
that sums up
a part of my teens.
Sweet sixteen and never been kissed.
Sad, eh?
And it's never
going
to change.
I won't ever
have a
first kiss,
a first boyfriend,
or get
married,
and have my
own children
to love.

Holly needs to
enjoy
being kissed.
I think ...
she can have
both
because she's met
the someone
who
understands.

Chapter 25

My alarm went off at four in the morning. I rolled over, shut it off, and picked up my laptop from the floor. I sat up and didn't turn on any lights. The volume on my computer was low, so I heard the knock. My door slowly opened a crack and I saw my mother's face.

"Come in," I whispered. Kash's race was about to start.

"What are you doing?" she whispered.

"Kash," I said, without taking my eyes off my computer. "She's racing in a few minutes. What are you doing up?"

"I couldn't sleep. Stew is snoring. Sounds like a duck blowing his nose. And I have the early shift today at the hospital, so no point going back to bed. Can I watch?"

I moved over, and she sat beside me on my bed. We used to sit on my bed all the time. When I was little, she read to me, and then in junior high, we talked, laughed, and she still read to me.

I snuck a quick glance at her stomach.

"You're getting a belly," I said. Since the day I'd been told, the day I'd been cut, we'd never really talked about her pregnancy. I think there were times when she wanted to talk to me, but she didn't, especially after the initial fiasco, that lack of proper timing. Maybe she was just waiting for me to say something first.

"I am," she said, patting it. "It seems to grow every day."

"Do you know the sex?"

"Not yet. I'm not sure we're going to find out."

The word "we're" made me cringe. I didn't want to hear her say that. That word was always saved for us. My mother had moved on from me.

"They're in lane six." I pointed to my screen. "They have Canadian flags on their oars."

Something inside me sank. I wanted to row with those oars: white with red maple leafs. So plain but so classy. All countries had their colors on their oars. What a proud moment. Good for Kash. The boats were lined up. Kash was three seat, wearing her Canadian singlet.

"Kash looks good," I said.

"You miss her."

"Yeah. I do," I said. I didn't want to talk about the

friend I was keeping a secret from, too. "Bit of wind. They said head."

"Here they go," I said. Louder than I wanted to.

"Shhh," said my mother.

I nodded. I didn't want Stew up, either. Eyes glued to the screen, I watched closely; we watched closely. The Canadians had a good start, and at the two-fifty mark were sitting in the pack. It was a close race. "Push it," I whispered.

As if they heard me, they pulled ahead, and within a hundred meters, they had a bow ball lead. They needed more.

"They're ahead," said Mom.

I didn't look at her. "Not by much," I said.

By a thousand meters, they were ahead by half a boat. They looked good. Strong.

Mom breathed beside me, and I knew she was really watching, not just sitting beside me. At twelve fifty, they pulled ahead a bit more. Just a little.

"Keep the power," I whispered.

Suddenly, the crew beside them moved on them, as they pushed through the fifteen hundred. "Great Britain is making their move in this first heat," said the announcer, calling the heat. "They're looking strong through the fifteen hundred. The Canadians seem to have overspent on their first three-quarters of this race."

"What happened?" my mother asked, when the Canadians crossed the line in third place.

I thought about everything that Alan had taught me, realizing that it had been a lot in such a short time. And what he had said about Lily, in that one race where she had lost.

"They raced it like it was fifteen hundred meters instead of two thousand," I said. "They used up all their energy. I'm sure their coach will work on that part of their race plan for the next race. It was just a heat, and the top three move on."

She nudged me with her shoulder. "Listen to you."

I glanced her way. "I want that, Mom."

"It's a lot of work to get there," she said.

"That's all you have to say?" I didn't close my computer, because I had more races to watch. Every. Single. Race. Until I had to row myself, later in the morning. The female single heats were coming up in two races.

My mother stood up, and the indent where she had been sitting was still beside me. She touched my hair. "Time might change that."

"What's that supposed to mean?"

She shook her head. "I don't know. I do want you to know that I understand that watching this must have been hard."

"But, see, that's the thing. I can do it next year. I can still be a junior next year. Rowers often compete well into their twenties, even thirties."

"Holly, that's a long shot. It's years of training every summer. Look at how you have a job this summer, and you're making money. You wouldn't be able to do that."

I frowned at her. "Don't you think I deserve to try?"

"Mary! Are you okay?" Stew's voice outside my door.

"I'm good, Stew. I'm coming."

Yeah, you go, I thought. But she turned to me. "I want you to think about this holiday that Stew wants us to go on. Maybe just ask for a few days off. It'll be fun for us to be together."

"And I want you to think about me and my goals, Mom."

She nodded. She had her hand on my doorknob when she turned and asked, "Would you like to come to my next doctor's appointment?"

I stared at her. "Um ... when is it?"

"August seventh."

"Sure ... um ... maybe," I squeaked my words out.

"It would be nice to have you there."

After she left, I leaned back on my headboard and closed my eyes. Shit. August seventh, I would be at the Royal Canadian Henley.

How was I getting out of this one?

"Did you watch the singles race this morning?" Alan asked, when I got to the rowing club.

"Yes. The girl from Germany was solid. She killed everyone. It didn't even look like she was trying."

"It's deceptive. The other rowers might have just let her go, once she was ahead, because three in every heat make the semi-finals. We'll talk about this before you race, because it will be a similar format."

Thinking about racing made my stomach do dangerous somersaults. "It's going to happen, isn't it?"

"We haven't been putting in all this time for nothing. Now get your boat out."

My boat? I couldn't believe he'd said that. As I carried the boat out, I heard him singing some Elton John song. I thought it sounded like "Daniel." He was in such a good mood.

Lorna Schultz Nicholson

Even though I was tired from the week of work, the row was the best one I'd had since I'd started with Alan. For some reason, I managed to do exactly what he wanted and, with good conditions, I shaved some time off.

I was turning the boat around, thinking the workout was finished, when Alan said, "Do you think you can row a full two thousand meters? I'd like to time you."

"Um … sure. I'm not sure how good my time will be."

"I want to get some sort of ballpark time. Then we can go from there. This will be something we will do at the end of every workout from now until you race."

I nodded. "What kind of start should I do?"

"Good question. Let's go with something simple. Singles are different from big boats. How about starting with a three-quarter stroke off the top. Then go to half, back to three-quarter, to full. That was Lily's start. Try to pry the boat through the water on the first stroke, then work on precision and getting the boat up to speed, then find quickness in the next ten to fifteen strokes, before you settle into a sustainable rhythm. And always remember to breathe on the start. It's easy to hold your breath, but you need to get oxygen to the lungs."

Once in position, I waited for his command. When

he yelled "Go," I did my first three-quarter stroke. Then the half. The boat moved forward. Singles were easier to get moving.

Finally, I got to full strokes and I just rowed. In my head, I figured I was at thirty-four strokes per minute.

"Thirty-three," yelled Alan.

Okay, I was close. But not close enough. I cranked it up a bit, and kept pushing back, stretching out a bit, lengthening. Chin up, chest open, I kept a spot in my vision, so I would keep the boat straight. It was all about focus. I crossed over the invisible finish line and let the boat run, leaning over the sculls, gasping for breath. In a way, I didn't want to hear my time, because I knew I was going to compare it to the rowers this morning.

"That was decent," he said. "Take the boat in."

"Are you going to tell me my time?" I called out. So much for not wanting to know.

"No."

"What? Why?"

"Meet you at the dock."

After I put the boat away, I said, "You're seriously not going to tell me?"

"No, I'm not. I will before you race. I promise."

"I guess you know what you're doing," I said.

"I do." He grinned.

"What's going on with you?" I asked, staring at his silly smile.

He shrugged. "I'm back in the mix. It feels good."

"Back in the mix!" I laughed out loud.

"What? Isn't that something you young folks would say?"

"Uh ... maybe."

He touched my shoulder, in a fatherly gesture, like Stew did with his boys. "Thanks," he said. "Your hard work has contributed hugely to this ... well ... this lightness I feel." He took his hand off my shoulder. "I like being out here."

"Me, too," I said. "Even if you're mean sometimes."

"Such is sport," he said, with a silly smirk.

"I'm looking forward to racing," I said.

"You're practicing to race. That's what it's all about."

"You think I can win?"

"Do you?"

I sucked in a deep breath, then exhaled. "Yes," I said. "I do."

"That's what's important. You're the one in the boat,

not me. I can only take you so far. The rest is up here."
He pointed to his temple. "Next week will be tough. I
would prepare. Rest this weekend."

I looked at him and, for the first time ever, I saw a
twinkle in his eyes. "I'm going to hate you. Aren't I?"

"Yes, Holly. That's a given." He glanced at his watch.
"I have to get going. My wife needs me to build a shelf."

"She's okay with this. Right?"

He sighed. "It's still really hard for her. She's trying."

As I was leaving the rowing club, I ran into Tessa and
Madison, again, out on a run. Good for them, getting
ready for Henley by pumping up the training. Bad for
me running into them.

"Hey," said Madison, "who's the guy you're hanging
with all the time."

"Excuse me?"

"The old guy."

"He's a friend."

"Was that you out in the single?" Tessa furrowed her
brows.

I shook my head. "Nope. Nice try." My heart just
started pounding in my chest. Like a hammer was hitting

it. I pretended to look at my phone. "I better go. Gotta work."

I rode off. I was freaking out, my blood racing through my body. They'd seen me. They couldn't blow this for me. My mother didn't know them, or their parents, so there was no chance they would tell her. But Bracebridge was small, and more and more people were coming to the park every day. What if someone said something to someone who knew my mother? What if someone came in the hospital, got her as a nurse, and just blabbed about seeing me on the river? *Oh, God, rumors had a way of swirling, finding that sweet spot.*

Once home, I looked at the calendar. We had less than two weeks of training. My plans couldn't blow up before then. They just couldn't. I had to race. I had thought over and over about how I was going to leave.

Pack my bags.

Write a note?

Leave it on the table?

All of the above.

That Night

You're probably wondering
how it
happened.
I was so mad
that night.
(Like Holly is
mad at
her mom,
but worse.)
I placed my boat on the water,
not caring that
 there were rules
for cold water rowing.
Stupid me.
 I got in,
and rowed,
and rowed.

Lorna Schultz Nicholson

The water flat at first.
Then a few
little waves
appeared.
Tiny. No problem.
My mind turned
inward
and I listened to
my breath,
go in and out.
I listened to
the bubbles under
my boat
too.
I calmed.
I would apologize
to Mom,
and Dad, too.
The sun lowered so
I stopped
and
sat
there.

Staring.
I'd never been
out at night like this,
and I was on
the other side
of the lake
A chill set in.
The sky darkened.
I turned the boat
around
and felt
the wind.

Chapter 26

Saturday was my one morning to sleep in, and my mother came in to wake me up for a family breakfast. Seriously? I was exhausted, even though I'd gone to bed at 9 PM. I'd had the night off with nowhere to go. Nowhere I wanted to go but to bed.

"I'll eat later," I said.

"Stew's made omelets. I thought since you went to bed early, you might be up early, too."

"Geez, Mom. I wanna sleep." I rolled over to face the wall. "I woke up to watch Kash's semi-final at, like, 4 AM."

"How did they do?" She sat on the end of my bed.

"They're in the finals." I pulled my duvet cover up under my chin.

"That's exciting," she said.

Now, I pulled that cover right over my head. The tears were hovering. It still stung. I wasn't in that boat. Was I not supposed to have these emotions? Stew, and his positiveness, sort of downplayed extreme emotions, or at least I thought so, anyway. You were always supposed to spin the emotion around and make it positive. And I sort of felt I'd been doing that with my own rowing, until I watched those races, and that slam of not being there came back. But maybe, just maybe, racing in Henley would stop the sting.

I tried to shrug my mother's touch off my shoulder.

She started to tickle me. "Come on. Join us."

"Mom, don't." I jerked my body away from her. "I'm not five."

I heard her sigh. "Sometimes I wish you were."

"Soon enough, you'll have a new five-year-old," I muttered.

"Lots of stages before then," she said. "And a lot of lack of sleep. You slept eleven hours."

"What are you? The sleep police?"

The bed springs bounced and I knew she'd gotten up. "See you at breakfast."

I didn't want to get up, but I flung my covers off and sat on the end of my bed. My legs felt like they had weights strapped around them, and not just little ankle thingies. Thinking of weights made me remember, I had one of my tougher weight workouts to do today, before my night shift at the restaurant. I'd been given all nights this week at work. God, I could have used the extra hour of sleep.

I went downstairs. The boys were up, in pajamas, playing Minecraft.

"We're like one big family," said Stew, in this super-jovial voice that hurt my ears so early in the morning. "I can't wait for Christmas morning."

"You can't seriously be talking about Christmas?" I rolled my eyes. "It's July by the way."

"Always a downer, aren't you?" Stew shook his head at me.

"Yeah, but at least I'm honest," I said. "Christmas is months away. You could always take the boys to Santa's Village if you're that eager for Christmas. But, FYI, count me out."

"You went to bed at nine last night, so you shouldn't be tired," he said. "Teens your age are supposed to stay out until their eleven o'clock curfew."

"Is everyone around here checking my sleep?" Then I curled my lip at him. "And eleven? Try midnight. Or even one."

"Not in this house."

"Excuse me. I just turned seventeen," I said. "What world are you living in? Times have changed, you know. Eleven o'clock is like a thing of the past."

"I guess I'm not up to speed on teenagers," he said. "Especially girls."

"You're telling me."

"Fill me in, then." He smiled at me. "I'm all ears."

Suddenly, there was screaming in the family room, and the sound of something being thrown. "Boys, I can deal with," he said, leaving the room. "This is to be continued."

"Later," I said. *Much later. Like, never.*

After eating (breakfast was good, I will admit) and cleaning up, I avoided the talk with Stew, and went straight back to my room and crawled into bed. I was almost asleep when my phone pinged.

Tim. He was texting about a party that was going on after work.

Sure, sounds like a plan

I had to do this, even though I almost didn't want to. Okay, yes, there was a part of me that did want to, because every time I was near the guy, I had such incredible feelings. But ... I had less than two weeks now before I left. That's it; that's all. I had to hold it together. I had to fool everyone, so I would go to the party for an hour. Here was me, a seventeen-year-old, who had to go out. *Had* to. Fake it until you make it. Maybe I should add that one to Stew's list of sayings. I was living a backward teen summer.

Done with texting, I curled into a ball and fell asleep.

My alarm went off at 1:30 and I groaned, but I got up and dressed in my workout gear, putting my work stuff in my duffle bag, and some clothes for the party after. I went downstairs and found my mother in the kitchen, baking something. She hardly ever baked. She didn't have time.

"Watcha making, Martha Stewart?"

She gave me a little smile. "Cookies." She lifted up the chocolate chips package. "Recipe from the back of the bag. So, not exactly Martha."

"But ... like, new passion?"

She shrugged. "Stew likes homemade cookies and so do the boys. And I finally have a modern kitchen."

I glanced around at the gas stove, gas oven, granite countertop. I knew all this stuff about kitchens because she'd filled me in. Stew's kitchen was supposedly a good one. "That you do," I said.

She plopped a spoonful of cookie dough onto the pan, before she glanced at me. "Honey, I want to talk to you about something."

"Sure," I said. "Fire away."

I tried to act all chill, but my throat dried. And my body was sweating. Had she figured it out? Had she heard something? She couldn't squash my dreams, but if she knew, maybe she could do just that.

She stopped moving and stared at me. "Are you doing okay? You seem so tired. You slept all morning. I'm worried. You're not rowing now, so you shouldn't be so tired. I'm wondering if we should get you checked for mono."

Mono? I almost laughed, as a wave of relief flowed over me.

"I don't have mono, Mom. I've got a job and I'm working nights. And I wanted to sleep in this morning, because I want to go out after work and have some summer fun. We're going to someone's house to play board games." *Why did I blurt that out? Board games?*

"It makes me happy that you're going out, meeting

new friends. But I want to meet them." She sounded adamant. She'd asked me so many times now.

I put my arm around her. "Soon. I promise. Can I have a midnight curfew? Or even one, seeing as we don't finish until eleven, sometimes." *Milk it, Holly.*

She leaned into me for a second, then went back to putting dough on a cookie sheet. "I guess," she said. "I trust you. But no later than one. And, again, I want to meet these friends. I really do."

I kissed her cheek. "Thanks."

Outside, I stood for a second with my hand against the brick wall, the heat from it going from my palm to my armpit to my heart. Whoa. I had to do better. And I wasn't bringing anyone home anytime soon.

At least, not for two weeks.

After work, Tim and I rode our bikes to the party. This time, there were tons of cars at Brendan's, and people hanging all over the front balcony, drinking, smoking, laughing in the warm summer night.

"Wow," I said. "Looks like a crowd."

"His parents are gone."

"He wasn't at work."

"Yeah, be prepared. Could get ugly."

"I think we should put our bikes in a safe spot," I said.

"Agreed."

We walked our bikes to a darkened side of the house and leaned them against the siding. "They're good to go here," he said.

We walked back around to the front of the house. I walked in the front door, and got knocked over by a couple who were falling all over each other in a lip-lock. The rap beat pulsed through the built-in speakers. People danced in the front room, gyrating and twerking. We headed to the back of the house, dodging bodies. Tim took my hand and I let him.

"Let's go to the pool," Tim yelled over the music.

I followed him, holding onto his hand, until we managed to get through the patio doors and out to the pool. Music blared through outdoor speakers.

"Great party," I said.

"You want something to drink?" He pulled out a bottle of something from his backpack.

"Sure," I lied. "Just a little."

We sat down on a ledge that led to a back garden, and he poured some booze in a cup and handed it to me.

"Thanks," I said.

Someone in the garden behind us puked.

"Gross," I said.

Tim laughed. Then he took a big sip of his drink, and I tried to look cool and do the same. Trying to be discreet, I spit it back in the cup.

He took another sip. "I got the okay, today," he said.

"Okay?"

"To start running again."

"That's fantastic!" I held up my hand for a high-five.

He gave a half-hearted pat back.

"What gives?" I asked.

"I thought I would be more excited." He shook his head. He took another huge sip, before he filled up his glass again and took another swig. He wiped his mouth and said, "I have my first practice in Toronto tomorrow." Another few gulps.

"Aren't you gonna feel like crap?" I tapped his cup.

"Probably. Or maybe I won't feel at all."

"Meaning? I'm kind of confused here."

"I'm not good enough." He sighed. "I have to accept my reality. It hurts so much, though." He punched his chest. "I had dreams. But they seem so far away."

"Keep trying," I said.

His shoulders slumped. "When I was a kid, I wanted to be this great hockey player. I was good, but never the best. Then in eighth grade, I decided to do some track events for fun. I killed it. Just like that." He snapped his fingers. "It seemed so easy. In high school, man, I killed it, too." He paused, and I felt the warm summer air circle around our heads. I knew he wasn't finished talking.

"Then college happened," he said. "Everyone on scholarship was as good as me. Some way better. I worked my ass off and shaved some time, and I thought I was getting there. Then I got this stupid injury, and that set me back."

"If you're that close," I said, "push through now. Again. You can do it."

"Thanks," he said. "Maybe I'm just scared to tank after being out." He gave me a gentle nudge with his shoulder, before putting his arm around me. I leaned into him.

"You gonna go tomorrow, anyway?" I asked.

He nodded. "Thanks to you, yes. Enough of me. What about your rowing?"

"I'm going to continue. Family support or not." *Maybe I should tell him? He'd understand.* Then I remembered the lies I'd told him at work. And Margo and her comment. That still made me feel sick every time I thought about it.

I saw Tessa coming over to us, weaving and looking completely gone.

"Where's your other boyfriend?" She slurred her words and broke out into hysterical giggles, as if she'd just said the funniest thing ever. Not.

I shook my head at Tessa. "What are you talking about?"

She held her stomach and laughed. "That old guy. At the rowing club."

"He's a friend," I said quickly. "Someone I make conversation with."

"You were standing sooooo close to him."

Alan and I kept our distance. Only once did he put his hand on my shoulder in a fatherly gesture. But he removed it quickly when, I'm thinking, he realized I wasn't Lily. This conversation was going nowhere. I had to get Tessa off Alan or she'd blow it for me.

Suddenly, sirens sounded in the distance. Tim and I stared at each other. They got closer and closer. My blood started to rush through my body at wicked speed.

"Oh, shit," said Tim. "Cops have been called. I don't want any part of this action. I get arrested, I don't get back into the States for school."

I looked at Tim and saw the fear in his eyes. "Come on, let's go." I grabbed his arm. I was underage, so I wanted to get away, too. I had a lot to lose as well. I glanced around, trying to figure out the best way out. I spotted a gated back door, behind the garden.

"Let's go through the back," I said.

"Good idea."

We bolted in that direction, leaving the lights of the backyard and moving into a darkened area. At least in the dark, we could squat down and hide. I sucked in a deep breath, smelling the fresh puke from God-knows-who, and just hoped I wasn't stepping in it.

"If we sneak around to the front, we can get our bikes and take off," he whispered.

I felt like I was in a bad mystery novel, as we tiptoed around the side of the house. My heart pounded like a drummer on a neverending encore. Oh, God. This couldn't be happening. But we both had to get away. Tim because of his situation. And I was underage. I wouldn't go to Henley, and I might as well kiss any type of scholarship goodbye.

But I also understood, at a moment like this, it was scarier for Tim. What if the cops caught him and put him in jail? We got to the side of the house, where our bikes were, and out front, I could see the red and blue flashing lights of the police cars that stood out against the dark sky. Throbbing. Pulsing. Flash. Flash. Flash.

"We'll have to be quick," he whispered.

We tiptoed to the bikes. I put my shaking hand on my seat and inhaled a huge breath, but it didn't seem to get anywhere near my blood stream. What if the cops saw us and chased us down? Knocked us off our bikes? Injured us? Arrested us? Beat Tim. I really didn't want to see how they would treat him. Like he said, there were a few on the force who were kind, but there were those who could be nasty to him.

"We can do this," I said quietly.

"I think the cops are inside already," he whispered.

"Let's go now," I said.

I hopped on my bike and pedaled hard, first over

grass, and then onto the sidewalk, all without looking back. Tim was beside me. I rode as fast as I could, my legs spinning, round and round, no stopping to coast. No siren sounded behind us.

After a couple of blocks, Tim said, "Slow down." I know he'd drunk a lot more than I had.

I did slow down but I kept riding. I glanced over at him. "I'm going home," I said. I was still shaking. Trembling from the top of my head to my end of my toes.

"Can we just stop, already?" he said.

Since we were far enough away, I did stop. I shook my head. "That was scary," I said.

"For sure. But we did it." He held his hand up for a high-five.

Halfheartedly, I tapped it. "This party is over for me," I said. "I'm going home."

He tilted his head. "I'm freaked. You're freaked. But something else is going on with you. I can sense it. Do ... you have a boyfriend? Is that why you're so hard to figure out?"

"No. Tessa is making things up." If only I hadn't lied to him at work. I could tell him everything right now. But if I did tell him now, I'd put him in an awkward position as a manager. He'd given me time off for a family vacation. Margo would have a heyday with this information. I couldn't do that to him. What if Bethany fired him for favoring me? Margo could spread lies, that he knew and accepted my lie. He needed his job.

"It's early," he said. "Let's go get some food somewhere."

"I can't, Tim." I shook my head. Then I blurted out, "And I can't go out after work anymore, either. I have something to concentrate on. I promise in a couple of weeks, things will be different. I won't be so confusing to you."

"A couple of weeks?" He frowned. "I don't get you. One minute you get close—then the next minute, you push back. I like you, Holly, but you're hard to get to know. Talk to me. Is it something I did? Or said?"

I shook my head. "It's not you. Not at all. I'm so sorry. I'll explain everything soon, okay? The less you know, the better. And just know it has nothing to do with you. It's all about me."

I didn't let him ask me another question. I took off, riding my bike as hard as I could, leaving him behind. I didn't even glance back. It wasn't fair of me to force him to keep a secret. This was the only way it could be for us.

As I rode, tears streamed down my face.

I liked him. I liked him a lot. I'd never felt for any guy like I did for Tim.

Did I just ruin everything?

Was this the sacrifice I had to make? My sobs continued.

End of My Story

I'll finish
my story.
No one else will
know
what happened
but you.
Not my parents,
or Holly.
Waves crashed
against my boat.
Strong winds blew.
I tried to row,
but went nowhere.
The lake turned to
whitecaps,
water seeped
inside my boat,

bitter cold water.

Dark skies raged above.

I talked to myself.

Push, Lily, push.

The water just kept

rushing over

the sides.

Think, Lily, think.

Get the boat over and

rest on the hull,

kick to shore.

I struggled with

my nameless boat.

Get over. Get over. Get over.

Cold water

splashed my face.

I blinked.

Cold water met my

warm tears.

I didn't know

I was crying.

Sobbing.

Roll over, boat. Please.

I got my shell upside down.

I held onto the

hull and

rocked with

the waves,

counting seconds.

Kick. Kick. Harder, Lily.

I couldn't see

shore lights.

Too much wind and rain.

Fingers cold. Legs numb.

Tried to wiggle

my numb toes.

I couldn't feel them

anymore

so

I started to sing.

You are my sunshine. My only sunshine.

You make me

happy

when skies

are gray.

I looked up.

It was a black sky
not gray.
You'll never know dear
how much
I love you.
I couldn't feel my fingers.
I tried to grasp my boat.
My brain went fuzzy
but was full of
song.
Please don't take my sunshine away.
The lullaby made
me warm.
My parents sang with me.
I didn't want to fall asleep.
I loved being on the
bed with
Mommy and Daddy
just the three of us.
You are my sunshine, my only sunshine.
I giggled at my
daddy's
bad singing.

You're going to
make me
pee my bed.
Was I peeing?
Is that why I felt
so warm?
No. The song made me warm.
My family made me warm.
Love made me warm.
My fingers slipped
off the hull,
my legs so heavy
they weighed
me down.
But I was warm
in the
freezing water.
Please,
don't take my sunshine
away ...

Chapter 27

"I have your schedule for Henley, your race times," said Alan.

"You do?!"

Even though I was tired from my grueling two-hour row, I jumped up and down. There really wasn't a lot of time left in the training schedule. In fact, after tomorrow's Friday row, I would start tapering. Just over a week and we'd be leaving.

"This is real." I almost squealed. So unlike me. I'd pushed through and got to this point. I'd managed to keep the secret, stay away from Tim, and just train. Tim had actually ignored me, too, so that part wasn't all that hard, except for the pain I felt every time I saw him.

Alan nodded and smiled, like he was happy that I was happy. Then he jokingly said, "Settle down. You're just like my Lily. Let me tell you how it all works."

I clasped my hands together in front of my chest

Lorna Schultz Nicholson

and did everything I could to stop jittering.

"You will race in the fourth heat on Friday, August ninth, in the under nineteen Junior Women's Single. Your time is ten-fifty-five and you've drawn lane four, which is good. It's a middle lane."

Sure, I was alive and buzzing, energy running like electricity up and down my veins, but I also knew there was a reality to this. "Do I dare ask how many heats?"

"Ten," he stated.

"Ten?! That's so many."

"Two from each heat move to the semi-finals."

"Oh, wow. That's intense."

"Your first heat is important. But we'll talk race plan at the beginning of next week."

"I saw that on the practice plan you gave me."

"Glad you're studying it."

"Of course."

"Your start is coming along."

"Thanks." I paused for a second before I asked, "How much did it cost?"

"For what?"

"My entry fee?"

"Don't worry about it."

"I've been saving," I said. "I want to pay."

"Let's work that out later. There's lots of other logistics that we need to work out first."

I nodded. "When will ... we leave?"

"I'd like to be there by the Sunday. Get you on the water for a few rows before your race. Just to feel out the course. We should pack up and leave Saturday at the latest. Is your mother coming?"

"Um ... I'm not sure," I said.

I couldn't make eye contact. No way. He would see the lie throbbing like a neon light in my eyes.

"I never missed Lily's races," he said. Then he laughed, as if he was remembering something. "Neither did her mother. She was her biggest cheerleader and, boy, was she loud. No cartwheels or flips, though. Sometimes Lily would come off and give her the 'really-Mom' look. She was so good at rolling her eyes."

Another long sentence about Lily. Every day he spoke about her more and more.

"My mom has never missed, either, but she's super busy this summer," I said. Understatement of the year. Busy being pregnant.

He nodded thoughtfully. "I understand. I'd like to

talk to her before we go. Maybe we can set up a meeting. I'm not going to take a seventeen-year-old off on a trip without the consent of her guardian."

"What about ..." I said as calmly as possible, when really my heart was thumping. How was I going to get out of this one? *Think. Think.* "If she ... uh ... signed a waiver form," I blurted out. "Like a trip form, if we can't find a good time for you guys to meet."

He eyed me and I tried to look nonplussed, cool.

"I think face-to-face is better. Just to sort it all out. I have a billet for you, but your mother should have all emergency contact information."

Tears welled behind my eyes. Someone had faith in me, and it made me happy and sad, all at the same time, because it wasn't either of my parents. I couldn't let him see stupid tears, so I just uttered the word, "Thanks," and stared at the ground. "I'll talk to her," I said.

"Great. Lily loved the Henley. It was one of her favorite regattas."

Tears sucked back into my skull; I lifted my head and said, "You're talking about her a lot today."

My dad probably never talked about me.

Then I saw his watery eyes.

"I am," he said. "I don't think it's a bad thing, though. Tough to do, yes. But bad to do, no. Do you know that for eight years now, I never said her name out loud? Except to Bella. I've said it my head, but never out loud."

"That's a long time," I said.

"It is." He nodded. "I blamed myself."

"It was a freak storm," I said.

Again, he nodded, and again, he blew out air. Wow, lots of stale stuff inside that body. "I should have been with her." His gaze moved to the water.

"I'm sorry."

He turned back and gave me a sad smile. "She was stubborn. Oh, boy, could she fight me on things."

"That's probably what made her so good, though," I said. "At rowing, anyway." I thought about that for a second.

This time he patted my shoulder, just two quick pats. "I should get going."

"Me, too," I said. "Thanks, Alan. For everything. I won't let you down."

Something jabbed me. Sure, I was going to race, but I might let Alan and my mother down, when they both heard the truth. Maybe Alan would never have to know

Lorna Schultz Nicholson

that I hadn't told my mother. And my mom wouldn't have to know until the race was over.

"When you get on that water," said Alan, "it's about you. Not me. Remember that."

I nodded. Good reminder. *This wasn't about my mother.*

"This is it," said Alan on Friday before our row. "Next week you start tapering."

I couldn't wait, my legs couldn't wait, or my arms, abs, or brain. Yes, my brain. My rowing future was still moving forward, and I was still heading to St. Catharines to race in a single. No one had stopped me yet. Huge inhale. Huge exhale. Alan was going to call my mom, but I told him she was out of town at a funeral. It was the best excuse I could muster.

The air was the muggiest it had been all year, and I had sweat running down my back, off my face, between my thighs, by the time I got the boat on the water. I hadn't even started my workout yet. The air had a stillness, and it was hard to breathe. The weather report was for a storm, but later, so I had to get through this row this morning. I stared up at the sky and saw clouds that I hadn't seen on my ride. Rain would be welcome to take away the humidity. But was it arriving earlier than expected?

"Let's get going to beat the rain," said Alan.

I nodded and got in the boat, pushing away from the dock.

Fifteen minutes later, warmup complete, I got prepared for my first sprint of five hundred meters. I completed it and two more. Then he made me row downriver so I could do a full two-thousand-meter race. I was well away from the dock when the sky suddenly darkened, like someone had just flicked off the lights and turned day to night. I kept rowing to get to the place where he wanted me to start. Along with the darkened sky came a blast of wind. The water had been so calm just minutes earlier, and now I was rowing through chop, trying to keep the boat upright. My hands smacked together but I took another stroke anyway.

Alan yelled. "Turn around and take the boat in. I don't like the look of this storm."

A loud clap of thunder bellowed through the air, and it felt like it was just over top of me. My heart rate accelerated. Waves splashed beside me, threatening to tip me over. Alan was right; I had to get the boat in.

Stay calm. I turned the boat around and took a stroke, missing water on my port side because of the waves jostling the boat. I was going to have to go against the river, and the wind was pushing it. Another huge bellow of thunder sounded above me. Lightning cracked and lit up the now dark sky. Rain started falling.

"Keep going!" Alan's voice sounded weird in the wind. "Take it slow. One stroke at a time!"

I tried to nod and keep rowing. The chop got bigger and bigger. Peaks going past me. I looked for landmarks to see where I was, how far I still had to go. At least a thousand meters. But then, only a thousand meters. I could do this. This was the choppiest water I'd ever rowed in. Water splashed over my gunwales. But the water was warm. Summer had warmed it; I would be okay, although I knew there were undercurrents to the river. The rain was now coming down in sheets.

I heard the motorboat moving toward me. Gas fumes. Getting closer.

"Stop!" Alan yelled. He was closer to me than he'd ever been, and I was worried about his wake being added to the waves.

"Why?" I yelled. "I have to get in! I can make it."

"I'll take you in."

"I'm fine. I can get in."

"Stop the boat!" he yelled. "Now!"

I stopped rowing and he chugged over to me.

"Careful," he said, holding out his hand.

"I can make it in, Alan."

"No. You can't. Take my hand."

How was I going to do this? I'd rather just row in, than try to jump into a motorboat from a single. But there he was, holding out his hand to me, totally freaked out. His eyes showed fear. Huge fear. Water dripped down his face.

I ripped the Velcro and slipped my feet out of the shoes in the boat. I pulled the sculls across the oaklocks. Now, I had to try and figure out how to stay balanced. I put both hands on the gunwales of the *Lilybean*, at first, just to get a feel for what I had to do. I couldn't stand up in the boat; it was too rough. Then I thought of another way. I stretched one leg over the side of the boat, and I took Alan's outstretched hand. It was shaking like crazy, and his tremors went from his skin into mine. He pulled me into the motorboat, then grabbed the rigger of the single. I undid the sculls and hauled them into the motorboat.

His eyes looked completely wild, and his body shook like he was freezing and we were in a snowstorm.

For a moment, we both just sat there. He was lost somewhere, and I was sure he wasn't seeing me at all. Slanting rain continued to fall from the sky. A huge downpour. Drops bounced off the seat in the motorboat.

"I'm in," I said loudly. "I'll hold onto the rigger. You drive."

I held onto the rigger of the single, trying desperately not to damage the boat. I couldn't race if the boat was wrecked. The rain drenched us, and it also created poor visibility. The motorboat bounced over the choppy water, but Alan went slow. Slower than I would have. But I was thankful, as his speed helped me hang onto the single, keeping it from smashing against the sides of the motorboat. I tried to look at him, get him to look at me, but he was gone, vacant.

We made it to the dock, and I carefully pulled the *Lilybean* around to the front. Holding onto the bow, I stepped out of the motorboat so that I could grab it, stop it from banging against the dock.

"I'll get the single and sculls out," I said. "You take your boat in."

He nodded, as if I was the parent and he was the child. Through the rain, I lifted the single. Water from the inside of the boat fell in one swoosh. I carried the boat on my side, instead of my head, because I was worried about the wind taking it from me.

I made it to the boat bay before Alan, and I stood there holding the boat. I wanted to tell him to hurry, but I knew I couldn't. Not in the state he was in. I waited patiently. He did attempt a little jog when he saw me standing in the rain, the boat resting on my hip bone. But when he tried to unlock the bay, it took three times to get the key in the lock, because his hands were shaking so much. Finally, I got the boat inside, and I was out of the pouring rain.

I racked it and came back to the front of the bay, where Alan was standing inside, out of the rain. It poured down in front of us. He was just staring. Out to the water.

I stood beside him.

"This is how it happened," he said, eyes on the water. "But it was cold. February. And she was on a lake. Way out in the middle. She would have been so cold."

"Yes," I said. I knew enough not to say too much.

The fact is: she would have been freezing. I was chilled, and it was summer and hot. I couldn't imagine being out there alone, in the dark, on a cold winter night, with wind howling around me. What had she been thinking out there? How long was she in the water? Had she tried to make it in?

"I should have been with her," he said. "I could have brought her in. We had a fight that day. I let her go. I shouldn't have let her go."

He didn't look at me but lowered his head, and then his shoulders just started shaking, the sobs in his throat animal-like. My eyes teared up; I couldn't help it. I knew that nothing I could say would help, so I remained silent, allowing a broken man his grief.

After, I have no idea how long, his sobbing subsided. He lifted his head and looked at me. "I can't."

"What do you mean?"

"Go on the water with you again. I just can't."

"What?" My stomach plunged.

"Holly, I can't go out there again. I'm sorry."

"What about the Henley?" I asked, shocked.

"I have to lock up now. I have to go home. I'm so sorry." He moved away from me, stepping outside to stand in the pouring rain. I watched the raindrops bounce off his slouched shoulders.

Then he turned to me and jingled the keys to the boat bay.

"I'm done, Holly."

"You can't do this to me," I said.

"I have to. I'm so sorry."

My eyes blurry, I ran to my bike, hopped on, and rode as fast as I could, rain splattering up from my wheels, creating ribbons of dirt on my body, my face.

I didn't stop pedaling.

I rode through the rain, my view hazy. The pelting rain still fell from a dark sky the way tears fell from my eyes.

Third Funeral

I thought
Holly had gotten
through to
 my dad.
This is like
another funeral.
My grandma
was my
first funeral.
I was my second.
Grandma, I watched from earth.
Me, I watched from above.
Heaven?
I don't want to be
in heaven
if my parents are
in hell.

Funeral number two
came months
after I died.
My parents wept.
Shoulders shaking. Noses running.
The deadness started
again.
I tried to reach
inside them
and say stop,
you have
to live.
They sat on my bed.
Stared at my walls.
Picked up my medals.
My mom lay on my floor
beside my bed
curled in a
tight ball.
 My dad went outside
and cut wood
with his electric saw,
making

nothing.

Then a For Sale sign.

Packed up my things.

Gave nothing away.

Not my dress in the bag,

or my socks.

They kept my

socks.

Moved to a small town,

clear across

the country

and stayed

because of Santa's Village.

Lily always

loved

Christmas, they said.

I followed them,

in spirit

but they couldn't feel me.

I called out,

but they

didn't listen.

My dad did odd

handyman jobs,
my mother worked
at a dental office.
And then my dad was
coaching again.
Excited. Even smiling.
Now this ...
a third funeral.

Chapter 28

"Are you okay?" Amaya asked me when I got to work. I'd tried to cover my swollen face with makeup. Obviously, I sucked at doing that. When the restaurant had called to ask if I could pick up a shift on my day off, I immediately said yes. I had to get out of the house.

"I'm fine," I said.

"O-kay." She paused for a second. Then she leaned forward and whispered, "A few of us are going down to the river tonight for a bonfire. We're going to keep it low key, though. Nothing like at Brendan's." It sounded like she was trying to cheer me up. I didn't want to be cheered up.

I shook my head and wouldn't look at her.

"Are you sure you're okay?"

"Stop asking me that. I'm fine." I know I snapped, but I just couldn't get hold of myself. Fortunately, people came in. I picked up the menus, forced a smile, and rattled off the specials like a robot, as I seated the table.

When I came back, I was happy to see more people lined up. If it stayed busy, I wouldn't have time to think. All day I'd sat in my room, thinking, pacing, thinking, pacing. I didn't want to think anymore.

Halfway through the night, Tim came out to see how we were doing.

"How's it going out here?"

"Good," I said, barely looking at him.

"We're fine," said Amaya. I knew she was boring holes in me, but I refused to look at either of them. I'd almost bumped into Tim when I first came in, but we barely spoke, and for good reason. I'd basically shoved him away. The party had been shut down, parents phoned, but no one arrested or anything like that.

Who cared? Not me. Right now, I cared about zilch, nothing. My body felt heavy, weighted down. I had been abandoned again, only this time, I was old enough to remember. Alan was no better than my non-existent father.

I picked up some menus. "I have to seat this table," I said.

As I recited the specials to the hungry customers, I thought about going to the beach tonight. Maybe I should go. Get fucking drunk.

"I'm coming with you guys," I said to Tim. My shift was over, and I didn't want to go home and ... do what? Sleep, so I could be prepared to row? Work out? I was doing none of that now. I wasn't rowing or going to Henley. I could sleep in, be hungover. Who cared? No one. No. One.

Tim gave me a look, and I wasn't sure what it meant, so I said, "What?"

"You're so confusing."

Since no one was standing near us, I whispered, "I have tip money. Can you buy me some booze?"

He furrowed his eyebrows. "Seriously?"

I nodded.

"Um ... don't worry about it. I have enough."

"I want my own."

He held up his hands. "Hey, whatever you want."

"Great. You riding over?" I asked.

"Um ... yeah. That is my transportation," he said.

"Can I ride with you?"

He shook his head at me. "Whatever."

"I'll wait for you outside," I said.

I gathered my belongings, shoved everything in my backpack, and headed to the door. Amaya tugged on my T-shirt and I turned. "You're going?"

"Yup," I said. "Just want to have some fun tonight. Like everyone else." I gave her the same smile I'd given Tim.

Outside, the rain had cleared the air, and the humidity was gone, the sky full of shining stars. As I stared upward, the anger that helped me through the night flip-flopped and, suddenly, I could feel the tears stinging behind my eyes again.

Get a grip, Holly.

By the time Tim wheeled his bike over to me, I was standing tall with my chin up.

I'd get through this, too. I would. And I could. But not before I got completely drunk.

Tim and I didn't talk on our way to the beach, except about work. When we got to the river, I saw the fire. I headed straight to the logs to sit down. No heavy conversation for me tonight.

My first gulp—and I mean gulp or chug or whatever

it's called—went down my throat like an animal screeching in the jungle. It burned and landed with a thump, in the bottom of an empty stomach. I hadn't eaten a thing since my row.

"You might want to slow down," said Tim.

"Says the guy who pounds it back."

"Am I supposed to take that as a compliment?"

"I dunno." I took another swig. It burned the same. Landed the same. And was as gross as the first. This time I coughed, it stung so much. He patted my back.

"What's up?" he asked softly.

I shook my head. And took another swig, draining the cup. I held out my red cup.

"Come on," I said. "Fill 'er up."

"Not a good idea."

"What? It's okay for everyone else, but not me?"

"This isn't like you."

"You don't know me," I said. "I can be fun." Since I was starting to feel the effects, I leaned into him. "Pleeease."

When he wouldn't do what I asked, a girl beside me offered, so I gave her ten bucks, and she filled me up. The booze glugged into my stomach. Rock bottom again.

And again.

And again.

My vision got fuzzy, but I liked the numbness that went along with the booze. When Amaya told a joke, I howled in laughter and it felt good. "You're so funny," I said.

"And you're hammered," she said.

"Maybe." I held out my cup and more money, and someone, I don't even know who, filled it up again. I didn't need to save my tips. I slugged it back like it was water. The burn went from my tongue to the bottom of my stomach. "I felt that land." I giggled.

Everything got blurrier and blurrier. I tried getting up to dance but my body felt mushy. I fell into someone who gave me a little shove. I glanced around and saw a grassy area. Maybe if I just sat down.

I was sitting on the ground when Tim came over. "You okay?"

I waved my hand in front of my face. "Stooooop asking thaaaat." My words were coming out of my mouth, but it was like I couldn't control them. I started to giggle. And I couldn't stop.

"You're totally wasted." Tim took my cup and I tried to hold onto it, but I fell backward onto the ground. I lay on my back, staring up at the sky. The wind was gone. The stars shone. "I can see staaars," I said. "The Biiiig Dipper."

My stomach started to roll and then, suddenly, I was spinning, like I was on a ride at the fair, going around and around. "Uh-oh," I slurred.

Tim held out his hand and I reached for it. I tried to sit up, but my body was bending in all the wrong directions, like an elastic band. He sat beside me and I fell into him, liking how hard his chest muscles were and how warm he felt. I looped my arms around his neck, and he smelled so good that I wanted to kiss him. I leaned into him, trying to press my lips to his. He dodged me, and he tried to pry my arms off him.

"What's your game?" he asked me.

"I wanna kiss you. Remember that niiiiight? We almost had seeeeex in the park!" I laughed.

"Wow," he said. "Um ... the other day, Holly, you rode away from me."

"That was beeeeefore." I pushed my body against his, wanting to feel him close to me.

He held me at a distance. "What changed?"

"Nuttin."

"Coulda fooled me."

"Nope. Nuttin." I leaned into him again. "Kiiiiss me."

"I'd love to kiss you, but not when you're like this," he said. "And only if you really want to kiss me back."

"I do."

He held on to my forearms and stared at me. "I really like you, Holly, but it's like you're using me. I don't think you mean this."

Suddenly, my vision blurred, and my stomach heaved. "I don't feel very good."

"Put your head between your legs," he said.

I did what he told me to. Everything swirled around me. He was right. I was using him to avoid my pain. I started to cry.

Finally, he said, "I'm going to get you home." He helped me stand up.

"I caaaan ride my biiiike." I stumbled up, holding onto Tim's arm, then his shoulder.

"Oh, my God," said Amaya. "She's so drunk."

"I ammm not," I said, pointing my finger at her. "You are."

Amaya laughed.

"I had the shhhittiest day ever." Was I going to cry again? Drunk girls always cried. Now I was one of them.

I started singing, "Like a Virgin." That old Madonna song.

Then I puked.

Tim got me home by walking my bike and his bike, while trying to hold me up. I babbled all the way home, telling him about Alan and rowing and not rowing. I stopped to cry on the curb. I think more than once. I had no idea what time it was. Nor did I care.

The lights were all on in my house.

"Uh-oh. I'm in trooooouble. And guess what?" I tried to look at Tim. "I don't giiive a flying shiiiit." I laughed. "Can you imaaagiine if shiiit did fly?"

"It's already two-thirty," he said. "Do you want me to come in?"

"You're a niiiiiice guy," I said.

"I try," he replied.

"Dooon't come in. I wanna be in trouble. Then I get grounded, and I can staaaay in my room foooorever. My whiiiite room. I have a poster of Serena Williams on my wall. And Christine Sinclair. And Silken Laumann. Do you know a boat hit her?" I tried to clap my hands, but it didn't work, and I almost fell.

"I'm sorry for what happened to you today with your rowing," he said.

"How do you know what happened?" Did I tell him? Oh riiiiight. I did. "Yuuuup. It suuuucks. What did I tell you?"

"I'll text you tomorrow," he said.

"I'd liiike that," I said.

"Would you? Really?"

I touched his cheek. "Why are you so nice to me?"

"I like you. We connect. Understand each other. Why do you push me away?"

I shrugged. "I doooon't know. Because I'm such a liiiiiar. I liiiied to you at work, and I didn't want you to ... lose ... your job. That bitch Margo would have got you fired, because she's a ...biiiiitch. I wasn't going anywhere with my stupid family. You would have got fired."

"I don't think Bethany would have fired me."

I tried to give him my sexiest smile. "Are you going to kiiiiiss me gooooodnight?"

He shook his head. "Not tonight."

He helped me put my bike away, and I went in through the back door, knocking over something in the mudroom on my way in. No idea what.

My mother met me before I walked into the kitchen, and took me by the shoulders. "Holly! Where have you been? It's almost three o'clock." She paused. "Are you drunk?"

"Noooope. I don't think sooooo."

"You are."

"Maybe. You said get out and have fun this suuuuummer. So … I did. And now I'm going to bed."

Suddenly, Stew appeared, looking like a big blob in the doorway. I started laughing, because he looked like a really blurry blob.

"Holly, you're way past your curfew," he said.

"Soooooo. You're not my faaaaather."

"Not now, Stew," said my mother. "She needs to go to bed."

"My faaaather left me." I started crying. But I wasn't crying about my biological father. I was crying about Alan.

My mother put her arm around me. "You need to go to bed. We can talk in the morning."

"I dooooo," I said. "I need to go to beeeed."

"She's drunk, Mary. This is not a good example for the boys."

"We can deal with it in the morning," said my mother.

I wagged my finger at Stew. "Leeeet it go, Super-Stew. Be-cause I'm druuuunk," I said. Then I barked. Then I howled like a basset hound.

And then, there was more puke. But this time, all over Stew's expensive sneakers.

Lorna Schultz Nicholson

Grief

My dad took
every coaching
certification course
available.
Our den
had bookshelves
full of
coaching manuals.
There isn't any
manual
available
for
grief.
He can't sit down and draft
a daily schedule
for his
grief.

It's not as if he can
cry
for a minute one day
and ten the
next,
have a rest on
Sunday.
For his sake,
I wish
there was
a manual
like that.

Chapter 29

"Holly."

My mother shook my shoulders. I slowly opened my eyes. Sunlight streamed through my window, little slats that landed on my floor and on my oh-so-sore eyes. I immediately closed them. I felt awful. Like, really awful. Headache, parched throat, sick stomach.

"What?" I grumbled.

"You have to get up. We want to talk to you."

"I don't want to talk to anyone."

Last night was hazy at best. What had I done? Oh, right. I'd gotten drunk. And now I had my first hangover. God. I wanted to puke again. Never again. Never again. I seemed to remember being in trouble.

"Come on," said Mom.

"Why?" I moaned.

I rolled over to face the wall. "I got drunk. Ground me." I wanted to be grounded, to give me a good excuse to be a recluse in my room, to wallow in my sorry life.

"Please, come downstairs."

"Only if you don't make a huge deal of this. I don't care if I'm grounded for the rest of the summer. I really don't. Ground me, already, and let me sleep."

"We will decide what to do."

"Why does he have to be involved?!" I sat up so fast that my stomach churned. "Uh-oh," I said.

I hopped off the bed—wearing pajamas I don't remember putting on—and, holding my mouth, ran to the washroom, where I puked up the water I'd drunk when I'd woken up completely parched. Oh, God. This was the worst.

"Holly." My mother stood outside the washroom.

"Go stand by your man."

"Meet me downstairs."

I wiped my mouth and passed her to go to the stairs.

"You coming?" I asked her. I might as well get it over with. When I entered the kitchen, Kevin looked up from his bowl of cereal and grinned at me. "You got drunk last night?"

Stew glared at me. Then he turned to Kevin. "Finish your breakfast."

God, I felt ill. I went to the fridge and opened it, searching for something that looked appealing, something that might not make me puke again.

Nothing. I turned back to Stew. "Sorry," I said. That was the best I could do.

"Holly, we need to have some rules in this house. I know it's hard for you here, an adjustment, but the boys heard everything. They're still young."

"You were barking like a dog." Kevin started barking.

"That's enough," said Stew to Kevin.

"Whatever," I mumbled.

Suddenly, I needed a toilet and soon. I ran from the room, and into the powder room. I was never, ever, going to get drunk again. When I came out of the powder room, my mother was waiting for me. "I'm going back to bed," I said.

"Can we talk?"

"Not now. I can't. Lecture me later, okay?"

The next time I woke up, it was noon, and I was actually feeling a little better. My stomach was empty, but at least I didn't want to puke. After I showered, I went downstairs. I guess I didn't have to do a weight workout today. I wasn't going to Henley. The stabbing pain returned. I still couldn't believe it was over. Alan had left me high and dry, just like my father.

My mother came into the kitchen when I was eating some toast with peanut butter.

"Holly," she said. "You're up."

"Yeah. Where's Stew?"

"He's out with the boys. I've decided this is a matter between you and me."

She sat down across from me, clasping her hands in front of her. "What do you have to say for yourself?" She spoke softly.

I couldn't look at her. "Not much."

"Talk to me."

I stared at my plate, the half-eaten toast. "What's there to talk about? I got drunk. Ground me."

"I think we do have things to discuss," she said. She reached out to touch my hand.

"Is it an apology you want?" I asked.

"Only if it's sincere," she said.

Would it be sincere? Probably not. I still hadn't lifted my head to look at her. I shook her hand off mine.

Instead of an apology, I just blurted out, "Why

didn't you tell me about the baby as soon as you found out? You should have told me." *Why was this what I wanted to talk about? Because it had been eating at me.* "That really hurt, you know. We were always us. You took that away from me."

"I'm sorry for that," she said, reaching out again for my hand, and this time squeezing it. I let her, for some reason.

"Holly, I was scared to tell you," she continued. "And scared, period. I was single once with a baby. You. I didn't want that again."

I finally looked at her to see if *she* was being sincere. And I didn't pull my hand away this time, because my heart almost broke when I saw that look in her eyes, of hurt and pain. She did feel bad. And she did have fears, too.

"Okay, then I'm sorry for last night."

"It's not the drinking I'm worried about, Holly. You just seem so unhappy."

"It's hard living here."

"I know it's an adjustment," she said.

"It sucks," I said.

"Okay. Fair enough. But you keep pushing Stew away. He's not your father."

"You got that right."

"That's not what I meant." She paused. Then she continued. "What I mean is, he's not *like* your father. He wants to try and have some sort of relationship with you. I know he's over the top sometimes, and I've talked to him about that. He's trying too hard."

"He's never going to be my father," I said.

"He knows that. But maybe, one day, he can be a man you trust. Stew is kind and caring. He loves me, which means he wants to love you because you're a part of me. I'm not scared anymore about this baby, because it'll be loved by both a mother and a father. Your father left you, but that doesn't mean every man will."

I slouched in the chair and stared at the toast on my plate. My dad left me. Never to return. Now Alan had left me, too. Thoughts of being in that single, rowing, hearing bubbles under the boat, bubbles that sounded like music, made my throat tighten, my heart collapse.

"Give him a chance," she said. "Give us a chance."

I ripped the crust off my toast.

"Maybe we can do more things together this summer," she said. "I'd like that."

I shrugged again. "Like what? You're always too busy. Couldn't even go for ice cream."

"I would have gone with you that day. I told you that. But I also knew it was a moment where Stew was really trying to bridge the gap between you two. Yes, he tried too hard. But we can go to a movie. Or maybe we can go shopping." She squeezed my fingers again. Gently. "You can help me pick out some maternity clothes."

My eyes started to well up with tears.

"Holly, it's okay. You're allowed to have feelings about all of this."

"You're having a baby." Snot ran out of my nose and I wiped it with my arm.

"Talk to me," she whispered.

"It's just ... I had a dream for my summer, and it didn't come true. It hurts so much." My shoulders started shaking. "And your dream is coming true, even though I didn't even know you wanted another baby." I wiped my nose. "And I'm trying to be happy for you, but it's so hard."

"You will have many dreams come true, too. I love you, Holly. I loved us when it was just us. But sometimes things change. You're going to be gone soon. I didn't want to be alone, but I also wasn't looking. But then Stew came along, and I got pregnant at the age of forty-five. I feel blessed and so grateful for this one last chance. I wasn't expecting these changes, but they came my way. And I'm happy they did. But it makes me sad to see *you* so unhappy."

I kept my head down, my hair falling in front of my face. Should I fess up about the rowing? Yes. I definitely needed to.

I looked at her and was about to speak, when she touched my hair.

"And we'd used a condom," she said with a silly smile. "I guess it had expired."

I laughed a little because she looked like Mom. My old mom. The one who had been, like, my best friend since I was born. The slightly sarcastic one, who I'd taken after. "Condoms expire?"

"Apparently." Suddenly, she touched her stomach. "Ohhhh, I felt a kick."

"You did?" I stared at the round bump.

"Oh, another one." She grabbed my hand and, before I knew it, my hand was on her belly.

The kick was small, just a little movement, but I did feel it. That foot belonged to my little brother or sister.

And it reminded me of something. Bubbles. It reminded me of bubbles. Under the boat. I had to tell her.

Suddenly the doorbell rang, interrupting our moment. "I'll get that," she said.

"I can get it, Mom." As soon as the door was answered, I would tell her about the rowing. I really wanted to make everything go back to the way we used to be. Honest and open.

"It's okay. Let me get it while I'm still walking, instead of waddling. Stay here," she said. "I'm enjoying our conversation." She was up before I could get up.

I was taking a bite of my toast when I heard Alan's voice. I almost choked. What was he doing here?

Then I heard my mother. "Holly, someone is here to see you."

Sorry

It's funny what
I remember about
my earthly life.
My dad sat
on my bed.
I was little. Maybe four.
I pouted. Arms crossed.
My favorite
stuffed green
crocodile
in my arms,
pressed against
my chest.
Daddy is sorry, he said.
I shouldn't have raised
my voice
but

Lorna Schultz Nicholson

you did
throw milk
on my training plan.
Lower lip pulled down.
Daddy, you weren't
listening
 to me.
He touched my cheek.
I'm listening now.
My dad always
said sorry
when he was wrong.
               Now, it's my turn.
Sorry for
               dying, Dad.

Chapter 30

"Alan!" I said. There he was, standing at my front door. "What are you doing here?" I quickly glanced at my mother, and she had this totally confused look on her face.

"I came by to apologize, Holly."

"Um ... okay," I mumbled. "How did you know where I live?"

"You're registered with the Muskoka Rowing Club. I needed your address to fill out the Henley registration forms."

"Would you like to come in?" my mother asked. She wasn't going anywhere, and I didn't dare ask for privacy. She moved aside and gave Alan her polite smile, even though that frown was still flashing, like a neon light.

"Holly," she said. "Mr. Coleman and I have done our introductions, and he says he's your rowing coach."

I nodded. Still avoiding direct eye contact.

"Mrs. Callahan, your daughter has talent," said Alan,

moving into the house. "In all my years of coaching, I've only ever known one other athlete who works as hard as she does."

"Interesting," said my mother.

I knew she was boring holes in me with her gaze, so I shot her a glance. I had to. I'd obviously lost my moment to tell her in private. She raised her eyebrows and I shrugged. Then she turned back to Alan, plastered that polite smile back on her face, and said, "Let's go to the kitchen."

Mom went first, and I ushered Alan forward with my hands, so he could go next. As I followed him, I saw the file folder tucked under his arm. We got to the kitchen, and Mom did her usual fussing with drinks. I cleaned up my embarrassing dirty toast plate, putting it in the dishwasher. Alan opted for a glass of water and I did, too.

"Holly," he said, when we were sitting across from each other at the kitchen table, "I would still like you to compete in the Royal Canadian Henley."

I wanted to jump up and down, hug him, squeal, but then there was the little issue of my mother, hovering over the conversation like a Queen Bee ready to sting. And my hangover. Couldn't forget that.

"I think you deserve this," he said.

"I'd like to know more about this," said my mother, from the outskirts of the conversation.

Now it was Alan's turn to furrow his eyebrows. "Did you not tell your mother about training in the single?"

"In a what?" my mother asked.

Okay, I had to do this. Now. Give her the goods. Fess up. I turned to look at her.

"I've been training in a single since the beginning of summer," I said.

"Excuse me?" Now she had a deep eleven etched between her eyebrows.

I sucked in a big breath. I had nothing to lose now. "Every morning after you go to work, I go to the rowing club and Alan coaches me." My words were coming out fast and furious. "I'm lucky, Mom, because Alan is a former Olympic coach. I've learned so much from him. And I've been rowing in ... his boat." I just couldn't say, Lily's boat. I would tell her about Lily after Alan left.

"How did this all come about?" My mother, who still hadn't sat down, now stared at Alan.

"It's a long story, Mom," I piped up. "We can talk later."

Alan looked at me, shocked. "Why didn't you tell your mother?"

"I wanted to," I said. I looked at my mother. *Just be honest, Holly.* I sat tall. "I thought she might not support me. And she does have a lot on her mind right now. Other, more important things than me rowing. Like having a new baby, a new family to think about."

"Oh, Holly," said my mother.

Alan spun his glass around, and it made a screeching sound. No one said anything.

Then Alan looked over at my mother. "I'm really sorry about this. I had no idea."

"Join the club," said my mother.

"We just met by chance, Mom," I said. "At the rowing course after a run, after I got home from St. Catharines. This isn't Alan's fault. I'm the one who kept this from you."

"And you've been rowing ... for how long?"

"Pretty much since I got back," I said. "Alan has helped me so much. You have no idea."

"The thing is, Mrs. Callahan," said Alan, turning to my mother again. "Holly has helped me as much as I've helped her."

"How so? And, please, call me Mary."

"Mom. Please. I can tell you everything later."

"It's okay, Holly," said Alan. He stood and faced my mother. "I met your daughter at the rowing club, and she was upset about not making the junior team."

Upset? Nice choice of words. I'd screamed like an idiot.

Alan continued. "I hadn't coached since my daughter died eight years ago. But Holly and I talked, and she seemed to be so passionate about the sport, that I asked her if she wanted to try the single, my daughter's boat. I don't know why I asked her, but she just seemed so curious, and my daughter had been like that. And then ... Holly was a natural."

"A natural?" My mother gave a small, sad smile.

What was she thinking with that smile? Did she like hearing I was a natural? Or sad because she might not let me do this?

"And your daughter showed me a work ethic I hadn't seen since my daughter rowed." I heard Alan's voice catch a little, but then he exhaled. This was a lot of words for him, unless he was in his motorboat. "The more she rowed, the more I wanted her to race."

"And you want her to race in the *Henley Regatta*?"

"Yes," he said. "Well, I did. I have to admit, I'm not

happy about her not telling you. But, in a way, this is something that my Lily might have done."

"I'm so sorry," I blurted out to Alan. "I still want to race."

Alan looked me right in the eyes. "Lily never had a second chance. So, I will give one to you, because you've worked hard. But this will only work if it's okay with your mother."

"Can you give me a few details?" my mother asked.

"My wife and I can drive her to St. Catharines," said Alan. "My wife, Bella, loved watching Lily race. I have a billet for Holly to stay with, a wonderful family whose son is on the senior National Team, which I organized, because Holly told me you would be too busy to come. Which is understandable when you have other children. I saw the hockey net outside." He looked at me. "I was under the impression Holly was an only child." He looked back to my mother. "We only had Lily."

"I was an only child," I said. "I now have stepbrothers and a soon-to-be sibling." I hung my head.

My mom didn't say anything. My heart thumped inside of me. I wanted her to answer, say I could go. Alan wouldn't go against my mother. Not now.

Say something, Mom, please.

Alan looked from my mom to me and back to my mom. The tension in the room loomed like the angry gray cloud that got us in this mess. I stared at the floor. I'd lied. Avoided telling the truth. This was a done deal. So much for my summer.

"I'm so sorry for your loss," she said softly.

"Thank you," said Alan.

"Would it be too late to get a hotel room?" Mom asked.

Mom and I made eye contact. The look in her eyes sent shivers through my entire body. Some disappointment for sure, but also this look of love that I hadn't seen, or maybe hadn't looked for, in months.

"You'll really come?" I blurted out.

"Yes. I will."

"But what about—"

"Alan," my mother cut me off, "let's have a look at the schedule. The sooner I ask for time off work, the better."

The rest of the conversation with Alan was business, and my mother responded with all the necessary answers and signatures. Then Alan talked to me about my/our rowing schedule, and how next week we would taper. Hungover or not, I was going to the gym today to

Lorna Schultz Nicholson

do my last weight workout, which was also, fortunately, a taper workout.

Alan finished, and I told my mother I would walk him out. At the door, he turned and said, "I wish you had told your mother."

"Me, too," I said.

"You put me in an awkward position."

"I know. I'm so sorry. But she's pregnant, and I guess I didn't want to complicate things. But I know it was wrong."

"Pregnant." He gave a sad, rueful smile. "That's exciting. I'm happy for her." The sadness in his voice matched the sad smile on his face.

Then he shrugged. "I'm glad it sorted itself out." He paused. "And I'm sorry for the other day."

"Alan, it's okay," I said quietly. "You were thinking of Lily."

He sighed. "I was. But I can't allow her death to dictate my life anymore. You've given me life again, and I don't want to lose it. Lily would want me to move on, coach you like I coached her."

"You've helped me, too."

Then he gave me his funny little smirk. "This doesn't

mean you're off the hook. Get that weight workout done today. And I'll see you Monday morning." He paused. "No more boozing, though."

My eyes bugged out of my head. How did he know?

"You show up to workout looking like you do, and we won't be tapering. I will put you through the hardest row you've ever had."

I nodded. "Promise," I said.

I shut the door and leaned my forehead against it, knowing I had a lot of questions to answer.

As predicted, my mother was waiting for me in the kitchen, leaning against the kitchen counter, holding a coffee mug.

"That was a shock," she said.

"I'm sorry, Mom," I said. Serious sincerity.

"Have you really been rowing every day?"

I nodded. "Not Saturday or Sunday. That's why I'm tired. I don't have mono, Mom, I'm training."

She just gave one big nod, and her lips were in a tight line. I knew better than to say anything, so I just stood there, waiting. A few seconds passed before she asked, "Were you ever going to tell me?"

How to answer this one? *Tell the truth.* The little

voice in my brain spoke. "I wanted to," I said. "I practiced up in my room what I was going to say to you, but ... I really didn't think I had your support. I was going to leave a note."

"*Leave a note*, Holly? Where? On the kitchen table?"

I sighed. "Mom, you didn't tell me about the baby for over a month. You kept that a secret with Stew. Not with me. With Stew. So, I kept a secret, too, but for different reasons."

"Well, aren't we a pair." She sighed. "We're both being pushed out of our comfort zones here, and neither of us knows how to handle it."

"Yeah. I guess we are. The thing is, Mom, I don't know Stew all that well, so I thought ... what if he said no? I'm not sure you would have had my back. I didn't know if you'd side with me or not. And I want this. Alan has faith in me. You don't—or you didn't until now. Until someone told you I could do it."

"Holly, that's not true."

"Do you think I can do this? Do you want me to do this?"

"All this mother wants is for her daugher to be happy. You were so crushed after St. Catharines, I didn't want to see you like that again. I guess I was just feeling mama-bear protective. Then you went out for the recreational program and quit. That's why I suggested the running and the Orillia Lakehead, and I thought a car might be an added bonus. I'm worried about what happens if you don't get a scholarship, and I was just trying to give you options."

"I'm an athlete, Mom. I'm going to have setbacks. I'm not going to be happy all the time."

"Maybe I'm just a little over-protective and hormonal."

"And from being with Stew, who is happy all the time."

"Holly, that's how he copes. His life with his ex-wife was tough. This works for him. It may not work for you, but we're all different in how we cope. He needs to be positive. It keeps him alive and functioning."

I thought about Alan. And Bella. How she was still stuck in her grief. But how being on the water with me had pushed Alan through some of his grief. People did cope in different ways. "Fair enough," I said.

I looked at her. "All the stuff about Lakehead University." I paused. "Is it financial? Did you give Stew all the university money you said you'd saved for me?"

"Oh, Holly, no ... no. I'm really sorry if that's what you thought." She shook her head. "I selfishly suggested

Orillia because I wanted you around me and the baby. I wanted you here to help me and to bond, to see him or her take first steps. I guess I don't want you to miss all of that. The thought of you leaving is tearing me apart. And I thought, if you weren't rowing, it would be perfect. Plus, this house has so much male testosterone." She gave me a funny smirk.

"You got that right," I said.

She put her hand on my shoulder, and her touch felt good. "But I know now, I need to let you move on, and go away to a university with a rowing program."

"I do, Mom. But I promise you can come visit me." I grinned at her. "Maybe you'll have a girl to ease some of that testosterone."

"Hey, I'm going to hold you to that visit. I may need a getaway."

I laughed. "No matter where I go, my dorm room will probably be small."

"I'll get us a hotel. With room service."

I laughed. "Sounds good to me."

She tilted her head. "I do have one more question. If you're training, I'm a bit confused about why you got drunk last night."

"I had another setback." I sighed. "But maybe I would have figured it out. I'd like to think I would have." I paused. "Can we sit?" I'd kept the toast down but now I had a splitting headache. I needed to finish my water and go do my last weight workout.

She'd asked a good question. Why *did* I drink last night? To forget. What an idiot. Plus, I had treated Tim like shit.

We sat down and I told her everything. The day I met Alan. Going in the boat for the first time. She even asked me if I had been scared. We laughed a little. Then I got a bit excited and told her how much I loved rowing in a single. She listened and nodded. And I told her how sad Alan had been, how he struggled with his daughter's death, and how, when the storm came up, he'd freaked out, canceled our trip. That's why I got drunk. I also told her about Tim, and how he'd been the one to walk me home last night. As I was talking, I heard a car in the driveway.

I sat up, my heart suddenly pounding against my skin. "It's Stew," I said. "What are you going to tell him?"

Pride

My dad was
always
proud of me.
Now,
I'm proud
of him.
I'm proud of
Holly, too.
For finally
talking to her
mom.
My time to
talk
is
over.

Chapter 31

The car shut off outside. I heard doors slam.

"I will tell him the truth," said my mom.

"Do you think he'll freak?"

"Holly, I'll deal with this. You are going to row, and I'm going to watch you row. Why don't you go up to your room? You have a workout this afternoon, and you still look awful. Get a little rest before you head out."

"What about that doctor's appointment? It's the same time as the regatta."

"I can reschedule." Then she grinned. "You realize you have to come now. You're not getting off the hook."

I laughed. Now this was my mother. "Yes, I'll go. It's not going to creep me out, is it?"

"That's what you think?" She laughed.

"I dunno." I shrugged. "Is it like an internal? When you have to open your legs for everyone to see your vagina. That happened on *Friends*. I don't want to see

Lorna Schultz Nicholson

your private parts hanging out. You're my mother."

She laughed. "It's an ultrasound, Holly. It won't creep you out. It might surprise you. You might hear a heartbeat."

A heartbeat? The voices got louder and louder.

"You can ground me," I said. "I'll do my workouts and work and do nothing else. Don't let him take this away from me."

She reached out and hugged me, her arms wrapping all around me, holding me, giving me comfort, making me safe. And I allowed her to hold me, loving every second.

"Don't worry," she said. "You are going to race, and I'm going to St. Catharines to watch my girl, and that's that." She pushed a strand of hair off my cheek. "And you are grounded."

"Thank you," I whispered. *Did I seriously just thank my mother for grounding me?*

The back door opened; she gave me one last squeeze before she said, "Go on. I'll deal with this."

As soon as I got to my room, I closed the door and punched the air. That is, until my head felt like it was going to burst open. I glanced at my watch, and knew it was around dinner time where Kash was training. After winning bronze in their last regatta, they were traveling to Lucerne for the World Championships. I picked up my phone and texted, hoping I'd catch her.

News flash! I'm racing in Henley! in a single

Text came back right away.

What? OMG. What? How? Whose boat?

Long story

Single? That's crazy, girl. Single??????

Yup

Tell me everything

I got under my duvet cover and sent her off a too-long text. Of course, I left out a lot, like me getting drunk. I wasn't doing that again anytime soon. No more parties until after race day. I would tell her that when she got home.

We texted back and forth and then she had to go. Then I knew I had to send another text.

Thx for last night & so sorry

I had just added some funny, green-faced emojis to the text when there was a knock on my door. I pressed SEND and, expecting Stew, I sat up on my bed. "Come in."

The door opened and there was my little buddy, Curtis. I instantly relaxed. I'd tensed up, preparing for an argument. My phone dinged, and I stared down at it and smiled at Tim's funny emojis that he'd sent back. I quickly fired a text back.

Hey, can you meet before work for coffee somewhere? Something I want to tell you. I'd understand if you can't but ... I need to say sorry in person

He answered: Sure

I wanted to beg forgiveness. The weird thing about this "relationship" with Tim was that ... it was like my sport. Backwards. Rowers went backwards down a course. Tim and I had done the make-out session first, now we were going for the coffee. I guess I hoped for the middle to be there, too.

"Hiya." I patted the end of my bed for Curtis. "Sit down, take a load off."

He almost skipped over, and the smile on his face was from ear to ear.

"What's up?"

"You're rowing again!"

"What makes you say that?"

"I heard your mom. I missed the beginning of them talking, because when we got in the house, I had to run to the bathroom. I had to take a poop after so much ice cream."

"Too much info, Bud. What did you hear?" I nuggied him. "Spill."

"Your mom is going to support you. My dad asked about some person named Alan. Do you have a boyfriend?"

"No." I shook my head. Then thought, *well, hopefully. Not Alan, though.* "Keep talking," I said.

"You're being pushy."

"You got that right. I'm almost like your big sis, so it's my job. Come on, give me the goods."

"My dad said he wasn't sure, because of the lying, and last night when you barked like a dog, but your mom held up her hand." Curtis held up his hands, palms out, for a dramatic demonstration.

"Then she said NO," said Curtis. "Her mind was made up. Then my dad said, okay, Mary, let's just discuss. And she said, 'NO DISCUSSION.' Then he looked at her and said, 'Okay, I agree. You know what's best for your daughter.'"

"Anything else?"

"Oh, he said he's trying to understand you. But doesn't really get teenage girls. That's you, by the way. You're the only teenage girl in this house. My dad only has boys. And you're grounded. What's grounded?"

"I'm not allowed to go out much."

Lorna Schultz Nicholson

"Oh, yeah," he snapped his fingers, "and I think she kinda started crying, so my dad hugged her. That's when I couldn't stick around. I didn't want to see them kiss. Yuk."

"I'm going to row a single at the Royal Canadian Henley in St. Catharines."

"Cool? What's a single?"

I opened my computer and showed him still shots and a video of the best female sculler in the world, racing in the Olympics. He watched, totally interested, and kept saying *wow* and *cool* and *soooo cool*.

"I love having you as a fan." I tousled his hair.

He laughed and held up his hand, so I high-fived him.

"I like having you live here," he said. He glanced around my room. "But your room sucks. It's white. But I like the posters. Well, sort of. They'd be better if they were all hockey or lacrosse or basketball players. You should paint it."

"How about," I said, "when I get home, you help me paint my room?"

"I don't know if my dad would let me do that. I might spill. He probably won't let you, either."

I laughed. "True enough. Maybe if we put down tarps."

Stew had said he wanted to paint my room when Mom and I moved in, and I was the one who refused to let him. "Maybe you can help me organize shelves and put up all my medals. And pick out the color. What color do you think it should be?"

"Not pink. You're not a pink girl."

I laughed again. "I know, right?"

I made myself do the workout, then I showered at the Sportsplex and headed to the coffee shop where I was meeting Tim. He'd already texted to ask me what I wanted to drink. Water and black coffee. I was still working on the hangover. When I saw him, he stood up and waved at me.

"Hey," I said, sitting down. "Thanks for the coffee and water."

"No problem," he said. "You get in trouble last night?"

"Oh, yeah. I'm grounded."

I reached across the table for his hand. "I'm so sorry about last night. And for pushing you away. I really am."

"It's okay." He squeezed my fingers but withdrew his hand. "I'm confused. You give such mixed signals."

I clasped my hands in my lap. "You have a right to

be confused. I know I mumbled incoherently last night about what was going on, but I'd like to tell you the story sober."

He nodded. "Okay. I'm all ears."

The words poured out of me, and I told him everything that had happened, including Alan and Lily, and then Alan showing up at my house today, wanting me to race again.

"Wow, that's a story and a half." He shook his head. "Hard to believe the guy's daughter died like that."

"I didn't tell you that last night."

"You weren't making a lot of sense."

"So sorry about that."

"It happens."

"I can't imagine what she went through that night."

"It'd be awful," said Tim. "Makes you think we're lucky. We're alive."

"Exactly." I paused for a second. "I'm so sorry I pushed you away. I just didn't know how to handle what was happening. And I'm so sorry I lied about getting time off for work. I wasn't going on a family holiday. I just wanted to race so badly. I've been worried that Margo will make trouble for you."

"I'll deal with that," he said.

"No, I'll tell Bethany."

He smiled at me. "Your mom is going now, so it kind of is a family holiday."

I smiled back. "Yeah, I guess so. I'll still talk to her."

He tilted his head and looked at me. "I'm an athlete. I would have understood."

I nodded. "I know that. This was all about me being cut and feeling shitty about myself. And, of course, my mother and this new family I have." This time when I reached across the table, I touched his cheek. "There's a reason why I met Alan ... just like ... there's a reason why I met you."

He took my hand and kissed my fingers. Then he laughed as he looked at my knuckles. "They look like shredded cheese."

"Hazards of the sport. But easier to deal with than an injury." Suddenly I remembered. "How was your first workout?"

He nodded his head, huge smile on his face. "It was great."

"I'm so happy for you. Tell me more. Tell me all about it."

"How about ... we go on a real date?" he asked. "No more parties. Let's hit a movie. Or dinner somewhere, or even just go for ice cream." He squeezed my fingers.

"I'd like that," I said. "I'd like that a lot."

"What do you think your mom and her boyfriend will say about us dating?"

"You mean ... because you're Black?"

He nodded and said, "And older."

"My mom will be cool. I've got this great-uncle who married a Black woman. They live on the east coast. My mom grew up with my grandpa supporting them. All good. As for Stew ... I don't know the guy well enough to know how he'll react, but knowing him, he'll freak over the age deal." I stopped talking for a second and thought about this. Then I said, "But ... I know my mom will support me on both." I smiled at him. "How about your parents?"

"They'll be cool." He smiled. "It's a date, then." He kissed my shredded knuckles.

Tingles flowed through my entire body.

A Letter

I wish I could
send
my parents
a letter.
Snail mail.
Okay, okay, I know
snail mail
is outdated.
Humor me, anyway.
It would be something
they could
keep.

Dear Mom and Dad,
Thank you for everything.
I truly mean that.
I want you to
give away

Lorna Schultz Nicholson

my socks.

Please. Get rid of them.

And give away that

blue dress

in the bag.

I hated dresses, anyway.

Give it to Holly.

Okay, keep my rowing singlets,

and your favorite

baby clothes.

Maybe the little

baby sweater

Grandma knit.

That pink hat

I loved so much

when I was five.

The gray sweater

I wore almost

every day

in high school.

But everything else goes.

Oh, you can keep my medals,

and newspaper write-ups.

Just not the ones

about

my death.

Keep my elementary

school drawings.

My Mother's Day cards.

My Father's Day notes.

The hand I made in plaster.

Let Holly have my boat.

Mom, cheer

for her

at the

finish line.

Snap away if you want

 but get rid of the

honking

big camera.

It's outdated, so

just use a phone.

Dad, coach her like you

coached me.

Only, don't ever,

ever

throw your megaphone.

That's outdated coaching.

Just saying.

Love you both.

Now live.

xoxox Lily.

That's what I would say.

Did I forget anything?

Chapter 32

"Remember your race plan," said Alan in this super calm, low voice. "Row your race. Don't let the other boats get to you. Just focus inside your boat. Keep your chin up, chest open, and row."

Good thing he was calm. Because I wasn't. I sat in the boat at the dock. At the St. Catharines Rowing Club. My heart was thumping. My palms sweating. Throat parched. I exhaled, loudly, and nodded, staring straight ahead.

"You've done the work. Now enjoy."

He took the blade part of my scull and pushed me off. I rowed, arms only, until I got away from the dock, then I lengthened. I knew the course. I rowed by the bulrushes on my left, heading toward the big bridge, only I wouldn't go that far. The starting gates were before the bridge. The Martindale Pond water was calm today, the air humid. Ontario summer air.

I had my race plan cemented in my head. My four-stroke start, then a hard ten, and when that was done, I was to get in a rhythm I could sustain. We'd worked on that, over and over. So far, the plan had worked, because I had come second in my heat to make it to the semis. Then third in the semis to make the finals.

This was it. My final race.

I rowed to the start line, running through my race plan in my head. The marshall running the race gave us our five-minute warning. I paddled over to lane two. I'd had four and three in my heat and semi. I would only be able to see the one boat on the one side, and the boats on the far side were hard to see, unless you were way ahead. Didn't matter. I had to follow the race plan.

The boatholder got hold of my stern and held onto my boat. I breathed out and leaned over my sculls, trying to get oxygen in. Every muscle was tensed. My blood raced through my body. Butterflies flew like they were jets inside my stomach, banging against the wall. I wanted to throw up.

But I didn't.

I sat up tall. Blew out air. Focused. Focused. My eyes on one spot.

The aligner held up his white flag to signify that all

boats were in alignment. I was straight. I waited. Nerves buzzing like live wires.

Focus, Holly, focus.

Beep!

The sound of the horn blasted through the air.

I pushed back, prying the boat through the water with my three-quarter stroke. I pushed through a quick half-stroke, another three-quarter stroke, and into a full stroke.

One. Two. Three.

I counted to myself.

Ten.

I got through the hard ten.

Lock, load, and send. Around the finish. Move with the boat. I passed through the two-fifty-meter mark and, out of the corner of my eye, I could see that I was ahead of lane one and three, but there was no way to know where I was with the other lanes. Not yet.

I kept pushing.

Feeling good, I threw in a hard twenty at the two-fifty. I counted in my head. Every stroke was hard, but I kept pushing. And breathing, too.

Breathe out. Breathe in. Suck in that air. Breathe out. Breathe in.

My legs snapped down.

At twenty, I was gasping, so I tried to get back into the rhythm. I needed to not fade. I could do this. Another stroke. And another.

Pushing through five hundred, I felt okay, but the race still seemed long. Still fifteen to go. Don't think like that. No, I can't. I have to just keep going. My lungs were bursting. I had a boat on lane one. Two on lane three. And I could also see four behind me.

Chin up. Chest open. Focus on the horizon. Feel the boat. I heard Alan's voice. I sat tall, looked out past my stern and, suddenly, the boat lifted.

One thousand meters. Halfway. I knew I needed a solid twenty. Again, I counted in my head. Pushed the puddles further and further. And I worked with that energy, taking my stroke rate up, but not rushing. Up. Up. Not too high. Remember what Alan said.

Bubbles sounded underneath.

Okay, I was coming up to fifteen hundred. I had to dig deep, like, real deep. Go somewhere I'd never gone. Push past my comfort zone and into the next zone. The higher zone. Feel the rhythm. The music of the stroke.

Just like life. Feel it. Open up to it.

Seventeen-fifty. Last two-fifty. I'd done it. I'd made it through. I could see boats behind me. Last twenty strokes. I pushed like I'd never pushed before. Stars swam in front of my face. My lungs hurt. My legs hurt. My arms hurt. My head hurt. Everything pained.

I crossed the finish line. Heard two horns within seconds of each other.

I let the *Lilybean* run, leaning over the sculls, panting, like a dog left in a desert with no water. Panting. Sucking for air. I leaned back and tried to breathe, get air to my burning lungs. I closed my eyes and squinted, hoping that would relieve the pain.

Then I heard the announcement.

I'd come second!

By how much? I looked up at the big board that had the times. I saw my name. I'd lost by 1.25 of a second.

My heart sank. One second. It hit me. I'd lost by one second. Was I okay with that? I wanted to be but ... I lost by probably a half a boat. Maybe not even.

Could I have won with one more push? The Henley Regatta only gives medals to the winner. The person who won gold. But placing second allowed me to stand on the podium.

I glanced over at the podium and, yes, I had come second by a second, but I got to go over there, get out of the boat, and stand in front of everyone. I slowly rowed to the podium and docked the *Lilybean*. My legs almost gave out on me when I stepped out of the boat, but I managed to right myself and walk to my place on the stand.

I stepped onto the second-place finish box and immediately saw my mom, because she was in the front row with her phone, snapping pictures. Really, Mom. My grandparents were beside her, having driven hours to get here. My mom lowered her phone and stared at me with this huge smile on her face. Of course, she waved in overly large gestures. And then Grandma whistled. I laughed. Like mother, like daughter.

I lifted my hand and gave them a little wave. Then I saw Bella come up to my mom, and they hugged. That made my heart expand.

As I watched the winner get the medal put around her neck, I heard a loud voice yelling, "Way to go, Holly!!!!"

Oh, my God. That was Curtis's voice. I quickly scanned the rest of the grandstands. Then I saw him, too, in a middle row, his hands cupped to his mouth. And I also saw Kevin and Stew. No one told me they were coming. And I saw Tim, too, standing beside Stew. He'd told me he might take the day off work, and he would try and borrow his parents' car, but he wasn't sure if that was doable. He'd come over to the house last week, before our ice cream date, and Stew had given him an over-the-top welcome. It'd been pretty funny, but Tim had actually liked the guy. Go figure. Now here they were, standing together. Tim nodded an acknowledgement to me, athlete to athlete.

"YEAH, HOLLY!" Curtis yelled. "WHAT A RACE! PHOTO FINISH!!!!"

I waved at him. When he saw me waving, he jumped up and down and waved back. By now, my breathing had returned to semi-normal. I laughed.

Since it was time to get back to our boats, I stepped down and walked back to the *Lilybean*. Once back in the boat, I slowly rowed to the boathouse. I didn't sing. I didn't win.

Alan was waiting for me on the dock. He held up his thumb when he saw me, and he was smiling, too. Huge. He was happy. I can see my mom being happy, but I thought Alan would be disappointed. I'd lost. I docked the boat and got out.

He looked me right in the eyes. "You raced that well, Holly. Really well. That was excellent!!"

"Thanks," I said. "I didn't win."

"You came second! When I first suggested you race here, I wasn't sure if you were even going to make the finals," he said. "You've rowed for such a short time in a single. It was a gamble to even enter you. To make the finals is a huge accomplishment. Ten heats of seven lanes! You beat out sixty-eight other boats. I'm so proud of you. You should be proud of yourself. You pulled that silver placing together in a short time. You have next year to win gold!"

Said that way, in such a lot of words, I knew I had to be happy. "You believed in me," I said.

"Yeah, but you did the work." He extended his hand and I shook it. "We make a good team." He gave me a lopsided grin. "We could continue to train for the rest of the summer. Doesn't have to be as intense. A few times a week. And if your school crew doesn't race in the fall, we could go to a few fall head regattas. Maybe even drive to Boston for the Head of the Charles."

His enthusiasm was infectious. "I'd love that," I said.

"And to think it all started with a scream."

I laughed, big belly laughs.

He laughed, too. "I think I can hug you now. I always hugged Lily after she raced. Can I hug you? I have to ask first; it's protocol now with Safe Sport."

"You sure can." I put up my hand. "Fyi, I'm sweaty."

He took me in his arms and gave me a big fatherly squeeze, which lasted a nano-second, before he let me go.

"Boat stretchers are up on the lefthand side," he said. "Take the boat up, and we'll get it ready to go on the trailer. We'll head home tomorrow."

Home. The word sunk deep inside me, but it didn't cause pain.

"My ... um ... family is here," I said.

He smiled at me. "I know. Your mom just texted me. Apparently, we're all going out to dinner tonight. Your mom organized the restaurant. We can celebrate your race."

"I'd like that," I said.

"You have to celebrate every moment," he said, "because you never know how long they'll last."

I nodded. I would text Tim and invite him to come, too.

Then I carried the *Lilybean* up to the waiting stretchers.

Lorna Schultz Nicholson

Rowing Glossary

Blade: This is the part of the oar or scull that enters the water and gathers water, to help the boat move. It is curved to grab onto the water.

Bow: The first part of the boat to cross the finish line. A **bow ball** is on the very end of the boat. Bow also refers to the person in the seat closest to the bow, who crosses the finish line first. Since rowers go backwards, it may seem as if this is the back of the boat, but it is called the bow, the front of the boat.

Bow coxed boat: A shell in which the coxswain lies in the bow of the boat instead of sitting in the stern. This lowers their center of gravity and is better for balance. They have an unrestricted view of the water way for accurate and safe steering. These boats can be pairs or fours.

Button: A wide collar on the oar that keeps it from slipping through the oarlock.

Catch: This is the point in the rowing cycle where the rower puts the blade in the water and catches the water. The push begins after the blade is loaded with water.

Coxbox: Is a microphone within the boat that enables all the rowers to hear the cox as clearly as possible. Speakers are mounted under the seats in the boat to project the voice through the microphone.

Coxswain: Is the person who steers the shell and is the on-the-water coach for the crew. A cox steers the boat with a rudder. They also help to motivate the crew and offer feedback after the race.

Ergometer: Rowers call it an "erg." It's a rowing machine that closely approximates the actual rowing motion. The rowers' choice is the Concept2, which utilizes a flywheel and a digital readout, so that the rower can measure strokes per minute, the pace, and the distance covered.

Feathering: This is when a rower turns the oar or sculling blade from perpendicular to a position parallel to the water.

Finish: The last part of the stroke where the oar/sculls come out of the water.

Gate: The bar across the oarlock that keeps the oar in place.

Head Race: These are races that are longer than sprint races, and have staggered starts instead of boats lining up and starting together.

Let it Run: This is a command given by a coach or coxswain that tells the rower(s) to stop rowing.

Oar: Apparatus used to drive the boat forward. Oars are hollow and can be made of wood or of a synthetic material like carbon fiber. Rowers do not use paddles.

Pitch: Pitch is the angle of the blade to the water. Incorrect pitch can cause the blade to dig or wash-out.

Port: Left side of the boat, while facing forward, in the direction of movement.

Power: A call for rowers to do their best, most powerful strokes. It's a strategy used to pull ahead of a competitor. This can be a power ten, twenty, even just five strokes. The amount of strokes is up to the coxswain, or in a coxless boat, one of the rowers.

Puddle: When the oar or scull exits that water, it creates a puddle. A rower can figure the run of the boat by looking for the distance between the puddles made by the same oar or sculls.

Rigger: The metal device that is bolted onto the side of the boat and holds the oars.

Run: The run is the distance the shell moves during one stroke.

Sculling: When each rower uses two oars or sculls. Single (for one person), double (for two people), quad (for four people).

Sculls: Oars used in sculling boats. They are smaller than sweep oars, and the rower has one scull in each hand. Sculls are used in singles, doubles, and quads.

Seat Race: This is used for crew selection, and is an evaluation of one rower against another rower by comparing them. A coach lines up two or more boats, has the rowers row a measured interval (either distance or time), and notes the difference between the boats at the end. Then the rowers make a switch. The coach will then row an identical piece and note the difference again. If one rower continually makes the boat go faster, then they will be the one chosen to make the crew. Coaches can keep notes about any irregularities, like changes in water conditions or stroke rates. A coach may also ask the coxswains to take notes about stroke rate, steering, and how the feel of the boat may have changed.

Shell: Can be used interchangeably with boat.

Slide: The set of runners for the wheels of each seat in the boat. The rower slides toward the stern and puts the oar or sculls in the water, and once the blade is covered with water, the rower pushes back, and the seat moves on the slide toward the bow.

Starboard: Right side of the boat, while facing forward, in the direction of movement.

Stern: The rear of the boat. Stroke seat, the person who dictates the stroke rate, sits in the stern of the boat, and all rowers behind the stroke seat follow. Since rowers face backwards, stroke seat may seem like the front of the boat.

Straight: This refers to a boat that operates without a coxswain.

Stretcher or Foot-stretcher: This is where the rower puts their feet when they get in the boat. The stretcher consists of two inclined footrests that have special shoes for the rower. Most rowers do wear socks. Footstretchers are adjustable for the height of the rower.

Stroke: The rower who sits closest to the stern. The stroke sets the rhythm for the boat; others behind him/her must follow his/her cadence.

Sweep: The type of rowing where rowers use only one oar. Pairs (for two people), fours (for four people), and the eight (eight people) are sweep boats. Pairs and fours may or may not have a coxswain. Eights always have a coxswain.

Lorna Schultz Nicholson

Acknowledgments

Like rowing in a race, getting a book across a finish line is a tremendous amount of work and requires a crew. It takes a lot of synchronization, and there are a lot of "let it run" moments. After those stopping moments, it takes a lot of pushing and grunting to make it move forward again.

I was lucky to have a wonderful team help me get across the finish line. My first thank-you is for Tanya Trafford, for the initial talks about the sport of rowing, and how it would make a good subject for a book. Then there were those first readers of that horrible first draft. My very first reader was Dannica Valent, a beautiful (inside and out), talented, young woman I met at the Forest of Reading event in Waterloo, Ontario. In this story, the poem "Connections" is dedicated to her. Natasha Deen, Barbara North, and Karen Spafford-Fitz, and Debby Waldman—all fabulous writers—also read early drafts and gave me character and story advice. My rowing recollections needed some updating, and Michele Fisher and Lesleh Anderson Wright were hugely helpful in making this book correct. Michele Fisher (we both won our first medal in a coxed four), and Lesleh Anderson Wright (a tough-as-shit cox who made us work), brought me into the modern world of rowing. I have a BIPOC character in this book, and Tololwa Mollel was a wonderful sensitivity reader, adding so much insight to the interracial romantic storyline between Holly and Tim. My agent, Amy Tompkins, was the first to believe that this book was saleable. I thank her for finding it a home, a really great home. My Red Deer Press editor, Peter Carver, deserves a massive thanks, because he believed in this project, saw the beauty of the sport, the characters, and the structure of the novel. He understood what I wanted to do, and his approach was that of a coach, but no yelling, just encouragement.

A book, like a race, has so many behind-the-scenes people involved. Red Deer Press publishes beautiful books, and there are people behind the cover art, design, copy-editing, marketing, social media, sales. I thank both Red Deer Press and Fitzhenry & Whiteside for getting this book out in the world as an actual book, instead of a manuscript on a computer.

Many thanks also to Tricia Smith (she picked me up at 5:30 to go to Burnaby Lake Aquatic Club), Alan Morrow (hired me as a coach at the University of Victoria), and Hadley Dyer (my very first book editor), for their wonderful endorsements. I'm so honored.

Years ago, I was a rower, and I want to thank everyone I had the pleasure of rowing with at my high school, the St. Catharines Rowing Club, Burnaby Lake Aquatic Club, and the University of Victoria. After I stopped being an athlete, I moved on to coaching, and I want to thank my mentors (two Alan's—thus the name—Alan Roaf and Al Morrow), as well as all the athletes (male and female) I had the pleasure of coaching, especially my men's novice team. This is a work of fiction, but often stories are created from life; writers dig into that past, to bring up memories, some happy, some painful, and they rework these memories and emotions, adding fictional characters and plots. I've done that with this book. Everyone in my rowing world helped me create this story, from coaches to athletes to parents to mentors. Thank you for being a part of my life.

Of course, in the end, when you cross the finish line, a book is about the reader. Please enjoy, and I hope you learn something about this beautiful sport, and love my characters as much as I loved creating them.

— Lorna Schultz Nicholson

In memory of:
Darryl Smith (March 14, 1968 – January 15, 1988)
Gareth Lineen (January 17, 1968 – January 15, 1988)

Interview with
Lorna Schultz Nicholson

What was it that made you want to tell this story?

I was a rower in my teens and a coach in my twenties. I wanted to highlight this beautiful, physically demanding sport in a novel.

But I also went though something when I was a coach that has been inside of me since 1988, and it needed to be told. Let me lay my cards out here: as a coach, I was involved in a situation where I had crews on the water, (two eights and a pair); the wind came up, and a Friday afternoon row escalated into a horrible tragedy. Two boys passed away during this incident, and it was an absolutely horrific time for so many people.

For years, my thoughts have been with the families of the boys. When I had my own children, I thought about the pain they must have felt, are still feeling, and it has been eating away at me. I guess I needed to get it on paper.

Lorna Schultz Nicholson

From the outset, there is an intriguing voice that comes through the poems that accompany Holly's story. Why did you want to include this voice, and why in this form?
Alan's story is about grief. As I said, for years I have thought about those families, and the grief they went through and are still going through, I'm sure. I didn't want to write a teen book that had a voice from an older person's point of view, so I thought a lot about how I could get Alan's story across. Then it hit me to write it from Lily's point of view. I wanted to keep the voices in the novel teen voices, but I didn't want to do alternate chapters as this is not Lily's story. It is Holly's story to tell. So, the verse sections were a way to bring out Alan's story without writing full chapters about him or going into his point of view.

Holly is a teenager who is becoming part of a blended family—which she is not pleased with, to say the least. Why did you want to explore this theme?
When my children were in their teenage years, they had numerous friends who were in blended families. I would hear the teens talk, and many were having issues with new stepparents and siblings, new living

arrangements, new everything. Many of them struggled with their arrangements. Teens actually like structure, and change is difficult for them, so I wanted to put that in the novel.

In Holly's world at this time in her life, it seems many people fail to understand each other—mis-read each other's intentions or attempts to reach out. Why was this something you wanted to focus on?

Sometimes I think adults don't always listen to teens and have the tendency to dismiss a teen's problem as minor. Adults feel they know the answer to the problem (maybe they've been through it before) so they don't allow the teen to go through the pain of the problem to grow. It hurts to see them in that pain so it's easier to offer solutions to fix the problem.

Holly's mother doesn't want to see Holly hurt, so she tries to fix her pain instead of allowing her to feel and grow and have an experience that will give her wisdom later in life. I did this with my own children. There were times I didn't listen and just tried to give opinions and solutions because I thought I was doing what was right. In this novel, I wanted to show how misguided intentions can happen when you think of yourself and not the other person.

Holly chooses not to tell her mother, her best friend, or anyone else about the rowing experience she's having with the mysterious Alan. In the end, do you think her keeping this secret helped her achieve what she wanted it to—or was it a mistake?

It's hard to say, because it was a secret, and I'm not for teens keeping secrets from their parents, but ... I'm not sure her mother would have allowed her to do what she wanted to do. Her mother wasn't an athlete and didn't understand what Holly wanted to achieve. She was also being Mama Bear protective, when she saw how devastated Holly was after being cut. She might have said no, thinking she was actually helping Holly deal with her pain.

With this book, I wanted to write about an athlete and how hard it is to excel, compete, get to the top, and how difficult that can be for a teen who doesn't have a support system. Holly's mother didn't understand her pursuits, because she saw Holly was devastated about being cut. She was trying to "fix" the situation, when Holly really needed to work through her pain. Holly was stronger than her mother gave her credit for. Yes, she was in pain, but that didn't mean she was giving up. So, I guess my answer to this question is, the secret did indeed help her achieve her goals. Ouch. I can't believe I just said that.

In telling this story, you have chosen to use real locations rather than fictitious ones. Why was that important to you?
The first draft of this novel had fictional towns. I think I was trying to skirt over what had happened in 1988. With my wonderful editor's advice, I dug deeper into this story and decided that real places showed the real rowing world. Now, I've only seen the Muskoka Rowing Club once, and never rowed there, so that one was different, but I wanted to use it to show that there are smaller cities with rowing clubs.

Your own experience as a rower and a rowing coach created a good deal of the energy in the story. Briefly, what do you find so compelling about this sport?
Rowing is a sport that is about beauty and pain. It all looks beautiful when the boat is moving, the oars going in the water at the same time, exiting perfectly, but the

Lorna Schultz Nicholson

training is brutal. It takes guts, raw hands, burning lungs, and hard work to be a rower ... but the result of winning and being on that team, making the boat move together is beautiful. And rowing a single is so serene and powerful, being out on the water, just you and the boat. When the boat does get that synchronicity, it is a wonderful feeling. I'm gushing here, but I think it is such an amazing sport.

Alan is a coach who works Holly hard during their training and tends to withhold his praise of her. Is that typical of rowing coaches—or athletic coaches in general?

Yes. Being an Olympic athlete, or having those aspirations to be at the top, is not an easy road. If coaches were easy on their athletes—offering praise all the time, not calling the athlete out on mistakes, or what they need to do to get better—the athlete wouldn't be able to excel. Some praise is necessary, and Alan does praise her, for the most part, at the appropriate times. I didn't want to make him this warm and fuzzy coach because to constantly praise, especially if the athlete hasn't succeeded, is just giving false hope. But ... I don't believe in abusive coaches; that is unacceptable.

I have to say that rowing, and getting the coaching I got over the years, helped prepare me for the writing world. I look at editorial advice like coaching. The art world can be a harsh too, like sport, and it is full of rejection and dismissals and criticism.

Holly is not the only person who keeps things secret in the story. Alan is another—and when we learn what his tragic secret is, we care about him even more. Why did you want to include Alan in Holly's story?

For over thirty years, I have thought of those parents losing their boys. Alan was a way for me to honor that grief. I'm a writer, so words are a way for me to do that. Alan is a composite character for me, though. He's a parent who lost a child, but he also has characteristics of coaches I had as an athlete, and of coaches who mentored me in my own coaching. I combined a lot of people to create Alan. I had two amazing mentors in Alan Roaf and Alan Morrow, thus the name Alan.

Holly spends a good part of the summer feeling that she is alone, that no one really understands what she is dealing with. To what extent do you think this is

really the case for her? Do you think this is a common experience for many people her age?

Anytime a teen feels a loss, I think they can get that sense of loneliness. Years ago, one summer, I was a teen athlete who got cut from the Canadian National coxed four that was going overseas to the World Championships, and it was just a few weeks before the team was leaving. I was replaced after a seat race, after training all summer long. I was devastated and felt so alone. My parents didn't understand (this is not a criticism, just a fact), because they weren't athletes. I had to read and hear about the crew racing well in Lucerne, Switzerland while I was at home. I used this experience to understand Holly and her loss.

What is your message for teenagers who find writing their own stories a challenge? Might they think that the opportunity of telling stories of their particular athletic experiences makes them better writers?

Absolutely. Write what you know, and what you experience. Look at how I'm writing about things that happened thirty and even over forty years ago. And don't be afraid to take your experiences and twist them to make up the characters and story. I twisted a lot of people into Alan. As I mentioned earlier, he's a composite character. Holly's being cut is my pain when I was young, but her family life isn't. My parents were married for over sixty years. I took a part of my experience, but added more to her that had nothing to do with me.

Think of the good and bad experiences you've had on a sports team, or in an individual sport, and take all that emotion to paper. Maybe someone was mean to you, said something rude. Or maybe you found your best friend on a team. Or ... maybe, you actually don't even like sports. That's okay, too. Write about that experience, of trying out for a team, and being the worst. Or maybe wanting to try out but being afraid. I think writing about experiences you've had can enrich your writing. And sport is full of so much emotion that you can add all of that to your story, too!

Thank you, Lorna, for your honesty and your many insights.